MW00891627

ONE BAD DECISION

LINDA MCCAIN

PAGE PUBLISHING, INC.
New York, NY

First originally published by Page Publishing, Inc. 2018

ISBN 978-1-64350-242-7 (Paperback)
ISBN 978-1-64424-240-7 (Hardcover)
ISBN 978-1-64350-243-4 (Digital)

Printed in the United States of America

Dedication and Acknowledgments

In loving memory of the beautiful Sylvia Swann.

To Tim Pool, my friend whose words "finish it" added greatly to my motivation to complete this book.

Also, special thanks to the following for their help and encouragement:

Daniella Farmer
Fatima Cone
Genae Finney
Celia Pool
Peggy Pritchard
Evelyn Thompson

CONTENTS

CHAPTER ONE

SHELBY MALLOY MOVED TO THE center of the platform on a Friday morning at rush hour in Washington, D.C. A crowd of commuters waited along with her, hoping to be one of the lucky ones to get on a train into the city to meet the demands of their job. This meant they ran, pushed, sighed heavily, did whatever they had to, to get on a train. She kept asking herself over and over, why hadn't she gotten up earlier? Why hadn't she set her alarm clock? She lingered on the thought of setting her alarm clock, then said softly to herself, "It's because you don't own an alarm clock, you idiot, but you do have a cell phone you could have set an alarm by." *What a bright idea*, she thought to herself sarcastically. *Still, I am going to get an alarm clock.* She decided right then and there that as soon as she left work that day, she'd head straight to the drugstore to buy an alarm clock, then life would be grand. She glanced at her watch anxiously. It was seven fifteen and she was due at work by eight.

If a train came now, right now, she reasoned, not only would she make it to work on time, but she'd also be able to quiet the growling in her stomach with a bagel from the bakery on the way to her office. She hoped a less-crowded train would come soon; she'd already passed up one that was packed tight with commuters.

Shelby began to pace up and down the platform. She didn't care how she appeared to others. So what if she hadn't had time to comb her hair, put on lipstick, or find a pair of matching shoes. She couldn't believe she'd actually left her apartment with a red shoe on one foot and a burgundy shoe on the other. "Honestly, Shelby," she said to herself. She said a silent prayer that she wouldn't see anyone she knew or even thought she knew.

Just when she thought her morning couldn't get any worse, she turned to look into the face of Paula Queria. Not only was Paula beautiful, but she was beautiful in all the right places. Her beautiful oval face would rival that of any who chose to challenge it. Her small but shapely frame was always clad in the most fashionable attire. Any color she chose to wear accented her beautiful deep complexion. Shelby often wondered how she kept her short, dark, wavy hair so together all the time. Everything about her was right, Shelby thought to herself.

"Hey, Shel, what's up?"

"Hi, Paula." Her cheerful greeting was forced while desperately trying to hide her feet so Paula wouldn't notice her mismatched shoes.

"Too late," Paula said with a smile.

"Excuse me?"

"I've already seen the shoes, Shel. Rough start this morning? It's all right. I have about one hundred pairs of shoes under my desk. You can borrow a pair for the day," she said with a smile.

"Thank you, Paula."

"Sure, I can't let my girl walk around looking crazy even though she is." They both laughed before getting into a conversation about the woes of womanhood. When the train finally pulled up, both of them determined to get on, forced their way in the door. The train ride was miserable, but they realized it was this train or suffer the wrath of their office administrator, Helen Spell. "Shel, do you have any mints on you?"

"No, I'm sorry, I don't. What about some gum, I do have that."

Paula hesitated before saying, "Well, okay, gum might work. Didn't have breakfast, and my mouth feels dry."

"Excuse me, miss, do you happen to have a dime?" Shelby turned in the direction of the voice, a voice so weak she thought for a second that she might have imagined it. A little lady who looked to be in her late seventies stared up at Shelby with sad gray eyes. She was dirty, smelly, and her dingy gray hair was matted; what wasn't matted hung heavy and long, almost covering her tiny face. The woman's hair looked as if it hadn't been washed in months. Her hand shook as she held it out to Shelby, expecting her to drop something in it.

"Please, miss, just a dime, that's all I need. I'm homeless and my cat needs food. I'm short a dime. I have just enough to take the train back to where I am staying for the night and short only a dime to get my Mittens her food."

"Mittens?" Shelby asked, trying to figure out if that was the woman's cat's name or if she had misunderstood what she'd said.

"Mittens, yes, Mittens is my cat, and she is all I got in the world. She's hungry and I have no more food for her."

"Shelby, come on, this is our stop. We've got to go." Paula's words encouraging her to get off the train were pressing but she refused to get off without giving the woman at least five dollars. She looked like she needed a meal too. She quickly looked through her wallet for a five-dollar bill, finding only a ten-dollar bill. She handed it to the lady and was out the door.

"You know, that woman just took you for ten bucks, Shelby. You've got to stop being so gullible," Paula said while walking so fast Shelby had to run to keep up with her.

"The woman clearly needed help, Paula. You saw her. There was no way I could get off that train without giving her something." As Shelby's anger got the best of her, she stared at Paula, daring her to deny what she'd said was true.

"You know what, forget it. Let's just change the subject, okay?" Paula said while rolling her eyes and throwing her hands in the air. "So what's going on with you these days? We haven't had lunch in almost a week," Paula said in an effort to put their conversation on a lighter note.

"Nothing much," Shelby replied while trying to conceal her mismatched shoes from the rest of the world by walking very fast so no one would notice them. She was also trying to keep up with Paula who seemed to be running now instead of walking.

"So do you want to have lunch today?"

"Sure, that's fine. Where should I meet you and what time?" Paula studied Shelby for a second before asking her if she were sure. "Of course, I'm sure. Why would I not be? Besides, I need some fresh air, will help clear my head."

"Okay then, great! Why don't you meet me downstairs in the main lobby of our building at twelve thirty?"

"I'll be there."

Shelby and Paula walked the rest of the distance to their office, taking in the beauty of the September morning and going on about their lunch plans.

Shelby arrived at her desk with five minutes to spare and bagel in hand. "Good morning, Helen," Shelby said with a sly smile. Helen Spell was the office administrator at Cordial Law Firm where Shelby worked and had been there for five years prior to Shelby. She had the reputation of being a stickler for being on time.

"Morning, Shelby, how are you?"

"Good, thank you." Shelby knew she was on time even with the train delay this morning. Helen probably wondered how she always seemed to make it with a few minutes to spare.

"Shelby, we have a few new people starting on Monday of next week. I'll e-mail you some necessary information. However, one person in particular… Alex Manson, a partner voted one of the best criminal lawyers in the world, brings with him a very large clientele, and we want him to be happy and comfortable."

"I see, I'll certainly do my part, Helen."

"I know you will, of course. You always do, don't you?" Shelby didn't know if that was a compliment or a bit of sarcasm. She decided to just smile and pretend she was happy to start her day with Helen breathing down her throat.

"Well, I've got a lot of work to do, always busy for me. I'm sure you'll find something to do with yourself today."

"Excuse me?" Shelby once again tried to determine where Helen was coming from with her remark.

"Oh, I just meant, you've been an office assistant for so long, you're probably used to the boredom that comes with your job."

"Boredom? I can only become bored if I have nothing to do. I have enough to keep me busy. Well I guess I should get right to work and I don't want to keep you from *all* that work you have waiting for you in your *office*." Helen attempted to smile, but failed, instead it turned into a look of regret and shame.

"I didn't mean to offend you in any way, Shelby!"

"No offense taken, believe me. I have learned to endure the worst conditions of my job since I've been here." Helen stared at Shelby for a second before turning on her heels and walking quickly away.

"Hey, Shelby!"

"Hey, Ricky, how long have you been standing there and how much did you hear?"

"A long time, and all of it. I'm glad you put her in her place, what an—"

"Stop!" Shelby was able to stop him before he got the word out. "Ricky, don't say it if it's not nice."

Ricky laughed. "Nice! I call it as I see it. What's going on, beautiful, and when are you going to let me take you to lunch again?"

"When you get some money to take me to lunch," Shelby said while logging on to her computer.

"Now see, did you have to go there?"

"You took me there. Ricky, what's going on?"

"Twenty bucks, Shel, that's all I need. I promise you, it's only until we get paid."

"My point proven. Oh, all right, but remember, this loan is good only until payday," Shelby said while handing Ricky the twenty-dollar bill.

"Thanks, Shel, thank you… I won't forget your kindness or to repay you," Ricky said while backing away from Shelby's desk and almost colliding with Helen in the process. "Sorry, Helen," he said as he turned just in time to avoid bumping into her. "I'm very sorry," he repeated, then raced out of the room with a quick wink at Shelby.

"How much did he borrow this time?" Shelby wanted to ask Helen to mind her own business, but thought again. After all, she did have rent to pay, a car note, and the list went on and on.

"Not much, you know Ricky, Helen, he's, well… Ricky. The day wouldn't be right if he didn't need something." Shelby smiled as she shook her head.

"I guess you're right, but still you'd think he'd get tired or embarrassed. I know I would." Helen walked over and dropped a pile of folders on Shelby's desk. "These are the profiles of those starting next week. Give special attention to the one on Alex Manson, picture included." Helen watched Shelby's reaction as she glanced at the photo of Alex Manson. "Handsome, isn't he?" Helen's slow smile made Shelby's stomach churn.

"He's not bad if you're into the pretty-boy type." Shelby closed the folder and turned to her computer in hopes of ending her conversation with Helen.

"You know, I'm not a bit fooled by your nonchalant attitude toward men. You and I both know that if the right one comes along... well, anyway, I've got to get back to work."

"I'm married, Helen, remember?"

"Well, you have to admit, he is definitely a looker!"

"Not bad! But I'm still married."

Helen studied Shelby for a second before asking her to make sure Reba got the profiles before three. Shelby watched Helen walk away with a combination of like and dislike. She had to admit that Helen, although a pain at times, had been very supportive of her during some very sticky situations, always making sure she was treated fairly. Even in her middle fifties, Helen was a very attractive woman with her beautiful olive complexion and large brown eyes. *Oh well,* Shelby thought, *there is something about her that I find very puzzeling for some reason.*

Shelby's morning flew by, and before she knew it, it was twelve twenty and time for her to meet Paula downstairs for lunch. She situated things on her desk to start on when she returned from lunch, picked up the pile of profiles, and dropped them off to Reba with a quick hello before dashing down to the main lobby.

"Hungry?" Paula asked with a big smile. "Oh, try these shoes on. I think they'll fit you."

"Perfect, thanks, Paula, I love them."

"Just don't get too comfortable, my friend. I want them back tomorrow morning. Give me your old ones. I'll put them in this large bag of mine for you. Hungry, right?" Paula asked a second time with a large grin.

"Starved!"

"So where to?" Paula asked, looking excitedly at Shelby. "I could eat almost anything. What about you?"

Shelby thought for a second before saying with a chuckle, "I know just the place!"

"Where?" Paula was hungry and didn't really feel like playing guessing games.

"The Barbecue Pit over on Madison Street. I hear the ribs are the best!"

"Okay, let's go," Paula said as she linked her arm in Shelby's and they headed for the Pit.

Shelby and Paula found a table near the center of the room and seated themselves. "Smells wonderful," Paula said as she picked up her menu and started glancing through it. She looked up to find Shelby lost in thought. "What is it, Shel?" Paula asked, as she reached across the table to place her hand over Shelby's hand.

"I was just thinking about life and how uncertain it is. I mean, one day everything seems to be falling in place, and the next day, things are all thrown off again. It's just so hard for me to get a firm grip on peace of mind these days."

"Thinking about the situation with you and Myron, the two of you being separated and all?"

"That and so many other things," Shelby said with a heavy sigh. "Paula, why won't Myron just admit he has been seeing someone, own up to it like any real man would?"

"You just answered your own question. He's no real man, honey. He's a jerk! I'm surprised you've put up with him as long as you have. I would have left him!"

"Am I supposed to be stupid, to believe that all those late hours he's been keeping are with his boys? All the times he had to rush out on a Sunday morning to buy a news-paper was the truth... I mean really? The Sunday paper is always delivered to our front door. Is he serious?"

"Listen, Shelby, if I tell you something, will you prom-ise not to be mad at me for withholding this information from you for the last month or so?"

"I don't know, Paula, maybe you'd better wait until after we've eaten. I may be in a better mood and less likely to smack you silly if I don't like what I'm hearing," Shelby said playfully.

Paula had to laugh, after all, that was the Shelby she knew. The five-foot-five bronzed beauty with long brown hair falling softly to her shoulders and framing her perfectly chiseled features. Her large light brown eyes were filled with sadness, but the fight was still there. Paula could see it. Large silver hoop earrings peeped from behind Shelby's thick mane and added to her fashionable silver necklace. She was down, Paula thought, but not out. That was evi-dent, not only in her eyes but in the way she carried herself, stylish and confident with her every move, even though her heart was broken. Battling her pain inwardly, she refused to let it surface, realizing life was too precious and too short to stress over the mundane.

"Really, Shel, I have something I have to tell you, something that, as a real friend, I think it's only right to tell you."

Shelby stared at Paula, a mixture of dread and fear made her nervous; however, she forced herself to remain calm. "Tell me." Shelby's words came out slow and uncertain. "Tell me!" This time they came out more forceful, more like a demand. Paula cleared her throat and bit her bottom lip as she looked Shelby directly in her eyes, her own eyes filled with pain and concern. She hurt for her friend, but she was determined to get it out.

"Remember…" Just then the waitress came to their table.

"Afternoon, ladies, ready to order?" she said with a cheerful smile. Shelby felt sick. She knew, even without Paula saying it, she knew what she was about to hear couldn't be good. She'd completely lost her appetite.

"I'm sorry, would you give us a few more minutes, please?" Paula asked the waitress while looking up at her with pleading eyes, begging her to leave them alone.

"Of course, I'll be back in about ten minutes. Take your time looking over the menu. There is no hurry." The waitress gave Paula a reassuring smile and walked away.

"Remember last Thursday when I left work early to meet someone?" Paula said cautiously and forged ahead. "I was with Myron."

"Myron?" Even though Shelby knew the worst was yet to come, she still couldn't seem to prepare herself for it. "You were with Myron, my husband Myron?"

"Yes," Paula said while looking down at the table. Paula thought, *yes*, such a simple word, yet right now it sounded like a word that shouldn't be used in public or in any decent conversation. Shelby stared at Paula for a second, narrowed her eyes, and smiled to herself.

"So what's this, Paula, an invitation to lunch to soften the blow?"

"What?" Paula said. She was a little offended by Shelby's reaction.

"Have you been seeing Myron? If so, it's over between us. It's just a matter of our taking that final step. I just need proof that he has been unfaithful, so if you've got it, by all means, give it to me."

"Seriously? We are friends! Best friends Shelby! I would never do that to you! How could you even think such a thing of me?"

"I know, I know," Shelby said while shaking her head and playing nervously with her silverware. "I'm sorry, Paula."

"Like I said, I was with Myron. He called and asked me to dinner. I was a little hesitant, considering what's going on with you two. My loyalty is to you foremost and always."

"I know, Paula, it's just that this thing with Myron and me has become so nasty. I'm on guard all the time, trust no one, and I hate it!"

The waitress reappeared and looked determined to get an order or kick them out. "What will it be, ladies?"

"I'll have the Cobb salad and iced tea," Shelby said.

"Same for me," Paula added quickly, in an effort to get rid of the waitress and continue their conversation. The waitress went off to put their order in, and they were alone once again. "Well, to make a long story short, he wants me to ask you to give him a divorce. He told me he was in love with someone else," Paula said, wiping away the tear that managed to spill from her eye in spite of her effort to stop it.

Shelby began to laugh, a laughter that kept coming and grew louder. Paula just looked at her, not knowing what to do. "Oh, goodness, Paula, I'm sorry." Shelby straightened up in her chair and cleared her throat. "Myron asking me for a divorce… the man I begged to set me free a year ago… you know the man, the one who sent me to work a few times with a black eye, the one who smacked me in front of you simply because I denied a lie he'd just told." Shelby's voice started to break, but she fought to hold back the floodgate of emotion, determined to make her point. "He asked you to ask me for a divorce? Well, I guess that tells you a lot, doesn't it?"

The waitress returned with their food. Neither of them felt like talking anymore. Shelby asked herself mentally why she had agreed to have lunch with Paula anyway and why decide on the Barbecue Pit for lunch only to have a salad? She now realized why she always lunched alone. It was safer. She didn't have to spend the rest of her work day worrying about some crazy conversation she'd been enticed into. *There goes my relaxing lunch*, Shelby thought while taking a sip of her drink.

Shelby left her office around six-thirty that evening, feeling a little depressed. She thought she'd overcome the heartbreak of being separated from her husband, but today's reaction to Paula's news concerning her dinner with Myron was sure evidence that she hadn't. She decided to put the day's earlier activities behind her and enjoy the rest of her evening. After a quick stop at the drugstore, she headed home.

CHAPTER TWO

SHELBY ENTERED HER SMALL BUT nicely decorated apartment after picking up the mail and collapsed on the living room sofa. She tossed her newly purchased alarm clock on the sofa beside her. The drugstore had been a little more crowded than she liked, and she'd almost left the store without it. The ringing of the phone made her moan with annoyance, but she reached over and answered it anyway.

"Shel, hey, it's Ricky and I'm downstairs in your lobby. Can I come up?"

"Oh, Rick... I just got in, just sat down, and I'm in no mood for small talk tonight. It's been a rough one."

"Please? Besides, I have the money I borrowed from you today. Come on, it'll only take a few minutes. I promise I'll be out of there in no time."

"What's up, Ricky? Why can't this wait until tomorrow? I haven't even had my dinner yet."

"Great, what are we having? I'm on my way up!" Ricky hung up the phone before Shelby could say anything more. Shelby hung up the phone with a sigh of defeat. It seemed Ricky's anxious knocking at her door came in less than a second. Shelby walked slowly over to the door and opened it. Ricky stood facing her with a sheepish grin on his face.

"You know, this had better be good and I mean it, Rick!"

"I'll try to make this quick. Oh, wait, didn't you say we were having dinner?"

"Ricky!"

"I'm hungry. Why don't you whip us up one of those nasty-tasting vegetarian omelets of yours. If I die after eating it, at least I can hope to die in your arms," Ricky said with a burst of laughter. Shelby just looked at him as if he'd lost his mind.

"You know Ricky, as much as I like you, it's not enough to allow you to stand in my living room and insult me, so you'd better be cool, or you're out of here on your head!"

"Man, wow, Shel, you really are in a bad mood." Ricky looked at her with concern, trying to figure out what had her so upset.

"I'm sorry, Ricky, it's just that I'm so tired tonight. Your visit caught me at a bad time. There must be something going on. You never stop by without calling."

"I did call."

"From home, Ricky, you know, before actually leaving your apartment to come here, not from the guard's desk in my lobby," Shelby said sarcastically. "Come on in the kitchen while I start one of those nasty-tasting omelets you love so much." Ricky followed Shelby to the kitchen with a big grin on his face, pulled out a chair, and made himself comfortable while Shelby busied herself with making dinner.

Shelby glanced up to find Ricky dozing off to sleep. She studied him for a while and wondered why he never mentioned a girlfriend. He was so handsome at all of six feet, with that nice honey brown skin. He had a very nice grade of hair and kept it cut very close and neat. For a man who seemed to be broke all the time, he was always very nicely dressed. Even the jeans and black leather jacket he wore tonight looked of good quality and taste. Ricky stirred and Shelby quickly turned away so he wouldn't catch her looking at him. She couldn't help wondering what his story was, why no one had swooped him up yet. Shelby had to admit she was attracted to him, but she reasoned, it would never work with them. Plus, she was still married to Myron.

Myron, she thought, why had she ever let herself get involved with him in the first place? She should've just kept walking the day he stopped her on the sidewalk and asked her if she had the time. Any man who couldn't come up with a better line than that had to be trouble and trouble was Myron's middle name.

Ricky and Shelby sat at her kitchen table eating the dinner Shelby had managed to come up with in about an hour. "You're not as bad a cook as I thought you were," Ricky said while lifting a fork full of omelet into his mouth. "I'm not really into vegetables, but they're okay. They taste pretty good all mixed up with the eggs and the cheese. These potatoes are not bad either."

"I'm glad you like it. Sorry I don't have more of a spread for you," Shelby said sadly.

"Shelby, you and I have known each other long enough to talk to each other about almost anything. I know something is bothering you, and I'm willing to listen if you're willing to share."

"It's nothing, really. I know you didn't come here to discuss my life's shattering events. What's going on with you, Rick?"

"I'm leaving the firm."

"Leaving! Why? What's going on? Why are you leaving?"

"Well, it's like this. I'm a thirty-two-year-old man, still living at home with my mother, no car, bank account, or money. I can't go on like this!"

"Wait, wait, wait! Think about all you just said, Ricky, and you are quitting your job? That makes no sense!"

"I'm in trouble, Shelby, big trouble!" Ricky didn't really know how to tell Shelby what was going on with him. He held his head down and continued to speak slowly and as clearly as possible. "I owe people, Shelby. I owe them big time. They're not involved in your friendly neighborhood bank business. You don't pay them, they hunt you down like a dog and take care of you… you know what I mean?"

"You can't be serious!"

"There are people after me. I've got to go! So I guess this is kind of a farewell dinner for us." Shelby could see the pain and fear in Ricky's eyes, saw them water. She jumped up and started clearing the table, as if doing so would erase what he had just said.

"How much do you owe them?" Shelby asked with her back turned to him, facing the sink full of dirty dishes. Wiping away her tears, she turned on the faucet to run water for washing the dishes. "I can get the money for you. You don't have to quit your job and leave everything."

"Shelby, baby, I owe people a lot of money, and I would never ask you to loan me that kind of money."

"I'm not worried about the money, Ricky. We are talking about your life here! Your life!" Shelby kept her back turned to Ricky while she spoke and started to wash the dishes. Ricky stared at his plate. When he finally lifted his head, he stared at Shelby's back and wished she was a free woman, free to be with him, free to be with anybody but that no-good husband of hers. Shelby's tears came in a rush. She gasped in an effort to hold them back, but they wouldn't stop. "We can work this out together, Ricky. We just need time," she said as she turned to face him.

"I don't have time, Shelby. My time is up. It's run or die." Ricky stood, wiped his mouth with a napkin, then slowly walked over and put his arms around Shelby. He just held her tightly for a while. He then buried his face in her neck and whispered, "I love you." Pulling away from her, he lifted her hand and placed a crumpled twenty-dollar bill in it, then turned and left, closing the door softly behind him.

Shelby sat at her kitchen table, letting her tears stream down her face. She didn't bother to wipe them away or blow her nose. How long she sat there like that she didn't know nor did she care. This was, without a doubt, one of the worst days of her entire twenty-eight years of existence. Not only did Myron have the nerve to go through her best friend to ask for a divorce instead of facing her like a man—the coward, she thought—now she was going to lose Ricky too. She loved Ricky. So what if he was always broke, always borrowing money from her. He was still one of the sweetest friends she ever had. She could tell him anything, call him anytime day or night. She'd shared things with him that she hadn't even told Paula.

Shelby finally slowly pushed herself away from the table, cleared it, and dropped the rest of the dirty dishes in the sink. She walked to her bathroom, turned on the water, and washed her face, then went to her bedroom and fell across the bed, not even bothering to take her clothes off.

CHAPTER THREE

THE SOUND OF THE RAIN brought her sleep to a regretful end. She'd been dreaming, dreaming of happier times spent with Myron. Times of laughter and surprises—where had those days gone? She wondered when the laughter had stopped and the abuse begun? What had made her husband's kind words turn to insults and malicious accusations? Shelby wondered why Myron used words to inflict pain upon her more than physical abuse. Sometimes, she felt she could endure the physical abuse more than the verbal. The few times he had struck her were fast and over. The sting of the blow lingered for a short while, but then it was gone. The words, the horrible words she just couldn't erase from her mind. He had called her a whore, a nut; he had tried to make her believe she was mentally unstable, but she knew she was the sane one and he the insane one. Things had gotten so bad, the abuse so painful, she'd decided to leave him or she was sure she would lose her sanity. She'd start to believe all the horrible things he'd called her and accused her of being were true. Glancing at the clock on her night stand, she thought about the time, eight twenty-three in the morning. She'd slept through the night, clothes and all, but she felt better, more rested than she'd felt all week.

All the things she needed to do that day raced into her mind. What day was it? she wondered. Saturday, it was Saturday. She remembered now and the fact that last night had been a Friday night when Ricky said goodbye to her. She forced herself to stop thinking about Ricky. There were a bunch of other things needing—no, demanding her attention. The one thing that seemed to overrule everything else right now was her meeting with Myron this morning. They were to meet at the Bradley Coffee Shop for breakfast and to discuss their separation.

The sun had come up; it looked hot out already. What to wear for her meeting with Myron? What did it matter? He wouldn't notice or care. In all of their three years of marriage, he'd never complimented her no matter how hard she'd tried. However, if an attractive woman entered the room they were in, he'd make it perfectly clear to her that given the chance, the woman would be in her seat and she out on the street.

Myron paced back and forth in front of the coffee shop. Was she late? she asked herself. She shot a quick glance at her watch, ten thirty-eight. They were to meet at ten forty-five, so what was the problem? Why was he pacing and looking as if he was angry at the world? she wondered.

"Hello, Myron," Shelby said while trying to muster up a smile and sound as pleasant as possible. Myron turned in the direction of her voice, studied her for a minute before offering his hand to her. Shelby looked at it, confused, trying to figure out the meaning of this seemingly kind gesture of his.

"I promise not to break your arm, Shel. Take my hand. I'm your husband. There is no need to fear me." Shelby stared at Myron. All the pain he'd inflicted on her, all the unwarranted pain she'd had to endure from him came rushing to the front of her mind. Her words came before she realized what she was saying.

"Husband? Is that what you are to me, Myron? My husband? Wow! You know, it's funny, but for some odd reason, I'd always thought of you as more of my antagonist than my husband. She sighed before saying, "Look, I'm sorry, let's not bring up the old, the past. Why bother? It's over anyway."

"Over? Nah, Shelby, it's not over. It's not over until I say it's over."

"Wait, aren't you the one who asked Paula to ask me for a divorce? I'm not afraid of you anymore, Myron, so cut the bully boy crap," Shelby said as she pushed past him and headed for the door of the coffee shop.

"Not afraid of me, Shelby?" Myron said as he slid his hands into the pockets of his trousers.

"No, Myron, you don't have that kind of control over me anymore."

"Oh, really, then what kind of control do I have over you?" he asked with a sly smile. *I really think this man has lost his mind, I mean he really has* she thought while holding one hand on the door knob. Shelby turned to face him.

"I still love you Myron, sadly, I do. But I don't worship you and I'm strong enough to walk away from you. I'm here today because I chose to be here, not because of you having any kind of *control* over me so get over yourself! I want to believe I can find something worth fighting for in this marriage, but you are making it very hard for me to uncover it if it's there!

Let's just get this over with. I have better things to do today than to stand here and play mind games with you."

Myron laughed and followed Shelby into the coffee shop. Shelby chose a booth as far in the back and secluded as possible. If Myron got nasty, she didn't want it heard by anyone in the shop. Some of the people there knew her, knew him, and she just couldn't handle that. She was a very private person.

Shelby settled herself in the booth before stealing a glance at Myron. She had to admit, he looked good. His hair was cut close, tapered neatly around his ears and fore-head, framing his perfect mouth. His skin looked clean, clear, not a pimple anywhere. His eyes were beautiful, slanted eyes. Did she really find him unbearable, or was it her fear of being attracted to him that really bothered her? She played with the question in her mind. If she really dis-liked him then why did she find him so attractive, desirable even? What was wrong with her? She was here to discuss her separation from him not be turned on by him. She had to get a grip.

"So," Shelby said as she cleared her throat. "How have you been, Myron?" He smiled at her, then reached over to place his hand over hers. She didn't try to stop him.

"I'm miserable, Shel, I want… I need you back."

"Is that so? That's not what Paula said."

"Paula?" He was trying to figure out where the conversation was going.

"You know Paula, my co-worker, my best friend, the one you suggested I try to be more like, the one you said you'd trade me for in a hot second!" Myron ignored her remark and played with her baby finger.

"Must we turn this into a catfight, Shelby? Come on, give a man a break. I'm really trying here."

"Trying! Trying to do what, Myron, get me back in bed with you? Or do you really want to make it work with us this time, the way you said you wanted to work things out between us a month ago, only to turn around and hurt me again."

"Don't be bitter, Shel. It's ugly."

"Everything about our marriage for the last two years has been ugly, Myron. The women, the abuse, the lies!"

"All right, all right, stop it! I don't want to argue with you. I'd hoped that we could discuss things between us like two adults. Why I ever thought we could do that, I don't know, because I'm still dealing with a child. A child, Shelby, camouflaged by the lines of old age and too much makeup!"

Shelby picked up the glass of water the waitress had sat before her earlier. She slowly raised it to her mouth and sipped just a little of it. Keeping her movements slow and careful, she fought to maintain her composure. She took so long before she replied that Myron let out a loud sigh and began to move around in his seat impatiently.

"You know, Myron, it's remarks like the one you just made that has us in the situation we're in today. But it's okay. I know you can't help yourself. Men like you need to resort to juvenility at the expense of others, just so you can feel better about yourself. You have to feel superior to the woman you're involved with. It's your way of thinking you're in full control of her. But make sure you not only listen to me but that you hear me as well. You don't control me, Myron, not anymore. So go ahead and hurl your nasty little insults if it'll make you feel like a grown man, even though your mentality is that of a five-year-old throwing a temper tantrum because he can't have his way."

She picked up her glass for another sip of water. The waitress appeared to take their order. She looked first at Shelby, then at Myron. Her eyes lingered on Myron a little longer than necessary. Shelby smiled and shook her head while thinking to herself, *Honey, if you only knew.* Shelby cleared her throat loudly in order to break the spell Myron had obviously cast on the waitress, then said, "I'll have the special of the day." Myron turned to the waitress and gave her one of his million-dollar smiles. "Oh, heavens, I'm going to be ill," Shelby said too loudly.

Myron turned to her with a smirk before saying, "Don't be jealous, baby. You know you're the only one for me."

Shelby played into his sarcasm by saying, "You know, baby, I feel the same way. Every minute we're apart drives me closer to insanity."

"I don't think you two are ready yet. I'll just come back in about five minutes," the waitress said and walked away shaking her head.

"You know, Shelby, we were good together, you and I. Best friends who promised we'd always stick together, no matter what. I must admit we've had some pretty rough times, but we've always been able to work it out. Why can't we work it out now?"

"It's simple, Myron, you're not willing to change your horrible ways and I'm not willing to put up with them." Shelby's bottom lip trembled, her eyes watered, and she scolded herself mentally for being so emotional.

"I love you, I've always loved you. I tried to give you everything you wanted—the house, the clothes, the cars. What more could you ask for?"

"You. You gave me all of that, Myron. How you were able to afford it, I don't know, but I never really had you or your unconditional love, and without that, what good is a bunch of material crap that eventually erodes and fades away?" A tear rolled down one side of Shelby's face. She quickly wiped it away with a trembling hand. She simply had to get control of herself.

"Don't throw it all away, girl. We still have something left to work for." Myron's words were desperate, pleading even.

"I simply can't take it anymore. I was a good wife to you, did everything humanly possible to please you. I kept our home clean, worked a sixteen-hour-a-day job some-times, and still made sure you had a good meal for dinner. I starved myself right into the hospital, thinking I was too fat and undesirable to you. Come to think of it, Myron. You never even came to see me, not even once while I was there, not even a phone call.

Then when I returned home from the hospital, I went right back to doing the same things, things to please you, because I loved you and wanted to keep my husband, save my marriage. But nothing I did was ever good enough for you. You know what the really sad part about this is for me? she said while dabbing away the tears from her face and eyes. "The fact that I'm willing to work with you but you are not willing to work with me. It's taken me a long time to realize this and an even longer time to accept it. Although this realization hurts me very deeply, I've finally accepted it, and now it's time for me to move on. We are creatures of habit, Myron. You have a habit of inflicting pain on others. I'd fallen into the habit of accepting it—not anymore!"

Myron took both of Shelby's hands in his, pulled them to his lips, and lightly kissed them before saying, "I promise you, I will never hit you again, Shelby. I mean it this time. I'll get professional help, whatever, just let me come home, please, baby… I want to come home to you."

"Have you heard anything I've said to you? I can't do it anymore, Myron, I cannot do it!" They stared at each other, realizing their conversation was going nowhere fast. "It wasn't the blows that hurt me most, Myron. It was the words. Why did you say those awful things to me, try to make me doubt my sanity, why!"

Myron stared at the table before slowly dropping Shelby's hands, rubbed his head in frustration before saying, "Look, I know what I did was wrong. I'm not perfect and that's what you wanted from me, perfection!"

"Not perfection Myron, *effort*! You couldn't even give me that."

Myron stared at Shelby, he was getting angry but he suppressed it knowing he'd get no where with her if he allowed it to get the best of him.

"Listen, I don't feel very much like continuing this conversation right now. I'll call you later."

"I've changed my phone number, Myron. It's now an unpublished number." He looked at her in disbelief.

"You're kidding, right? So are you going to give it to me, Shelby, or do I have to beg for that too?"

"No, I'm not going to give it to you. I'll call you when and if I'm available to meet with you again, but until then, let me make it perfectly clear to you that I'm done negotiating our farce of a marriage with you. If you really want us to work then I'm on board, if not, please stop wasting my time with your foolishness."

Myron smiled and finished his water, stood up from the table, calmly buttoned the center of his expensive black suit jacket, and walked out without looking back. It took all she had not to go after him. He looked so good, so fit, so right. She wanted him, she wanted him bad, but she let him go, realizing that a few minutes of pleasure just wasn't worth a lifetime of pain.

Shelby got up from the table and walked out the door. Once she was sure Myron was nowhere around, she used her cell phone to call and schedule a hair appointment for the afternoon. She'd seen a pair of black pumps in the mall. If she ever needed them, she needed those shoes now. She felt she needed something to keep her from falling apart. She decided she would buy the shoes after getting her hair done. "It must be time for my cycle. All I seem to be able to do is cry here lately," she said to herself.

* * * * *

Just as she'd finished paying for her shoes, her cell phone rang and it was Paula.

"What's up, girl?"

"Hey, Paula, nothing much, I'm at the mall."

"You sound bad, like you've been crying."

"I just left Myron. We met to discuss our separation. I still love him, Paula. Isn't that insane?!"

"No, not really," Paula said, trying to show her support in her voice. She felt bad for Shelby because she knew she truly wanted to save her marriage, make it work. However, Myron, well, they both knew being married to anyone or how he treated them was not the focal point of his life because money was.

"He looked so good! Paula, it's just not fair. Everything about him was right today. His hair was cut close, his suit fell perfectly on that tall, lean body of his. I wanted to invite him back to my apartment, but I knew that would've been stupid."

"Shelby…" Paula's words were slow and cautious, but she had to say what was on her mind. "Shel, don't get me wrong. I'm on your side here. It's just that sometimes we can push a person to the point… do you understand what I am trying to say?" The silence between them hung in the air for what seemed an eternity.

"Paula, what do you mean by that? Come on, I know I have my moments just like anyone else, but what could I have done to deserve him hitting me, calling me names such as slut and dog? I'm a human being, Paula. I didn't deserve that. No one deserves to be treated that way. He hurt me, Paula! He almost destroyed me mentally and physically."

Shelby realized she was shouting into the phone, then remembered where she was and tried to lower her voice.

"Okay! Okay! I'm sorry! You're right. No one deserves to be treated that way."

"He cheated on me too, I may not have proof of it yet, but deep down in my heart I know he did." Shelby felt she had to get it all out, right there in the open, on the sidewalk for the world to hear.

"Do you want me to come over tonight? I can pick up some food and be at your place by seven. Is that all right with you?"

"No, don't come. I want to be alone tonight. I appreciate the offer, Paula, but I'm just not feeling very sociable today. I need some time to myself."

"I understand, then tomorrow maybe?" Paula wasn't giving up. She was worried that something bad would happen if she didn't get to Shelby soon. Something just wasn't right in her voice, she felt.

"I know what you're thinking. You're thinking I'm about to break down, lose it, aren't you? Well, let me tell you, a year ago, I may have, but those days are gone. I want to live. I want to thrive and I will. My pity party is over, so don't worry. I'll be fine, trust me."

"I'm calling you later and that's it. If you don't answer, I'm coming over, Shelby, and I mean it."

"Paula, I am fine, believe me!"

"Okay. Oh, by the way, did Myron find another job yet?"

"What?"

"He lost his job. Didn't he tell you?"

"As a matter of fact, he didn't. Paula, I've got to go or I'll be late for my hair appointment. I'll talk to you tonight." Shelby hung up before Paula could respond. She couldn't help wondering how Paula knew Myron had lost his job. She seemed to know more about her husband than she did. Jealousy was trying to raise its ugly head. She knew it and refused to give into it. She and Paula were best friends. She trusted her, believed she would never do anything to hurt her. *But how, how did she know Myron had lost his job?* she thought to herself? So that's why he wanted to come home to her. He was out of a job and probably about to be out on the street. Myron was never one to save money. He loved women and clothes too much for that. *I should've known something was up when he declared his love for me today.* Myron Malloy, without a doubt, is the perfect definition of the phrase *dirty dog*!

Shelby was pleased with her hair. She liked Fallen, who always listened to her and gave her just what she asked for in a haircut. Paula called around seven fifteen, and they talked about twenty minutes, long enough to assure Paula that Shelby was all right.

Although the thought of Myron losing his job and how Paula knew about it kept coming to mind, she refused to ask. Shelby squashed the desire to ask each time the thought tried to force its way to the surface.

CHAPTER FOUR

MONDAY MORNING, AS USUAL, CAME too soon. The only difference between this Monday and last Monday was her new alarm clock. Shelby set the alarm for six-thirty and it worked, too perfectly she thought as she reached over to shut it off. It was still dark outside as she rolled herself out of bed and made her way to the bathroom to shower. She let her oversized sleep-shirt fall to the floor as she reached up to turn on the shower. As the steam from the shower rose, she stuck her head in so it could fall on her face and help wake her up.

Today was the day the new people were to start in her office, she remembered, so she decided to put a little extra work into pulling her look together. She complimented herself on deciding to have her hair done over the weekend. Showered, partially clothed, and after putting on a little blush and adding a touch of lip gloss, she walked over to the bed and picked up the navy blue dress she'd chosen for the day. The dress was straight and complimented her size 8 shapely frame well. A pair of small pearl earrings were her only accessory besides a pair of slim navy blue heels.

Shelby glanced down at her feet before heading to the train station, a short walk from her apartment. Her shoes had to match today, she thought and laughed to herself as she remembered the mismatched shoes she wore to work on Friday. She had the ones Paula loaned her in her bag, ready to return. Finding a seat on the train easily, she felt good, confident, and ready to face the day ahead. Her morning was going well.

She pulled out her book and started to read. Just as she started to turn the page, she had a funny feeling she was being watched. She glanced out the corner of her eye, not wanting to give her suspicion undue attention. Why was she feeling this way? she wondered. She couldn't go back to her book without knowing for certain if she was being watched. Taking out her compact and pretending to fix her hair, she used the mirror to see who was behind her, then quickly glanced to her right then to the left. That's when she saw her, the lady, the dirty little lady she'd given the ten dollars to last week.

Was it a coincidence that she was on the same train this morning. Had she been following her? What? "Calm down, Shelby," she said quietly to herself. "You are being paranoid." She made an effort to relax and return to her book. Just when she'd gotten to the middle of the page, she noticed it, a smell that could not be ignored. What in the world, she thought to herself. Looking up, there she was, standing by her seat. Shelby thanked goodness there was someone sitting beside her.

"Morning, miss, it's me. Remember me from last Friday? I got my Mittens some food and had three dollars left, so I bought me some food too. Can't thank you enough, miss. Yes, ma'am, can't thank you enough!"

The passenger seated next to Shelby moved to another seat, and the little old homeless woman quickly sat down beside Shelby. Shifting her position so as to avoid contact and the smell as much as possible, Shelby managed to turn and give her a polite "you're welcome." Against her will, Shelby automatically put her hands to her nose in an effort to block the smell of the woman. "You're looking real nice this morning, miss. Yes, ma'am, you're looking real nice. Something bothering your nose, Miss?"

"Thank you, big day at work today. Thought I'd try to look a little nice, and no, my nose is fine, thank you."

"Oh, you are a pretty one, you are. Yes, ma'am, a real beaut. Bet your parents are real proud of you." Shelby just smiled at the lady and tried to go back to reading her book. The train approached her stop, and Shelby gathered her things to get off.

"Well, it was nice seeing you again…"

"Augusta, my name is Augusta. Thought I told you that."

"I'm sorry, you may have."

"Come to think of it, I didn't tell you, but what's in a name, right?" Augusta smiled, revealing her perfectly white even teeth. Shelby wondered how she was able to have such nice teeth when the rest of her was such a mess.

"This is my stop. Have a good day."

"You too, miss. I'll be seeing ya," Augusta yelled as Shelby quickly made her way through the crowd and off the train.

The walk to the office was pleasant. *September is a beautiful month*, Shelby thought, *not too cool and not too warm.* After stopping at the bakery and picking up breakfast, she took her time walking the short distance to her office. She had plenty of time thanks to her new alarm clock. Once at her desk, she found the folder on Alex Manson laying in front of her, placed there by Helen, no doubt. Shelby picked up the folder and slowly opened it. Leafing through it, she found a lot of impressive information on him along with his award-winning photo. He looked to be in his late thirties, light complexion, dark wavy hair, and deep-set eyes. She had to admit that he was a very handsome man. Shelby glanced up to find Alex Manson standing right in front of her.

"Good morning, I'm Alex Manson. I see an introduction has already been made by way of my profile."

"Mr. Manson, good morning and welcome. I'm sorry, I didn't hear you come in."

"Not a problem! I'm sorry, your name is?"

"I'm Shelby Malloy, office assistant." Shelby quickly closed the folder and extended her hand to welcome Alex Manson more warmly. "Please make yourself comfortable. I'll give Helen, our administrator, a call for you."

"Thank you."

* * * * *

"So you met Alex Manson this morning in the flesh. What do you think?" Paula asked as she took a bite of her sandwich.

"He's okay."

"Just okay? The way Helen described him, he is the best thing since sliced bread," Paula said as she laughed and winked at Shelby.

"Forget it. I'm not moved by money and looks. He is just another man to me."

"Whatever!"

"I mean it, Paula. I think Mr. Manson is more your type."

"Really, and what is my type?"

"Let's see," Shelby pretended to think for a moment. "Oh, he must have money, and then he must have money. Did I mention he must have money?" Shelby said as she burst into laughter.

"All right, all right… I get the point."

"I'm just kidding, Paula, but I do mean it when I say this one is not for me!"

"Whatever you say, my friend. We'd better get moving. We have exactly ten minutes to get back to our desk."

The rest of the day passed pretty quickly. Shelby didn't realize it was practically five o'clock. She was clearing her desk in preparation to leave when Helen walked up.

"Shelby, I realize this may be a terrible inconvenience for you, however, I still have to ask. Would you please join me and Alex Manson for dinner this evening?"

"What? Helen, I'm an office assistant. Why am I being asked to join you and Mr. Manson for dinner tonight?"

"Well, the invitation is at Mr. Manson's request, my dear. He figured you would know the ins and outs of the office better than anyone."

"Helen, you and I both know this is highly unusual. I don't mean to be uncooperative, but I have to say I don't understand his request and would prefer not to join the two of you for dinner tonight; plus, I have plans for the evening already, I'm sorry. You are the office administrator. You know this office like the back of your hand. I'm sure you can supply Mr. Manson with any needed information about our office."

"That may be true, but it's your company he is requesting. I think he only invited me out of courtesy."

"I'm sorry, Helen, but I must respectfully decline. I really do have other arrangements for the evening."

"What a shame. I'll apologize to Mr. Manson for you. Have a lovely evening and I'll see you tomorrow."

"Good night, Helen." After Helen left her desk, Shelby just sat there for a few minutes trying to figure out what had just happened. She decided she'd better not spend too much time thinking about it because Helen might come back and catch her still at her desk.

*   *   *   *   *

After unlocking the door to her apartment and kicking off her shoes, Shelby let out a heavy sigh. She walked over to the sofa and sat down, then thought it better to lay down. Grabbing one of the stuffed pillows, she buried her face in it, then turned on her side and was asleep before she realized it. The phone was ringing, or was she dreaming? It took her a few seconds to realize the phone was actually ringing. She ran to her bedroom and snatched up the receiver before it could stop. "Hello," she said, a little short of breath.

"Ms. Malloy, it's Alex Manson. You sound a little winded, hope I'm not disturbing you." Shelby looked at the clock on her night stand, ten twenty-five. Why was he calling her so late? she wondered.

"Mr. Manson?"

"Please call me Alex."

"Okay, Alex, is there something wrong? Can I help you in some way?" A thousand thoughts raced through Shelby's mind, foremost was how he'd gotten her number.

"As a matter of fact, perhaps you can be of help to me. You see, I'm trying to find an anniversary gift for my wife. It's this weekend, and I was hoping you could suggest a place to purchase jewelry. I hope you don't mind, but I asked Helen for your number. I noticed the pearl earrings you were wearing today and was hoping you could tell me where you bought them."

"I see, well, they were a gift to me from my husband, and unfortunately, I don't know where he purchased them."

"Your husband?" Shelby thought she detected a bit of surprise in his voice, but couldn't be sure.

"I could ask him if you'd like?"

"No, no, don't put yourself through any trouble, really. I'll work something out. Good night, Shelby, I'll see you tomorrow."

"Good night." Here lately, Shelby thought, her life was full of endless surprises.

The week was over. Alex Manson was settled in his office, and the rest of the new arrivals were all set. Helen,

Paula, and Shelby worked overtime all week to make sure everyone was happy with their new office assignments. It was now seven thirty and Shelby was more than ready to go home. She'd let Paula talk her into meeting her at Ravi's for drinks after work, but after that, she was determined to head straight home. As she stepped out of her building, she noticed a light rain, the air had a clean, washed feel and scent to it.

Sprinting the few blocks to Ravi's with her head down, she collided with Alex Manson. In an effort to avoid the collision, although unsuccessful, she turned her ankle while trying to move too quickly. Before she knew it, she was lying flat on her back, her dress twisted around her knees and one of her shoes had come off. Alex rushed to help her, asking all the while if she was all right. She knew he was genuinely concerned but also noticed the effort he made to conceal his amusement.

"Are you all right?" he asked as he reached out his hand to help her up.

"Yes, I'm fine, thank you." Shelby accepted his hand, and together, they were able to get her up off the sidewalk. She was embarrassed beyond description, but she smiled anyway and joked about having two left feet. "My shoe?"

"Oh, I see it." Alex ran over to pick the shoe up from the curb of the sidewalk. "Here you are. I'm afraid the heel is broken." Shelby took her shoe, her hand shaking a little. She felt like a child who'd just gotten caught with their hand in the cookie jar. She tried hard to hide her shame. "Can I take you somewhere? My car is parked on the lot the next street over. I can get it and be back in a second to pick you up."

"Thanks, but I'm fine. I'm meeting Paula just next door for drinks, but I appreciate the offer." Shelby prayed he would just turn and walk away without another word, but such was not the case.

"Listen, Shelby, I'm sorry I ran into you, and I've told myself a million times that I should watch where I'm going."

"I… Alex, please, this is as much my fault as yours. I should've just taken my time and walked. I knew the ground was wet. Please don't give it another thought. Good night and have a nice weekend."

"Good night, Shelby," he said and walked quickly away.

"What now? Did I say the wrong thing? Did I offend him? Go home, Shelby. You're standing in public, in the rain, talking to yourself." Pulling out her cell phone, she dialed Paula and explained what had just happened and that she didn't feel up to drinks; she was heading home.

CHAPTER FIVE

THE ROOM WAS SMALL, DARK, and smelled of urine. The door to the bathroom had either been taken off or knocked off, perhaps the result of a fight, Ricky assumed. He sat on the side of the bed in his rented motel room. His eyes were red and his head hurt from thinking too long and too hard about a woman he'd never have, Shelby Malloy. He missed her so much he felt he'd lose his mind. He laughed at the thought, him a grown man, going crazy over a woman. *Really*, man?

He'd worked with Shelby for years and had always felt there was something special about her. Her eyes, those beautiful eyes, the way she narrowed her eyes and stared down anyone who would dare challenge her opinion on life. When did he start to have feelings for her? Was it the day she bought him his first lunch or the day she loaned him that first twenty-dollar bill he'd borrowed from her? He knew now, he knew exactly when it was. It was the day the two of them went to lunch for the first time. He had just eight dollars to his name and could only afford his sandwich and no drink. He remembered how she had ordered a soft drink with her sandwich, looked at the drink, and said, "This is a regular. I asked for a diet soda," and then asked him to drink it so it would not go to waste, then paid for his sandwich and hers. That's when he knew, without a shadow of a doubt, that he had strong feelings for her. Her person, her kindness, her—period. However, he also knew she would never belong to him because she was married to Myron. The thought of Myron made his pulse speed up and his head hurt more.

Shelby had introduced him to Myron, invited him over to have dinner with them several times. One night, while he was over for dinner and Shelby had gone to the kitchen to stack the dishes, Myron looked at him and asked if he could use a little extra cash. Thinking back, Ricky knew it was wrong, all wrong, but he trusted this man because of Shelby. If Shelby was married to him, he had to be a good person. However, a dog was what Myron had proven to be, in his opinion. A low-down dirty dog.

Now, broke and on the run, he was sitting in a filthy motel room fearing for his life, wondering where his next meal will come from, or if he'll even be able to finish his next meal before being shot to death or worse. It was almost one thirty in the morning, but he didn't care. He had to talk to Shelby. He needed to hear her voice. Hesitating before picking up the phone, he thought the worst she could do was hang up on him. The phone rang only six times but it seemed like sixty-six times.

"Hello, Shel?" There was a pause before she answered.

"Ricky… Rick, is that you?"

"Hey, you remembered my voice!"

"Of course, I remember your voice, silly. Where are you? I miss you, come back!"

"I miss you too, but I can't come back, not yet anyway."

"Ricky, please tell me what's going on. It's been almost a month. I can help you if you would just let me. I can't believe how much I miss you, it's crazy! Ricky. I cried myself to sleep after you left that night. It was horrible!"

"You cried over me? No way, did you really?"

"Stop it, I love you. You're one of my best friends."

"I love you too, Shelby."

"Then stop shutting me out of your life, talk to me." The pain was intense, but he refused to let Shelby hear the emotion in his voice.

"Shel, listen, I've got to go. I'll try to call you again later. I love you, Shelby, I love you," he said quickly and hung up.

"Don't do this, Ricky. Friends don't hurt each other like this," she said just above a whisper, still holding the receiver, knowing he wouldn't hear. She looked at the phone to see if the number he'd called from showed, but it didn't. Sadly, she hung up the phone.

CHAPTER SIX

PAULA AND SHELBY STOOD IN front of Klein's shoe store, staring in amazement at the price of the shoes.

"Those shoes are hot! Expensive but hot!"

"I don't know, they look like something a hooker would wear, to me."

"Look, Malloy, you need to live a little, get that husband out of your head, and start enjoying life again!"

"I'm trying. Ricky called me last night."

"Ricky Clay?"

"Yes, Ricky Clay," Shelby said with a sarcastic smile.

"What a gorgeous human being. So where is he? How is he?"

"I don't know the answer to either of those questions. I wish I did." The sadness in Shelby's voice and eyes were evident to Paula. Paula felt sad herself. Not only was Ricky wonderful eye candy but he was one of the sweetest men she'd ever met.

"I know how you feel. If Ricky was about six years older and had a more stable job, I'd be all over him."

"Is that so, Ms. Paula?"

"Yes, ma'am, it certainly is," she said, smiling to herself.

*   *   *   *   *

"I didn't know it was supposed to rain like this," Shelby sighed, staring out at the weather.

"They are saying all day, fine by me. It's Wednesday, and at five thirty today, I'm out the door, headed for beautiful Honolulu, Hawaii!"

"Paula, if I had a dime for every trip you've taken to Hawaii, I'd be rich."

"Don't be jealous. I invited you to come, but no, it's always some kind of excuse with you."

"I guess you're right. I'm just not in the mood for too much of anything until I see which way things will go with Myron and me."

"What do you mean how they will go? I thought it was decided that the two of you are getting a divorce." Shelby didn't respond to Paula right away. She looked out at the rain. The sky was dark, and the rain fell heavily. Had she known it would rain like this, she would have eaten lunch at her desk. "Shelby, did you hear me?"

"I still love him, Paula."

"Are you kidding me? You're crazy! This man has abused you several times, both verbally and physically. He cheated on you, Shel, several times, though we have no real proof yet, we both know he has. Each time you forgave him only to have him repeat the same thing over again, and you still love him? It's the rain and the darkness of the day. I don't know what else to blame it on, but something is screwing up your head today because you are certainly not thinking right!"

"All that you say is true, still, I have to try! I have to try to work things out with Myron Paula, and I just can't simply forget what we had, our marriage."

"Now you're talking, what you *had*, Shelby, not have. It's gone. It's over. Myron doesn't love you. Hell, that idiot doesn't love anyone but himself. Don't second guess yourself on this, stick to your decision to end that farce of a marriage with Myron, or you will regret it for the rest of your life. Pack him up and change the locks on your doors and windows, baby! Tell Myron it's over and then show him it's over, by not responding to any type of contact he tries to make with you."

"That's easy for you to say. You don't understand."

"Oh, I understand. I understand he is a user and abuser."

"As I was about to say, I'm really hurting and trying to understand why Myron turned into this ugly person, a person I never saw when we were dating. Why did he do this to us? We had everything we needed to make our marriage a successful one."

"Sadly, Shelby, your marriage was missing two key ingredients to make it a successful one: communication and loyalty. You told me you tried to talk to Myron about the problems the two of you were having, but he never made time to listen. We both know he wasn't loyal to you, Shelby. He listened to his friends, his parents, everyone but you, when you tried to talk to him, reason with him on matters pertaining to your marriage. He would just get angry with you, shut you out, and take their advice over yours, his wife. I know, because I saw it first-hand a few times."

"Stop! Just stop, I get it, all right! I get it!"

"Do you, Shelby? I don't think so, because if you did, you wouldn't be giving Myron a second thought!"

Paula was angry, determined to get her point across, refusing Shelby the opportunity to respond. "Listen to me, I know for a fact that you don't need Myron's support financially. I know you make enough money to support yourself comfortably, and that doesn't include the money your parents left you. You don't need Myron. If anything, he needs you. Cut him loose, because he is drowning you physically, mentally, and most dangerously of all, emotionally. He can no longer abuse you physically, so now you are allowing him to abuse you emotionally. Don't give into it, Shelby. Fight him with all that you've got."

"Paula, you don't understand what this is like, what I'm feeling. You've never been married."

"True, but I do have enough sense to see when a person is toxic, trying to blind me to the happiness and success I deserve in life. I see what Myron is doing to you, Shelby."

"Look, I don't feel like discussing this anymore, Paula."

"One last thing, Shelby, he didn't meet you to discuss your separation looking like he'd lost his job, although he had. He made sure his appearance would pass the test of a magnifying glass. Myron knew no matter how the discussion between the two of you went, if you didn't remember anything else, you'd remember how good he looked. That is what he wanted to leave on your mind more than anything, because he knew if anything would break you down emotionally, that fact would."

"Paula, please! I get it!"

"You know why you make decent money? It's because we at Cordial recognize your value, your hard work, and your loyalty. Paying you that kind of money is our way of saying we appreciate you and we love you. My point is this Shelby, when someone loves and appreciates you, they don't serve you peanuts. They serve you caviar. They show it. They give you their best. Myron, for the last years of your marriage, has served you nothing but rotten peanuts spat out by his mistresses and presented to you on a silver platter to disguise his filth. Myron is a smooth talker, Shelby. You know it and I know it. That's why I say he doesn't love you. If he did, he wouldn't treat you like trash. You're a beautiful and kind woman, Shelby, and any sane person would be glad to have you. But we both know that Myron Malloy is anything but sane."

"Wow! I didn't know you felt so strongly about my situation."

"I do. I care about you, Shelby. I'd do anything to make you happy, always remember that."

"So that great review I just received, did you have something to do with that?" Shelby asked with a puzzled look on her face. "I know you're in a position to review me, Paula."

"I guess you will never know cause I'm not saying."

"Oh, Paula, come on!"

"As I said, I'd do anything to make you happy and you earned it."

Shelby kept waiting for Paula to smile, to take some of the seriousness away from what she'd said, but Paula didn't smile. Instead, she stared at Shelby, willing her to understand the sincerity of what she was saying. Shelby looked off in to space and shook her head slowly before saying, "Thank you Paula. I could not have asked for a better best friend, I know that. I'm just hoping that one day Myron will see that our marriage is worth saving. Is it reasonable for me to want this, probably not, but I do."

"Shelby, tell me something please because I am really trying to understand," Paula said with a look of frustration on her face. "Please help me understand and I'm being totally serious here. Help me understand why you are fighting so hard to stay in an abusive marriage? Women who try to stay in situations like yours often wind up dead Shelby, *dead* do you hear me?"

"Goodness, we'd better get back," Shelby said while glancing at her watch and totally ignoring what Paula had just said. "I didn't realize it was almost one o'clock."

"I'm sorry, I didn't mean to preach you a sermon."

"Don't be silly. I needed to hear every bit of what you said, and it won't fall on deaf ears, I promise you. We are going to need an umbrella. It's still coming down out there."

"Here, take mine. I'm stopping in the drugstore next door to pick up a few more things for my trip, and hopefully, the rain will have stopped by the time I leave the store."

"Okay, listen, if I don't talk to you before your flight leaves tonight, have a fantastic time and safe trip. Who are you taking with you?"

"Just me, myself, and I. You wouldn't take me up on my invitation, even after I offered to pay for everything. So there is no one else."

"Thanks again, I could really use a get-away right now but I'd better not."

"I'll call you when I land. I love you, Shelby."

"Love you too," Shelby said as she hugged Paula, then turned to rush back to work.

Paula stood there until Shelby disappeared, then said to herself, "I'd do anything to make you happy, to make up for what I've done. I'm so very sorry, Shelby. But I promise you, it will never happen again." She then turned and ran into the drugstore.

*   *   *   *   *

Shelby sat in her bathtub full of bubbles, the smell of lavender scented the air. The large pillar candles cast a warm glow on the rich fuchsia walls of her bathroom. Six candles, and she'd positioned each of them just so, to give the room the warmth and feeling she desired. Her mind wandered to earlier in the day when she'd had lunch with Paula. Paula's words came to mind—"I'd do anything to make you happy." Even as Shelby remembered those words, she couldn't deny that there was a hidden message or meaning to what she was trying to say to her. Paula was trying to tell her something and had been trying for the last few months or so to get a message across without saying it directly.

"What is it, Paula? What are you trying to tell me?" she asked herself. "What are you trying to say to me?"

Paula, what a beautiful woman. Beautiful hair, skin, very shapely, and very fashionable. What was her story? She could have any man she wanted. The physical was definitely there, the money too. It was rumored that she earned a seven-figure salary and had been with Cordial over ten years. Paula's home was beautiful, one of the largest she'd ever seen. There was enough room for two families to live there comfortably, yet she lived alone, how odd. She never spoke of family other than her dad, one of the founders of Cordial, Queria, and Stein. No mention of a man in her life. Shelby remembered the last time she'd mentioned a man to Paula; it had made her mad. She just stared at Shelby as if she had two heads, then told her she needed to be more independent. "We don't need them. They need us," had been her answer to Shelby.

Well, I don't need a man, this is true. But it would be nice to have a decent one, she thought to herself as she stepped out of the tub and reached for the towel. After drying herself off and putting out the candles, she walked to the kitchen to put on a pot of coffee. She then sat down and thought about calling Myron. Why couldn't she stop thinking about him? Lately, he just would not leave her alone, dominating her thoughts. She'd even been dreaming about him. What was wrong with her? Paula was right. Myron didn't love anyone but himself, and he was making her an emotional wreck. Still, she found herself picking up the phone.

"Hello." Myron's voice came through the receiver nicely, not a deep voice but sexy nonetheless. He sounded cool, confident in himself.

"Hello, Myron, it's Shelby."

"I know it's you, Shel. You're my wife, remember? What's up?" Her heart gave a start. The way he was talking to her as if she was some female friend he didn't feel like being bothered with.

"I was… I was wondering if we could meet this weekend?"

"This weekend?"

"Yes."

"What for? I'm actually a little busy this weekend."

"Saturday and Sunday?" Shelby asked while trying to hide her disappointment and keep anger from taking over. "We need to finish up our discussion about the separation."

"I could be available one of those days, that depends."

"On what?"

"On what day you'd like to meet."

"Saturday."

"Then I'm busy Saturday. Oh, and Shelby, your new number is showing up, but don't worry, I won't be using it. I no longer need it, found a new job. Oh, and my number, pretend you never knew it." Myron hung up on her before she could get out another word. Shelby slammed the phone down so hard she injured her hand.

She got up from the table, turned to her left then quickly to her right. "Don't you cry, don't you dare cry," she said to herself through clenched teeth. "You just got what you deserved. Paula told you. She told you! But, no, you had to learn the hard way! I hate you, Myron, I hate you!" She stood there, her body shaking from rage and hurt, screaming over and over, "I hate you, Myron!"

CHAPTER SEVEN

EVERYONE WAS RUNNING AROUND TRYING to get stuff done on a late Friday afternoon at Cordial. Alex Manson and his team needed the help of all available hands to get a filing completed before five. Helen was running in circles, getting in everybody's way more than accomplishing anything.

"Shelby, please! Time is getting away from us," Helen yelled as she ran down the hall to her office. It seemed Helen was back in less than half a second. "Where is Paula?"

"Helen, Paula is on vacation, remember?"

"Whatever, then get me someone else in HR and call the courier already, for heaven's sakes! Find me someone who can round up some more free hands!"

"Why is she asking me to call a courier when she's still looking for people to help complete the document? The woman is a nut!"

"I heard that, Shel, and although it's true, thanks to this job, it's not very nice. Now get that courier on the line, missy. I'll take you to lunch Monday if he's here in the next forty-five minutes." Shelby called the courier.

"Watch. The courier will be here, and they still won't be ready."

"I heard that too!"

*   *   *   *   *

60

The train was late, and Shelby was tired. By the time she'd reached her stop and walked the few short blocks to her apartment complex, she was irritable and hungry.

"Evening, miss!" Shelby couldn't believe it. No, it simply couldn't be. There in front of her door sat Augusta, just as dirty and smelly as ever.

"Augusta, what are you doing here? Who let you in the building?"

"That man did."

"What man, Augusta?"

"That real cute one that sits in that box downstairs," Augusta said with a sheepish grin.

"You mean the guard at the desk?"

"If he's guarding the desk down there, then that's the one I mean."

"Oh, Augusta, I'm so worn out. Do you need more money?"

"No, ma'am, I just wanted to see you. I missed you. I haven't been able to catch up with you on the train. Thought maybe I'd been getting on the wrong train."

"Oh, well, I've been leaving a little earlier than usual. It's been so chaotic at work lately. But that's a part of life, right?"

"Life, yes, ma'am, that's life, chaotic."

"How did you know where I lived, and how are you getting money to take the train?"

"I followed you home that day, got off the train right behind you, without you even noticing. I saves my money right here." Augusta proudly showed Shelby a jar with a rusty top on it full of pennies, dimes, and nickels. "This here is my emergency savings. My life savings I keep in a jar in me bag right here, see?" Augusta said as she raised a dirty plastic bag to show Shelby what she was talking about. "It has all quarters in it, yes, ma'am, all quarters. See, I've got good sense when it comes to me money, never spend me last dime. Beg for some and save some of what I get. It's just that when I met you that day on the train, I'd fallen on hard times and didn't have a cent to my name and my Mittens had to eat."

"You followed me home Augusta?"

"I told that man in the box downstairs I was your mother. He looked at me a little strange but let me in. Yes, ma'am, he let me in."

Shelby walked past Augusta to unlock the door to her apartment. Once inside, she turned and looked at Augusta. She couldn't, she just couldn't bring herself to leave her standing in the hallway. She looked so pitiful and so helpless. Her beautiful gray eyes glistened with moisture, her hair matted and dirty.

"Augusta, what's wrong? Have you been crying?" Augusta looked up at her with pleading eyes. She folded and unfolded her hands nervously, positioning them as if she was about to pray. As she spoke, her weak voice broke and she started to cry uncontrollably.

"Me cat, she died today, miss. She died. She was all I had in this world," Augusta said as she raised a trembling, dirty, and bruised hand to wipe her swollen eyes. "Nobody else, nobody, miss, do I have. Yes, ma'am, not a soul in this world did I have but my cat, and now she done gone and left me too. I don't know why, miss, don't know why.

I was good to her. Yes, I was good to her. There were days when I didn't eat, miss, but I made sure me cat ate, yes, ma'am. I made sure she ate." Augusta continued to sob and wipe her swollen eyes. Shelby rushed to console Augusta. Forgetting the filth and the smell, she wrapped her arms around Augusta and pulled her tight against her chest.

"Augusta, I know this is a hell of a time to mention this, but I notice sometimes you say *my* and sometimes you say *me* when mentioning what belongs to you. It's *my*, try to remember that. Try to speak clearly and properly when talking to people so they can better understand how to help you."

"Okay, I will try."

"I'm so sorry, it's going to be all right. Here, come in and sit down. I'll make you some hot tea and something to eat. Do you like tea?"

"Yes, miss, I do. I sure do." Shelby helped her into the apartment, then ran to her bedroom and brought back a warm blanket to place around her shoulders before going to the bathroom to wash up, then to the kitchen.

Her cell phone rang just as she was putting a tea bag in Augusta's cup.

"Hello?"

"Greetings!"

"Paula, hey!"

"What's going on? Are you okay? You sound a little rushed."

"Well, I sort of have company."

"Oh, who? Anyone I know… Is it a relative?"

"Not quite."

"Then who, silly, come on, we tell each other everything. Wait, Myron? Shel, is Myron there? Please, please tell me that scum is not there, please!" Shelby took a deep breath then hesitated for a second while thinking of all the times Paula could have called today. Why did it have to be now?

"You remember the little old lady from the train?"

"What little old lady? I don't recall you introducing me to any little old lady."

"I didn't introduce you. She just kind of appeared on the train one morning while we were riding into work together."

Paula paused and thought for a second before saying, "Oh no, oh no, no, no, no! You didn't!"

"Paula, I've got to go, I'm making tea and I need to decide what to fix for dinner!"

"You've lost your mind. I'm convinced of it! You're talking and acting like she is some long-lost relative that just showed up for an overdue visit! Do you know that woman could have some type of dreadful disease!"

"Stop it!"

"She is filthy and you know it. Heaven only knows what's growing under her skin!"

"I don't see filth. I see a mother, a daughter, a grandmother. I see years of sacrifice and hard work, sleepless nights and hunger. That's what I see, Paula."

"That woman is filthy! I don't care how you choose to look at it or see it and she stinks to high heaven! Before she leaves, your entire place will smell like an outhouse! Well, it's a good thing I'm still on vacation and I won't be coming over tonight."

"I have to go now. Augusta is here and I've kept her waiting too long as it is. She needs some tea and something to eat. Good night." Shelby hung up before Paula could make another argument against Augusta being there.

Come on Paula, don't be such a heartless snob. I mean it could be you in Augusta's shoes and she in yours, the roles reversed. Then how would you feel? Shelby continued to think to herself about how Paula was acting concerning Augusta. Why was she so against Augusta? Why? Because she was homeless? Why do people judge homeless people so harshly, as if most of them chose to be in that situation? *Well, I will say this for them, they will say good morning to you while there are those with a job and a place to lay their head at night who won't even give you the time of day. But I guess there is a good reason for that. Most of them have their noses so high in the air they forget to look down to see there is an actual human being in front of them. Heaven forbid they lower their nose long enough to speak.* Shelby was angry and continued to mentally scold Paula and the likes of her until she remembered Augusta was in the other room.

Shelby shook her head and walked briskly to the bathroom to wash her hands. While washing her hands, she glanced over at the bathtub surrounded by the candles she always enjoyed while bathing. *No,* she thought to herself, *absolutely not. You will never get that tub clean again. No way, can't do it,* she said to herself while shaking her head back and forth and reaching for the hand towel.

"Something the matter, miss?" Shelby jumped out of fear, not realizing Augusta had walked up.

"Augusta, you nearly scared the life out of me. How long have you been standing there?"

"I just walked up. Are you all right, miss?"

"I'm fine, Augusta, listen to me. Wouldn't you feel better having some dinner after taking a nice hot bubble bath?"

"Bath, me, miss?"

"Of course, you."

"Oh no, miss, I can't. I don't got no place to go and get me no bath. Plus, I don't have any clean clothes or underwear to put on once I've washed myself, so I hardly see the point of it all." Shelby considered Augusta's words for a moment.

"Augusta, you are taking a bath tonight. I've got some extra night gowns. I'm sure they will fit and cover you until I can purchase you some new things."

"No, miss, please no. It's been so long I done forgot how to wash myself properly."

"Don't worry, I will help you. Now go back in the living room. Once your bath water is ready, I'll call you." Augusta hesitated, looked up at Shelby, then slowly turned and walked back to the living room.

Shelby hurriedly rinsed out the tub, then she poured two caps of bubble bath in the water while it ran into the tub. Something else was needed, she thought. Oh, alcohol, just a smidgen. Once the water was ready, nice and warm, not too hot, Shelby lit the candles and gave the aroma from them a chance to penetrate the air. She then walked to the living room to get Augusta.

"Augusta, where are you? Come on, your bath is ready. Augusta, are you there?" Shelby stopped in her tracks once she noticed the front door was open and Augusta was nowhere in the room. "Oh, Augusta, where did you go?" Shelby walked slowly to the front door, shut it, and put the lock on it. She walked to the sofa and sat down with a heavy sigh, then noticed the blanket she'd used earlier to put around Augusta. Picking it up off the floor, it occurred to her that it wasn't warmth or tea Augusta needed that night. It was someone to listen to her about the loss of her cat and she had provided that. Smiling to herself, she walked to the bathroom, pulled off her clothes, and climbed into the warm bath herself.

CHAPTER EIGHT

"WHO ARE YOU LOOKING FOR? My goodness, you've looked outside your door five times in the last twenty minutes."

"Paula, look, you are really starting to bug me. Every time I get up, your eyes follow me!"

"I can't help it. You're getting up too often and you seem distracted. Are you expecting someone?"

"Yes, I am."

"Oh, should I leave?"

"No, don't be silly. It's not a man."

"Pity," Paula said with a smirk while leafing through a magazine she had absolutely no interest in.

"So your vacation was awesome! The pictures tell it all. Who is that gorgeous man you were having dinner with in that first picture you showed me?"

"Nobody really, just someone who was looking for a roll in the sack, and you know I wasn't having that!" They both burst into laughter.

Paula tossed the magazine on the coffee table, stood up, and stretched. "Listen, I'm a little sleepy. You mind if I nap on your bed?"

"No, be my guest."

"You know, Shelby, you look a little tired yourself. There's plenty of room on your bed for two."

"Thanks, Paula, but I'm fine. You go nap. Please help yourself."

"If you change your mind, you could take the top part, and I, the bottom of the bed. That way we both could get some rest."

"Thanks, but I have some things to do, but you go ahead. I'll be fine."

"Okay, well, I am on my way to dreamland. Join me later if you'd like." After Paula closed the door behind her, Shelby turned to stare after her. Walking to the window, she looked out at the night. Paula? Could she really trust her? Could she? She'd never given her any reason not to Shelby continued to tell herself over and over in her mind, trying to convince herself that Paula would never do anything to hurt her.

"Enough! You are being ridiculous. You think too long. You think wrong," she said to herself. "Paula has always been there for me no matter what. She would never do anything to hurt me," she said softly to herself. Ricky wandered into her thoughts. Where was he? What was he doing? Was he hurt? What if something terrible has happened to him? Her mind was about to explode with what-ifs. Questions and confusion about Paula and Ricky ran together in her head and crowded out reason. She tried to force herself to stop thinking about both of them and just relax.

It was nearing dinnertime, and Shelby didn't feel like eating. She felt the pangs of hunger but ignored them because she didn't want to eat and didn't feel like cooking.

It would just take too much effort right now. Her life was filled with too many unanswered questions. Why hadn't she heard more from Ricky by now? Had those people after him caught up with him? she wondered. Myron, why she still loved him she couldn't figure out, but sadly, she did and she hated the fact.

Then there was Paula's surprise visit this afternoon. Why wasn't she still vacationing? She wasn't due back for another few days. She looked great and well rested to Shelby. *I guess for some people a little rest was all that was needed.* Yet Paula was in her bedroom getting what she felt was more needed rest. This thought puzzled her the most. Shelby wondered if she'd spoken to Myron since her return from vacation.

The magnificent gold bracelet Paula brought back for Shelby lay in its beautiful black velvet box on the coffee table beside the discarded magazine.

Dinner, something had to be done about it. Maybe if she busied herself with cooking, it would take her mind off other things. Walking to the refrigerator, she stopped suddenly to strain her ears. There was a faint sound coming from her front door. A knock, yes, that's what it was. Someone was knocking, but it sounded more like a tap than a knock. She walked to the door to peer out of the peephole, but there was no one there.

The noise was back again. What on earth could it be? She simply refused to make another unnecessary trip to the front door. Trying to dismiss the thought of checking the door just one more time, Shelby opened the refrigerator to survey food choices for dinner. "Let me see," she said to herself as she picked up several containers of leftover food to examine, and as with container after container, nothing appealed to her. None of it sparked any excitement or desire, period! "I know. I'll order dinner from the new Chinese place down the road. I hear the food is fabulous!"

"Whose food is fabulous?"

"Hey, I thought you were napping."

"I tried, but my stomach kept waking me up. Heard you mention Chinese food. Sounds great. Is there a menu?"

"Sure, I'll get it. I picked one up at their grand opening last week."

"Okay, while you're getting it, I'll answer your door."

"There is no one at the door."

"Yes, there is. Don't you hear that? Is the noise coming from somewhere in the back?" Shelby listened for a moment, then she heard the sound she'd been hearing all evening.

"Oh that, it's nothing. I've been hearing the same noise, and like you, I thought, it's someone at the door. When I checked, there was no one there."

"Well, let me just see. Why don't you go ahead and get the menu and I'll check it out this time?"

"All right."

Just as Shelby walked through the bedroom door in search of her bag, she heard the sound of the door closing behind her, then instantly felt a hand cover her mouth from behind her. She tried to scream, to free herself! But the person's grip was too tight. No air was the message sent to her brain! Panic gripped her, and she began to struggle wildly! She managed to elbow her attacker in the stomach and fought even harder to free herself!

"Will you come on. I'm hungry," she heard Paula say as she walked toward the bedroom. The person loosened their grip on her, turned, and jumped out the window.

Shelby rushed to her purse, pulled out her cell phone, and dialed 911. Paula rushed in the door and was about to scold her for taking too long, but could see she was upset and stood in silence until she'd finished talking to the police department. After Shelby hung up, Paula rushed to her.

"What the hell! What is going on?"

"Someone was here, Paula, in the bedroom when I came in to get the menu out of my purse!"

"What! Who?"

"Paula! Do you honestly think they took the time to introduce themselves?"

"I was just in here sleeping, oh my god! I could have been killed, murdered in my sleep," Paula said as she put her hands over her chest as if she was about to have a heart attack.

"Calm down, Paula, it's okay. The police are on their way."

"You have to move. You can't stay here after what just happened. They may come back!"

"Paula, please!"

"That must have been the noise we kept hearing! Oh my god!" Paula said again, unable to calm herself. "Are you all right? Did they hurt you?"

"No, I'm fine."

After the officers left, Shelby ordered the Chinese food for herself and Paula. She was determined not to let the fact that there was an intruder that night ruin her entire evening. They ate veggie egg rolls, chicken lo mein, and salad that made their mouth water. Afterward, Shelby said good night to Paula and told her she was going to shower and go to bed. Shelby returned from the bathroom to find Paula curled up on her sofa under a comforter.

"I thought you were leaving."

"Changed my mind. I am not leaving you alone tonight. Not after what just happened, no way!"

"Paula, please, I will be all right. The windows are locked. I will make sure the doors are locked, and it's not likely that whoever it was will return here tonight. They have to know I've notified the police."

"I'm not leaving you and that's the end of it. Now shut up and go get me another comforter and a pillow."

"You're impossible, you know that?"

"Of course I am, and you wouldn't have it any other way. Someone has got to look after you."

"Thanks for staying. I do feel better knowing you're staying over. Hey, why don't you take my bed and I sleep on the sofa?"

"Oh, heck no, if whoever that was does decide to return tonight, it will be you they find in that room and not me!"

"Chicken!"

"Whatever!"

"Night," Paula said as she snuggled up under the comforter to go to sleep. "Oh, tomorrow we go apartment shopping for you."

"What! I love this apartment. I don't want to move!"

"Shel, you have to. It's not safe here. Plus, this place is a little outdated. A move will do you good." Shelby thought about what she'd said for a second. Things were a little run-down, especially the carpet.

"But this is what I can afford."

"You and I both know you can afford a lot better than this. Listen, it can't hurt to look. Tomorrow is Sunday. It will be quiet. We can have brunch, then start our search. I'll drive. Now get some sleep."

"Ok, I guess, good night and thanks again."

"Welcome, night," Paula said while waving Shelby away.

*   *   *   *   *

Shelby and Paula searched for a full five hours before they spotted something that made them both stop in their tracks. They'd parked Paula's truck after deciding to walk the wooded neighborhood with well-cared-for lawns and beautifully detailed brick buildings, spaced so there were only three townhomes attached for each section. Each section was spaced so you could barely see the next section of homes nestled in between large oak and crepe myrtle trees.

"These are amazing, but I can't afford one of these. Besides, they are townhomes, not apartments."

"We're going in," Paula said as she grabbed Shelby by the hand and ran toward the building advertising the open house. Just as they entered, they were approached by a tall, slender woman with blue eyes and thick red hair pulled back in a ponytail. She wore a white shirt, a straight black pencil skirt, and red patent leather stilettos that contributed to her height.

"Good afternoon, ladies. I'm Haverty," she said while offering her hand to first Shelby, then Paula for a handshake. "Welcome to the Green Oak." *What a fitting name*, Shelby thought, since there were what seemed like billions of oak trees everywhere. Paula sprang into action.

"Hello, I'm Paula, and this is my friend, Shelby. I realize it's a little late but could we possibly have a tour of the home?"

"Nonsense, my doors are open as long as there are guests. As I do with all my guests, I invite you to join me in the dining room before I start the tour." Paula and Shelby followed Haverty into a spacious room decorated in mostly golds and browns, with a large, deep orange accent wall. There was a wrought iron glass dining table filled with various salads, chocolate-covered fruit, several different cheeses and crackers. "Please help yourself. I'll be right back." Haverty returned carrying a tray with three tall wine glasses and a choice of white or red wine.

"My goodness, this is quite a spread," Paula said, reaching for a small plate to help herself.

"We treat those who choose to purchase one of our homes even better." Shelby stole a glance at Haverty. *What a beautiful woman, they hit the jackpot choosing this one to sell their homes. Beauty, brains, and personality, a win-win combination for a sell*, Shelby thought to herself. *She is perfect!* "So, eat up, girls, then let's take that tour! I've taken the liberty of starting your application process. Basically, after your tour is done, all you will need to do is sign on the dotted line."

"Don't you think you're getting ahead of yourself?" Paula asked while chewing on a piece of cheese.

"Absolutely not. I have no doubt one of our models will be just what you're looking for, and there is no better choice than Green Oak. If there were, I wouldn't be here. Your search stops here because, hands down, we offer the best in home amenities, luxury, and price. So shall we start our tour?"

"Would you excuse us for a minute, please? I need to discuss some things in private with Paula," Shelby said.

"Of course, please, take all the time you need. I'll be out front when you're ready."

Shelby pulled Paula into a corner of the room where she felt they couldn't be heard by Haverty. "Have you lost your mind? I can't afford a home like this on my salary!"

"Shelby, people who make a lot less money than you do can afford a home like this and do you know why? Because they want it, and they don't doubt their ability to make it in a home like this. Now woman up and let's go take that tour!"

"I thought the saying was man up," Shelby said as she tried to slow Paula down who had started to go in search of Haverty.

"Woman up, man up, whatever! Let's just get this party started, missy. No more stalling, and you are clearly not a man. Let's go find that redhead!"

Haverty expertly and professionally took them through every room, pointing out the spaciousness of the rooms, the beautifully detailed fireplaces in one of the three bedrooms and one in the family room off the well-equipped and well-designed large kitchen, with its stainless-steel appliances and granite countertops. When they reached the living room, which Haverty decided to show last, with its twelve-foot ceiling and large palladium windows, Shelby had made up her mind. She had to have it!

After following Haverty to her office and reading over the details of the buying process and price, Haverty handed them the escrow papers to start reading over and sign. Paula let Shelby accept them since she was the one doing the buying of the house.

Shelby read each bit of information carefully, and after signing the first form, she handed it to Haverty to review. As Haverty read it over. Shelby noticed a puzzled look on her face.

"Is something wrong?" Shelby asked.

"No, no, I was just noticing your name, Shelby Malloy, interesting… My fiancé's last name is Malloy. His name is Myron Malloy, any relation? Do you know him?" Shelby and Paula exchanged a quick glance at each other.

"We are familiar with him, yes, but we are not one of his closest friends," Paula said, forcing a smile.

"Oh, I will have to tell him you were here and applied to buy a home from me."

"Haverty, uh, I want to keep this a secret, kind of a surprise for my family, and I would hate for anything to spoil it, so would you please not mention our being here to Myron, I mean Mr. Malloy?"

"What a great surprise. Your secret is safe with me. My lips are sealed." *Okay, so maybe she is not so perfect,* Shelby thought to herself. *She is an idiot. She is engaged to Myron.*

CHAPTER NINE

THE SNOW FELL SOFTLY AT first, then as if it was bored with its calm settling upon the earth, the flakes grew bigger and came at a quicker pace. It was cold, crazy cold, Shelby thought. Where had the months gone? Already it was nearing the end of January. It was true, time stood still for no one and nothing, not even a broken heart. September turned into October. October seemed to have flown in and flown out, picking up November and December in its flight. January, a soon-to-be memory, and the holidays over.

She thought about learning of Myron's engagement and that they were not even divorced yet. When she'd asked him about it, he'd just laughed and told her he was no longer her concern nor she, his. He wanted to know how she knew about his engagement to Haverty, and she had simply told him it didn't matter how she knew, but she did.

As she hurried along the sidewalk leading to her new townhouse, she thought about other things, lots of other things. She and Myron had sealed the decision to divorce, allowing for no further discussion of the matter, destroying her hopes for a reconciliation with Myron and saving their marriage. Thinking about it, she finally realized that it wasn't Myron she wanted most. What she really wanted was to save her *marriage* because she'd always believed that marriage was something sacred. The new townhome and her move were the result of Paula's constant badgering, insisting that she couldn't possibly stay in her old place after the break-in. She smiled as she thought of the beautiful living room set Paula insisted on buying her. She certainly would never have been able to afford it.

Augusta, poor Augusta, where could she be? Every day, Shelby returned to her old apartment building in hopes of finding her there. But it was the same each time, no Augusta, and today was no exception. Tomorrow was a different day, and she would go again in search of her newfound friend. She had to find her, see that she was alive and well. The colder it got, the more determined she became to find her.

As she turned up the collar to her long black wool coat, Shelby spotted him. She'd know him anywhere. Traffic was heavy but she didn't care. Before she knew it, she was sprinting across the busy street and yelling his name at the same time. He had to hear her. Why wasn't he answering her?

"Ricky! Ricky! Wait, stop!" He turned in the direction of her voice, and before she knew it, she was there, right up on him. "Ric… Ricky! What in the world happened?" The sight of his bruised and battered face shocked her. "What happened to your face?"

"Shel?" He tried to smile, but she could see that even making the effort to do so was too painful.

"What happened? Who did this to you?" she yelled at Ricky. Ricky's right jaw was swollen and bruised. A cut ran along the right side of his nose, held together by three small stitches. His right eye was black and swollen shut.

"I was out walking one morning, heading to the grocery store, and all of a sudden these two guys came out of nowhere. Before I knew it, they were on me, hitting and punching me. But I got them, Shelby. I may look like hell, but they look a lot worse. I fought them, got in a couple of good jabs and kicks. Two teenagers who were walking by saw that I was being jumped, and before I knew it, they were all over those guys. They beat the crap out of them! When they were finally able to get up, they half ran, half limped away. Afterward, the two young guys came over, helped me up, put their arms around me, and walked me to their home. Their mom was there. They told her what happened, and she ran over to me saying, 'Poor man, poor man!' Then she started fussing and throwing her hands up in the air. If I wasn't so beat up and in so much pain it would have been comical seeing her do this. Then she was saying again, 'Poor man, poor man.' The next instant, she turned to her sons and told them to go quickly, get the car, and they took me to the hospital.

Shelby, it's cold out here. Let's go inside this bakery so you can warm up." They found a small table and ordered coffee. "Those two young guys saved my life that day, Shelby, and I will never forget it."

"Have you been in touch with them since? They sound like good guys."

"Oh yeah, they are great. One is named Diego and the other Joshua! Diego is sixteen and Joshua is seventeen. They were on their way to school that morning. Their mother's name is Agacia, which means kind, and that she is. They have the address to the motel where I'm staying. I told them what is going on with me. The boys drive there every evening after school to bring me a hot meal their mom has prepared for me. They are wonderful people."

"So do you think the guys are the ones after you, looking for their money?"

"I don't know, Shelby, I don't know," Ricky said and slid down in his seat with a sigh. "It's not safe for you to be seen with me, and I've got to go. I'm on the run. Listen, I will be in touch. You get home and get out of those wet clothes."

"All right, but promise me you will be in touch."

"I promise." Shelby reached in her purse to pull out money to pay for their coffee, but Ricky stopped her, saying, "No, this one is on me."

Shelby watched Ricky walk away from her; she stood there for a while just watching him, feeling scared and sad for him. Anger and determination kicked in, knowing that Ricky's life hung in the balance. Before she knew it, she was running again as fast as her feet would carry her in the same direction she'd seen Ricky head in. She had no idea where she was going, but she had to get to him before they did, whoever they were. As her body collided with some of the people she encountered, she excused herself but kept running. Where she found the energy, she didn't know, but she refused to stop. Several times she tripped over her coat, until it finally occurred to her to raise it to knee level before she landed flat on her face.

When she finally caught sight of him standing before her in the distance, she noticed another man with him whose face she could not see because Ricky was blocking him. Shelby stopped and tried to decide how to approach them. Suddenly, Ricky stepped back enough to expose the other man's face. "Myron!" Before she knew it, she was half running, half walking toward them. Myron called her name as she approached them, totally taken by surprise at her being there. Ricky swirled around to face her.

"Shelby, get out of here," Ricky said in panic.

"I'm not going anywhere! What is this, Myron? What have you gotten Ricky all mixed up in? What? So help me, Myron, you define the word *scum*!" Shelby said.

"I suggest you listen to pretty boy and make your exit."

"You know where you can go, Myron," Shelby shouted at him. Myron smiled and shook his head. "You low-down dirty dog, look at him, look at Ricky's face! Did you have anything to do with this?" Myron ignored her question as if she wasn't even there. "Answer me," she shouted. It was there, Myron's fury, but it no longer paralyzed her.

Myron stared at Shelby, silently warning her to leave before saying again, "Leave, Shelby. It will be the best decision you've ever made."

"I've made one bad decision in my life, Myron, and that was to marry you, because my life has been a living nightmare ever since." Just as Myron started toward Shelby, Ricky stepped in front of him.

"I'll kill you, Myron. Touch her, and so help me, I'll end your miserable life today!"

Myron swung at Ricky with a movement so fast Shelby couldn't think straight. Myron's fist landed on Ricky's already-bruised right jaw, causing blood to rush from a half-opened wound. Ricky staggered but was able to keep his balance. Shelby lunged at Myron, but he was too quick and jumped to the side, causing her to fall hard onto the pavement. Ricky grabbed Myron by the collar and threw him to the ground.

"Don't get up, man. Stay down or this will be where it ends for you. Right here, right now, it's your call." Myron and Shelby looked at Ricky, both knowing he meant what he said. Once Myron felt it was safe to get up, he did and brushed off his expensive gray coat.

"You will regret this, Ricky. Trust me, you will regret it," Myron said. Neither Shelby nor Ricky replied to him.

Ricky rushed over to help Shelby off the ground, then pulled her toward him and into his arms. Shelby looked up at Ricky's bleeding face before asking, "Are you okay, Ricky?" Then she turned and glared at Myron. Myron stared at them for a second, then turned and walked away, shaking his head.

CHAPTER TEN

"WHAT A BORING DAY THIS is. Yesterday was a lot more fun," Paula said while flipping through the channels on the TV.

"How was yesterday more fun? All we did was eat and put on about twenty pounds. Where is the fun in that?" Shelby said while taking the last bite of her cheesecake.

"And yet she continues to eat," Paula said while glancing at Shelby out of the corner of her eye.

"What? I love cheesecake. This is only my second and a half piece," Shelby said innocently.

"I've got an idea as to how we can wake this day up! There is a lot of snow on the ground and a huge hill in the back of your place."

"No, no way! What are we going to use to slide down the hill on?"

"I don't know! There are a bunch of kids out there. I've been listening to them slide down that hill all afternoon and it sounds like they are having fun!"

"Paula, you cannot be serious!"

"Totally serious, let's go! Let's go take over their sleds."

Paula and Shelby finally finished putting on what they felt would be enough clothes to keep them warm. For

Paula, always the fashionista, it was a ski jacket over a pair of thick leggings. She added a thick scarf around her neck, boots, and gloves.

"You could freeze to death out there trying to be cute, Paula Renae Queria, but at least, you're halfway dressed warmly."

"Fine by me, at least I will be cute when I do."

There were kids and teenagers everywhere. Some were sliding down the hill. Of course some of them, mostly teenagers, were huddled around a fire they had somehow managed to build. Three large opened bags of marshmallows lay by their side so they could easily pull the sweet treat from them to roast.

"Okay, I am going for the short, chubby kid's sled. I know he won't be able to catch me once I snatch it and run!"

"Paula! That's Jordan! You leave his sled alone. Plus, his older brother is over there, roasting marshmallows. Touch Jordan and you're toast!" They both laughed and went in search of kids who they felt would let them take a few slides down the hill on their sleds. The kids they asked were excited to let them use their sleds, even going out of their way to show them how to get the most fun out of their slide down the hill.

After an hour of sliding down the hill, falling off their sleds, and getting a few bumps and bruises from falling down while trying to get up the hill, Paula and Shelby were done. They accepted a few roasted marshmallows offered to them by the teenagers, said good night, and headed in.

"Now, that's how you wake up an afternoon!" Paula said while limping back to Shelby's place.

"Man! That was awesome! I think I broke my baby toe, but hey, it was so worth it," Shelby said while unlocking the door to go in. They struggled out of their wet clothes and replaced them with warm pajamas Shelby found for each of them in her drawer. They fought over who would get to eat the last piece of cheesecake. Paula won since Shelby had already eaten half of it, she claimed, then camped out in the family room.

"How about a glass of wine to finish off the day?" Paula suggested.

"Sounds great! Pop open a bottle and I'll get the wine glasses," Shelby said while walking over to the kitchen cabinet to get them. They finished about two glasses of wine each and fell asleep, Paula on the floor and Shelby in the big cushiony chair next to her.

* * * * *

It had been a hectic week at work, but as usual, life settled into it's normal pattern and pace over the weekend. Ricky wandered into Shelby's thoughts so she decided to give him a call. She dialed his number repeatedly only to have it ring repeatedly. *Where is he?* she wondered. Her patience had run out and she was tired. Finally, her call rolled to v-mail.

"Ricky, it's Shelby. Where are you? Please call me. We can't go on pretending everything is okay when we both know it's not. Call me... I need to talk to you." Leaving a message was all she could do, and that was doing nothing for her anxiety, worrying that something had happened to him.

She walked to the kitchen and stared out the window over the sink. Sundays always had a way of making her feel all was right with the world. Something about the slower, uncertain pace of a Sunday, the disappearance of your neighbors, and complete quietness. It was nearing 7:00 p.m., where had the day gone? Seemed she was just getting out of bed that morning. Now the day was done.

The ringing of the phone interrupted her thoughts and she knew it was Ricky even before answering.

"Hello!"

"Hey!"

"Hey! We need to talk. I'm going crazy trying to figure out what's happening between you and Myron. I know what you told me after we had that run-in with Myron a few days ago, but I still have questions, so many unanswered questions. Why did you let him talk you into getting involved with some risky money situation? He promised you money for something, Ricky, I know he did! You are smarter than that, Ricky. I know you are. Was it the money, or what were you thinking?"

"I guess I wasn't thinking. I was broke, Shelby. I needed money and I trusted Myron to be up front with me about everything involved. I trusted him!"

"Why?"

"He is your husband, Shelby. I just knew you would never get involved with anyone like Myron."

"Now let me get this straight. You trusted him because he is married to me?"

"Yes, and he told me there was nothing illegal going down, and before I knew it, I would have my money and could just walk away."

"Ricky, that makes no sense!"

"Shel, when I look at you, I see something beautiful. I'm not talking about just the physical. You're compassionate, open, and honest, and I expected the same from the man you married. Hold on for a moment. There is someone at my door."

"I thought you were staying in a motel. How could someone know where you are?"

"Just hold on a second. I'll be right back." Shelby heard a man's voice in the background. She wondered if it was Myron, there to make good on his threat to make Ricky regret throwing him to the ground that day the three of them got into a fight.

She put her ear as close to the phone as possible so as to hear what was being said, but she couldn't hear a thing. After the initial greeting between Ricky and the person who knocked on his door, there was nothing but silence. A good nine minutes, according to the time on her cell phone, had gone by and still Ricky had not returned to the phone. *Just calm down. Everything is fine. Maybe he simply forgot I am on the phone.* Still the fear of something more dreadful being the cause of him not returning to the phone would not let her be.

"Ricky, what's going on? Are you all right? Ricky!" Shelby hoped he'd hear her yelling through the phone, but still nothing. "Please let him be all right. Please, please, let him be all right," Shelby whispered to herself while still clutching the phone.

Suddenly, she hung up the call, she began to pace back and forth, not knowing what to do and not wanting to think only horrible thoughts. Images of Ricky came to mind. She'd go insane if she allowed herself to think of what may have happened to him.

Calling the police was her first inclination, then she remembered not having an address for him. A cell phone number was all she had and that's the way he wanted it. Paula, she'd call Paula. Why? She didn't know but she had to talk to someone. After about five rings, Paula answered sounding as if she'd just woken up.

"Paula!"

"What's up?"

"Paula, I need to talk to you, wake up!"

"What's going on?"

"I think something has happened to Ricky!"

"Ricky… What do you mean?"

"Well, we were talking on the phone when there was a knock at his door, and he went to answer it. I waited and waited for him to return to the phone but he never did."

"Maybe he just fell asleep or something."

"No, I don't think so."

"What makes you think something is wrong? I don't understand."

"It's a long story. I'll have to tell you about it later, but for now I need to know that he is all right."

"I could come get you if you'd like and we can drive over to his place to check on him if that would make you feel better."

"That would be perfect. There is a problem with that though. I don't have an address."

"So much for that. I don't know what you want me to do."

"I guess to just talk to me. Tell me he is okay."

"He is okay."

"How do you know?"

"I don't! I'm just telling you what you want to hear so you will leave me alone and let me go back to sleep."

"That's just great. I feel a lot better now. I certainly called the right person," Shelby said sarcastically. Paula hung up on her.

Shelby looked at the phone in disbelief, then hit redial. It seemed an eternity before Paula picked up, but finally she did.

"Did you just hang up on me?"

"Yes."

"Why?"

"Because you are a crazy woman, and you are not making any sense going on and on about something being wrong with Ricky. You don't have an address, you can't give me even an idea as to why you feel something is wrong, and more importantly, I'm sleepy. Listen, he is fine, just fell asleep or something, I don't know! Give it a little more time. It's eight thirty now. Give it until nine thirty. If you don't hear from him by then, call him, then let me know what happens."

"I guess, certainly makes sense."

"Of course it does, because I'm the sane one."

"Why are you sleeping? It's Sunday night. You're usually out or over here bugging me."

"I'm tired, need to catch up on my beauty rest. Now leave me alone. I have a nine o'clock movie I want to watch. I need to sleep a little more before it starts. You have a beautiful, brand-new townhome, go clean or decorate or something to occupy your mind. I'll text you later if I don't hear from you."

"Okay, thank you."

"Yep, later."

Calling Paula helped, but not much. The uneasiness in the bottom of her stomach was still there, and her head was starting to hurt. "Something isn't right. Something has happened to Ricky," she said to herself. Myron was the last person she wanted to talk to right now, but if he could give her the assurance needed that Ricky was not in harm's way, then she would talk to him. But would he talk to her after what happened the other day? She doubted it. Staring at the phone, she realized just how crippling pride could be. Myron might have the answer she needed to put her mind at ease. However, because of her foolish pride, she couldn't lift her hand to pick up the phone and dial his number. "This is ridiculous. Just pick up the phone and call him." Before she knew it, Myron's line was ringing. "There, was that so hard?" She let the phone ring ten times with no answer, not even an invitation from a machine to leave a message. Finally, she hung up the phone with a heavy sigh.

Walking over to the small desk in the corner of her room, she picked up her checkbook and tried to balance it. After a few minutes, she realized just how impossible it was to concentrate on anything or anyone other than Ricky.

"What is the matter with me? Why am I so upset that Ricky didn't return to the phone? Because I know he could be hurt, beat up all over again, or worse, dead. You are losing it, Shelby. Not only are you talking to yourself, you're answering yourself. Stop it!"

At about twenty after nine, she'd had all she could stand. Snatching up the phone she dialed Ricky's cell.

"Hello."

"Oh, thank goodness, where were you? Why didn't you come back to the phone? How rude, Rick!"

"I'm sorry, but one of my elderly neighbors here at the motel needed help with something. I was so eager to help him I forgot you were on the phone, I'm sorry. I was just about to call you."

"Well, just so you are all right. How are you able to afford to pay to stay at a motel? Are you working now?"

"This little old cheap, run-down, makeshift of a motel is only costing me thirty dollars a week, believe it or not. I do small, odds and ends jobs during the day to pay for my stay."

"Food, how are you eating?"

"At first, it was rough. I was about to starve to death, literally. But remember me telling you about the young guys and their mother? Well, the guys still bring me a hot meal every day and gallons of iced tea. Their mom packs it in a small cooler with lots of ice, I can keep here in my room. Man, that woman can cook, and she sends so much food it lasts me for two or three days at a time. She is wonderful! She also sent a box packed with clean sheets, towels, wash clothes, soap, and deodorant and enough toothpaste to last me for a month. When the boys come, they ask for my dirty laundry so they can take it back to their mom for washing. I told them they didn't have to do that, but they said their mom insists, and what their mom wants, she gets, so I send it." Shelby felt a little bit of jealousy at the fact that he thought Agacia was such a good cook, great person, and she was taking such great care of him. She scolded herself mentally for it.

"Oh, nice, sounds like you have it all under control. You know, this is driving me crazy."

"What is?"

"You know perfectly well what I mean. This whole situation. Your disappearing act, and now finding out you let that crazy Myron talk you into something that might cost you your life."

"Are you worried about me?" Ricky asked with a chuckle.

"This isn't funny, Ricky, and what do you think?"

"I don't know. That's why I'm asking."

"We are friends, right? Wouldn't you worry about me if I disappeared on you?"

"No, wouldn't have to because I would never let you disappear on me. I would always know exactly where to find you if you were with me, if our circumstances were different. But sadly they are not and we are forced to deal with the hand we've been dealt whether we like it or not." Shelby didn't know what to say, how they being friends became defined as their being together, but she knew she had to break the terrible silence between them at that moment that seemed to last far too long. She cleared her throat and said "Ricky, I've got to go. I got a lot to do tonight. I would like to help, give you some money, so can you meet me somewhere tonight?"

"I'm sorry. It's not safe, Shelby. Listen, let me talk to Agacia. Perhaps she can meet you. I'll call you right back."

"Agacia," Shelby said to herself because Ricky had already hung up.

In less than five minutes, he called back.

"Hey, Shel, it's all set. Just give me your address and Agacia will stop by tomorrow, okay with you?"

"Sure!" Shelby reluctantly gave him her address, upset that it would be Agacia coming tomorrow instead of Ricky.

"Did you move?"

"Yes, I did, bought a new townhouse."

"Man, Shel, they must be treating you real good at Cordial these days. Only the rich and famous can afford to live in your neighborhood, according to the address you just gave me."

"Well, you and I both know I'm not rich or famous, just fortunate I guess. Paula actually helped me find my new home, all thanks to her."

"Paula, how is that sexy half-pint?"

"You know Paula, never a dull moment with her." Silence hung in the air between them for a while before Shelby said, "Hey, Ricky, when this is all over, I can have you over for a real dinner."

"Sounds good. You know I love your nasty cooking," Ricky said jokingly. "You can expect Agacia around seven. Love you, Shel, and I appreciate you loaning me the money."

"It's not a loan, Rick. You don't have to pay it back."

"Text you later."

"All right, later, Ricky."

*   *   *   *   *

Shelby spent the rest of the afternoon after leaving work cleaning and doing laundry. She loved her new home and everything from her old apartment had fit in nicely. It was a lot more space than needed for just her, but she decorated it so it would have a coziness to it. She chose warm colors, lots of throw pillows, decorative rugs, and lamps. She loved lamps. She turned one of the three bedrooms into a TV room or office. Her fifty-five-inch television fit well in the room, and she still had plenty of space for a loveseat, a cushiony chair, and a desk. It was her favorite room in the whole house.

Around six, she started preparing for Agacia. She made sure she had the cash ready for Ricky, three hundred dollars. She also set out some chips, dip, and drink to offer Agacia when she got there. Just as she sat down to relax, she heard a knock at the door. *She is early*, Shelby thought to herself. *It's only six forty-five.* She checked her appearance in the foyer mirror, put on a big smile, and opened the door only to find Paula standing there.

"Oh, it's just you."

"Nice to see you too," Paula said as she waltzed in wearing sweats and a baseball cap.

"I'm sorry, Paula, it's just that I was expecting someone else."

"If it's a man and he is good looking, hands off, my friend. He is all mine," Paula said matter-of-factly as she noticed the bowl of chips and headed for them.

"Paula?"

"What, I'm serious! I can't remember the last time I've had the company of a fine gentleman," Paula said while taking off her baseball cap and fluffing out her hair.

"Didn't you tell me you went on a date last week?"

"Shelby Malloy, that man was no fine gentleman. All he did was whine all evening about his ex. If I'd had a pacifier, I would have stuck it in his mouth." They both burst out laughing while Shelby closed the door and warned her not to bother the chips. Of course, Paula ignored her and helped herself to a small plate of chips and a diet soda. Just then, they both turned in the direction of a knock on the door.

Shelby opened the door to a beautiful, big-eyed, voluptuous Agacia. Her long, beautiful, thick black hair fell in waves around her shoulders. Her honey brown complexion boasted just a hint of makeup. Full breasts and an amazing figure filled out her jeans and top perfectly.

"Hello," she said with a smile that emphasized her dimples and pearly whites. "I'm Agacia. You must be Shelby." Shelby was floored as she was expecting anything but what she saw standing before her. A short, motherly, and not-so-pretty woman, not a bombshell. It took her a second to pull it together before inviting her in.

"Hi, yes, I'm Shelby. Please come in," she said as she stepped aside to let Agacia in.

"Well, aren't you a beauty," Paula said as Agacia walked in the room.

"Agacia, this is my friend, Paula."

"Hello, Paula, nice to meet you."

"I'm not so sure it's so nice to meet you. No wonder there are no available men in this city. You probably have them all knocking down your door." Agacia laughed but Shelby and Paula didn't.

"Don't mind her, Agacia. She has had one too many potato chips," Shelby said while shooting Paula a warning glance. "Please have a seat, may I offer you some chips and dip, I also have some bottled water?" Shelby said while offering Agacia the bowl of chips. "Thank you, but I try to watch what I eat. If you have some carrot sticks, I'll take those with the bottled water, that would be nice; otherwise, I'm fine, but thank you."

"On that note, I will just take the entire bowl of chips and all the diet soda I can drink into the kitchen. Nice meeting you, Agacia." Paula said as she picked up the bowl of chips along with the drinks and walked out of the room, leaving Shelby alone to talk with Agacia.

Shelby invited Agacia to make herself comfortable after showing her to a small, smartly decorated room off the kitchen. Shelby liked to refer to it as the sitting room because she spent most of her time in the room after work reading, doing her bills, or just listening to music.

"Your home is lovely," Agacia said as she chose a seat in a plush, soft, and roomy chair in the corner of the room.

"Thank you. I hope you enjoy sitting in that chair as much as I do. I love coming in this room in the evenings because of the amazing view of the woods, and it's not a very small or a large room, just the perfect size for whatever you like to do."

"It's so comfortable and I love the color. It's like a salmon color that goes well with your cream-colored walls. Did you decorate your home yourself?"

"I sure did. I love to decorate."

"Well, you did an amazing job," Agacia said as she sat taking in the beauty of the room. "So Ricky told me the two of you have been friends for a long time."

"Yes, we met each other at work. We used to work together."

"You know, it's funny, but I met my ex-husband at work. A lot of romances start in the workplace," Agacia said, keeping her eyes glued to Shelby's face, looking to see how she would react to what she'd just said. *We are not going to play that game. Don't try to read me*, Shelby said to herself, realizing Agacia was trying to determine what type of relationship she had with Ricky.

"I've heard the same thing, but it's also true that a lot of great friendships start in the workplace, case in point, my friendship with Ricky."

"You are a good friend, willing to loan him money."

"Give him money," Shelby corrected her.

Agacia smiled before saying, "Forgive me, I thought Ricky said you were loaning him money. It's very kind of you. I'm sure Ricky will appreciate your generosity." It was something about the way she said Ricky's name that pissed Shelby off. Why, she didn't know but it did.

"Well, Ricky knows I'm here for him whenever he needs me. As he said, we have been friends a long time and I feel I need to help if I can."

"It's good to know you are friends. We all need reliable friends in our life," Agacia said as she stood in preparation to leave.

"Yes, we do."

"It's been nice meeting you, Shelby."

"You as well," Shelby said with a smile. Just as she'd finished her sentence, she heard Agacia's phone go off. Agacia dug in her bag for her phone to see who it was.

"Shelby, please excuse me. Ricky is texting."

"Of course, I'll wait for you by the door." Shelby left the room reluctantly, to let Agacia text with Ricky freely or call him if she'd like in private. Agacia walked up to Shelby after talking to Ricky with a smile on her face as big as a basketball field, and Shelby knew all too well it was the result of the conversation she'd just had with Ricky. Was she jealous? This time she didn't have to try to figure it out. She knew without a doubt she was jealous, very, and she hated to admit it.

She smiled at Agacia and tried to seem indifferent to her obvious pleasure as a result of hearing from Ricky.

"How is Ricky?"

"He is great! He is waiting for me downstairs. He said he was nearby and wanted to know if I'd found your home all right. I told him yes and that I was just on my way out."

"Oh, did he not want to come up?"

"No, he's tired, been out all day, job hunting. I told him to wait by my car for me. I'd take him home with me, make him dinner, and put him up on my sleep sofa tonight. I'm sorry, is it okay to get the money from you now?"

"Oh, of course," Shelby said while taking the envelope from her pocket and handing it to Agacia.

"Thanks again Shelby, got to run. You know, I'm really glad I got to meet you. It's nice to know you truly care about Ricky and want to help him as a friend, unlike some empty headed women who use their money to try to buy a man. I'll tell Rick you said hello. Good night." Agacia was gone before Shelby could even respond to her. She stared at the back of the door after Agacia had closed it softly behind her. "If she is so great, Ricky, why didn't she give you money?" Shelby said to herself angrily.

"I can't believe you let her get away with that," Paula said as she walked back in the room with her arms folded. She then mimicked Agacia by saying *It's good to know you are not one of those empty headed women who tries to buy a man.* It took all I had not to come in here and make her choke on those words. She is after your man."

"He is not my man, nosy, and how long have you been standing there?"

"Long enough to know that Ms. Agacia has it bad for Ricky, and if you want him, you'd better get busy, real busy and real soon!"

"Paula, I don't want Ricky. We are friends, that's all. He can see and be with whomever he wants. I don't care!"

"Sure, you don't," Paula said sarcastically.

"Look, I'm tired so I'm kicking you out."

"Don't get mad at me just because I'm stating the obvious. I've got to get up early in the morning anyway so I'm out," Paula said as she walked past Shelby to the door with a new bag of chips in her hands.

"Leave the chips, missy."

"Nope, see you tomorrow. Nighty-night!"

CHAPTER ELEVEN

WEDNESDAY AT LAST, SHELBY THOUGHT, *and thank goodness for it!* She had to admit that the day had gone by pretty quickly, and for that, she was grateful. Just three more minutes and she'd be out the door.

"Hi, Shelby!" Shelby looked up to see Alex Manson standing before her in all his glory. His wife was a very fortunate woman, Shelby concluded.

"Mr. Manson, how are you?"

"Please call me Alex. Besides, I can't be that much older than you. I mean you are what… twenty-five, twenty-six?"

"You are close," Shelby said with a chuckle.

"I just wanted to thank you for being so nice to my client. He was in around three today and mentioned how polite and helpful you were."

"Thank you. He made it easy for me. He was very nice. Mr. Conte, right?"

"Yes, he has been a client for many years. So it looks like you're wrapping things up for the day. Can I perhaps buy you a drink, just to further show my appreciation? My wife will be joining us. I'd like you to meet her."

"Thank you, that is very kind of you, but I'm really drained. I think it best I head on home." Alex Manson looked at her. His disappointment in her not accepting his offer was obvious.

"I'm sorry, some other time?"

"Yeah, sure, some other time, then."

"Have a good evening, Shelby."

"You too, Alex."

The man obviously was not used to having his invitations turned down, Shelby thought. Finding Augusta meant a lot more to her than spending the better part of her evening opposite Alex Manson, sipping on some expensive wine she didn't even like. It was true, she was drained and needed to head home, but first she would stop by her old apartment in hopes of finding Augusta there.

Walking the short distance from her job to her old apartment took longer than usual it seemed. She was glad she had parked her car there so she could just hop in it and drive home. It was so cold she felt her hands and feet would freeze before she got to the apartment building. So much for leather gloves. They looked good, but that's all they did. Just as she rounded the corner, she saw Augusta huddled beside a trash can in the park opposite her old apartment building. She had a cardboard box surrounding her in an effort to keep warm, no doubt. Her beautiful gray eyes peeped over the top of the box. Shelby would know them anywhere. It was those eyes that told the story of her unfortunate journey on the streets, yet Shelby also saw strength in them, a determination to survive against the odds. *The will to live can be a strong weapon against anything that threatens to take life away from you*, Shelby thought to herself as she slowly approached Augusta.

Augusta stared straight ahead as if she was in some sort of trance, not even seeming to blink.

"Augusta," Shelby called to her as she approached the box surrounding her, but there was no response. "Augusta!" This time Shelby reached out to her. Just as she did, Augusta jumped. "Augusta, darling, it's me." Augusta turned to look in her direction but didn't speak, just stared at her. "Augusta, don't you recognize me? You remember me, don't you? I gave you ten dollars that day on the subway train." As she spoke, she tried to reassure her with a smile but failed; instead, her lips quivered and she had to turn away quickly so Augusta wouldn't notice.

Shelby knelt down beside her, not giving up. Tugging gently at the cardboard box, she tried to get closer to Augusta to see what she looked like under all the layers of rags and blankets she had covering her to keep from freezing to death. On her head was a funny-looking black velveteen hat with a bunch of torn bright flowers on it. Where she'd found that, Shelby had no idea. But if it kept her head warm, who cared?

"Augusta, listen to me. You can't stay out here. It's horribly cold. You will freeze to death."

"I stayed out here last night, and I didn't freeze to death," Augusta said matter-of-factly. "I went to your place last night, and you didn't come to the door. After all that begging I did, finally that stupid guard let me up and you didn't come to your door. So I stayed out here last night and it was cold then too, but I'm still here. Yes, ma'am, I'm still here."

"I'm sorry, I'm sorry I wasn't there for you last night. I've moved, Augusta, that's why I wasn't there. You should see my new place. It's beautiful, and there is an extra bedroom for you, and you and I can decorate it any way you'd like."

"I don't have no money to earn my keep, miss, no money at all. That's why I'm on the street."

"Well, you could earn your keep."

"How?"

"Can you cook? You could cook, prepare our meals for us."

"You're too trusting, miss. How do you know I won't try to poison you or rob you blind?"

"Because, somehow, I just know you wouldn't do either of those things. Now come on. Let's go home. My car is right over there."

"Why you being so nice to me, miss? I ain't got nothing to give ya, nothing! You treat me better than my own daughter." Shelby was shocked at this revelation. Augusta had mentioned only having a cat once, not a daughter.

"You have a daughter? Where is she? I thought you told me you had no one after you lost Mittens."

Augusta was quiet for a long time. Shelby didn't rush her to answer even though she was beginning to lose the feeling in her ears. Instead, she tugged at the cardboard box, but every time she did, Augusta pulled it back toward her. Finally, with all the strength she could muster, Shelby yanked the box away and threw it to the side.

"You are crazy," Augusta said and rolled her eyes at Shelby.

"Well, that makes two of us, because only a crazy person would want to stay out here in the freezing cold when they are being offered shelter and a warm bed. I'm leaving now. It's your choice. Either you are coming with me or you're not." Shelby turned and walked away, knowing Augusta would follow her. After she had gone some distance, she turned to see if her plan had worked, and sure enough, Augusta was slowly following her, dragging her dirty blankets and trying to keep her hat on her head. Shelby slowed up to give her a chance to catch up to her. "Come on, we are almost there. The car is right in front of us."

"I'm dirty and you want me to get in your nice, clean car?"

"It's material, you are a human being and of much greater value than this car," Shelby said as she pointed to her car. "The seats are leather, easily cleaned. Listen, don't worry about my car. Worry about yourself."

When they got to the car, Augusta hesitated, stared at it as if it was something forbidden to touch or be near. Shelby walked around to the passenger side and opened the door for her, then waited for her to get in. Instead, Augusta turned and ran.

"Augusta! You come back here right now!" Augusta just kept running. Shelby slammed her car door shut and took off after her. Augusta tripped over the blankets and fell, her hat flying off her head. As Shelby approached her, she heard her saying over and over, "My hat!" Shelby stood over her with her hands on her knees, trying to catch her breath.

"Augusta, listen to me. It's cold as hell out here. You will surely catch your death if you try to stay out here tonight.

One night, just give it a try for one night. Please, Augusta, that's all I ask. Then if you still want to leave, go back to the streets, you can. But please just give it one night, okay? Deal?" Shelby said, reaching out her hand to Augusta to help pull her off the ground.

"Oh, all right," Augusta said, taking Shelby's hand and struggling to get herself off the ground, picking up her hat as she did so.

They rode in silence, except for Shelby constantly asking Augusta if she was warm enough. For some reason, she felt she had to turn the heat up to the limit in order to keep Augusta warm.

"Oh, I am warm enough, about to darn near burn up in here. Will you please turn that button down some?" Shelby smiled to herself and did as Augusta asked. Snow had begun to fall softly as they neared the townhouse. Shelby pulled into her reserved parking spot, then went around to help Augusta out of the car. It took some effort getting inside with Augusta still clinging to her blankets and worn hat. Shelby slowly opened the door, not knowing if Augusta would actually go in or turn and run. She prayed she would just walk in without effort because she was tired and had no energy to fight with Augusta in any way to get her inside.

Augusta stood in the middle of the living room, taking in its massive size and beauty.

"Come on, love. Let's go have a look at your room," Shelby said, motioning for Augusta to follow her with her hand. Augusta did as she asked, still dragging her blankets with her, clutching them tightly in one hand and holding her hat on her head with her free hand.

The bedroom was medium-sized with a large walk-in closet. There was plenty of room for a queen-size bed, a TV stand, dresser, and small desk. The walls were painted an eggshell white and the carpet was just a shade darker. "Well, what do you think?" Shelby asked, standing in the room with her hands on her hips and surveying Augusta's expression to see what type of reaction she was having to seeing her very own room.

Augusta didn't say anything right away, just turned and stared at Shelby for a minute before saying, "Mittens would have liked it. The carpet looks so nice and soft. She would have loved laying around in it, but she died. She died, miss."

"I know, you told me, remember? So sorry, Augusta. We will get you another cat, okay?" Augusta just shook her head in agreement. "Well, let's get you showered and into some clean things. I'm sorry I don't have your bed yet but we can go shopping for it tomorrow after your doctor's appointment."

"Doctor, am I sick, miss?"

"No, I just want you to have a physical and some blood tests ran so we can be sure you're all right and you don't need to be on any type of meds. You are no spring chicken, you know," Shelby said with a chuckle.

"Yes, ma'am," Augusta said softly.

"My mom was ma'am. I'm Shelby or, as my friends call me, Shel." Again, Augusta just shook her head in agreement.

After Shelby had gotten Augusta in the shower, showed her how best to wash herself and made sure she stayed put, she went to the dresser drawer in her room and pulled out new underwear and a new pair of pajamas. Augusta was just a bit smaller than she was, but she was sure the clothes would at least be able to stay up on her.

"Miss?" Shelby turned from the dresser to stare into the small, timid face of Augusta.

"Oh, look at you, Augusta! Look how pretty you are!" Augusta's nice olive skin was flawless, and her big beautiful gray eyes stood out from her small heart-shaped face. Her thick gray hair was a mass of endless curls, her hair now washed and clean.

"Pretty, who me miss? Nobody ever called me that before," Augusta said while holding her towel tightly around her, trying hard to conceal her small five-foot frame.

"Well, you are absolutely stunning. Here, try these things on while I go get clean blankets and pillows to change my bed so you have a comfortable and clean bed to sleep in until we get your bed, okay with you?"

"Oh no, miss, I can't take your bed for the night. This is your bed and you should sleep in it. All I need is a few blankets and a pillow. I will be fine right here on the floor," Augusta said while pointing to a spot on the floor right next to the bed.

"Augusta, listen. I am sleeping on the floor tonight, right in the spot you are pointing to." Augusta didn't say anything. She just turned and stared at Shelby.

After Shelby had given Augusta a cup of soup and a sandwich, cleaned the bathroom, and gotten Augusta down for the night, she called and left Helen a message that she wouldn't be in the next day, something had come up.

CHAPTER TWELVE

AUGUSTA LOOKED A LITTLE OUT of place sitting in the doctor's office in a size too-big jeans and a T-shirt that almost came to her ankles. *We really have to go shopping for her today*, Shelby thought to herself. Shelby had called ahead earlier that morning and scheduled a noon appointment with her family doctor since she was a little girl.

Dr. Rosenbloom had, as a favor to her, agreed to give Augusta a thorough physical, complete with blood work to include tests for everything from high blood pressure to HIV. Dr. Rosenbloom was not only her family doctor, but he and her dad had been best friends and had performed surgery side by side for years before his passing. Not long after her dad died, her mom died suddenly. Dr. Rosenbloom promised Shelby at her mother's funeral that if ever she needed anything, all she need do was ask. Ever since that day, this was the only thing she'd ever asked for, a complete physical for Augusta. He agreed to it without hesitation and without charge.

After leaving the doctor's office, Shelby and Augusta stopped at a small diner nearby for a salad and a cup of coffee. It was even colder today than yesterday, but Shelby made sure Augusta was all bundled up in a warm coat from her closet with a scarf and gloves. Augusta insisted on wearing her black velveteen hat with the torn flowers on it. Shelby could have sworn she'd thrown it in the trash with the dirty blankets and clothes Augusta had worn the night before.

After eating, they walked the short distance to Shelby's car. The first stop they made was at a furniture store where they picked out a white queen-size bedroom set for Augusta, with matching dresser and desk. Shelby let her choose a medium-size TV stand in silver and white for her room. The sales person agreed to have everything delivered, mattresses included, by three the next day. Afterward, they stopped at a few clothing stores to pick up some things for Augusta to wear. The day ended with them both exhausted from endless shopping for Augusta. By the time they got home that night, they were both so tired they had a sandwich and went to bed.

Shelby woke the next morning to the smell of bacon, eggs, and hot coffee. She rolled out of bed and staggered to the kitchen. There stood Augusta with an apron around her pajamas, a pair of her new slippers, and her beautiful curly hair piled high on top of her head.

"Is that lipstick you're wearing, Augusta?" Shelby asked with a smile.

"Sure is. I borrowed it from your bathroom. Hope you don't mind. It matched my new pink slippers, so I put some on. You like it?"

"Yes, you look lovely."

"Thank you," Augusta said with a sheepish grin. "Now come sit. I've got breakfast all ready for you. I hope you like it. I figured it was time I start earning my keep."

"Well, it certainly looks delicious." Shelby glanced at the clock hanging over the refrigerator. "Augusta, you do realize that it's only five-thirty. I don't have to be at work until eight."

"Good, give you plenty time to shower, read the paper, and do your makeup before you leave the house. I ironed your blue skirt and white blouse for you to wear today, I found them in your closet while you were sleeping last night. Did it when I noticed you hadn't laid out anything for the day."

"Wow, thank you so much. Well, I'd better get washed up for breakfast real quick before it gets cold. Be right back."

Shelby and Augusta ate breakfast and talked about the activities of the day. Shelby explained where she would leave an extra key for her in case she wanted to walk out for the day, what time her furniture was to be delivered then gave Augusta her cell and work number in case she needed anything. A little after seven, Shelby left for work, promising Augusta she would call her in the late afternoon to see how she was doing.

*   *   *   *   *

Shelby hadn't been at her desk five minutes before Paula showed up, asking all kinds of questions.

"Well, good morning! I sent you a million text messages yesterday, called twice as many times, and not a word back from you. I was beginning to get worried. Are you all right? You were out yesterday."

"Sure, I'm fine."

"Well, where were you yesterday?"

"Oh, I just had some things I had to take care of is all. I'm perfectly fine." Paula stared at her, then walked around to feel her forehead.

"Are you sure you're not sick? You never take off from work."

"I am not sick."

"Good. Well, what do you say I pick up some Indian food tonight and we hang out at your place and watch a couple of movies?"

"Not tonight. I was hoping to get to bed early tonight."

"Oh, okay, tomorrow night then?"

"Paula, I have a lot going on this week, not a good week for hanging. Maybe we can do something this weekend." Paula wasn't buying a word she said, and quite frankly, she was feeling a little put off.

"What's going on, Shel? What do you mean? There is something you're not telling me. Did that no-good Myron get on your nerves yesterday? Did he come by demanding sex?"

"Paula, really! Myron knows better than to ask me for anything. I just have a lot going on this week. Now, I've got to get these files taken care of. Call you later to see if you're up for lunch?" Paula just rolled her eyes and walked away. Shelby shook her head and returned to doing her work.

She was anxious to finish up her day and return home to make sure all was well with Augusta. She did not want to have to stay late that night under any circumstances. She loved Paula and she was her best friend, but she had no time right now for her dramatic episodes.

Shelby typed the last three lines of an e-mail to Helen, explaining she'd be a little late Monday morning and why, logged off her computer, and headed out the door. She hoped her elevator would keep going without stopping on any floors, but such was not the case. The elevator came to a halt two floors down, where the majority of the attorneys were, and in stepped Helen.

"Hi, Helen, I uh, I sent you an e-mail letting you know I will be just a little late Monday morning. I have an appointment, but will be in right afterward."

"Fine by me. Everything all right? Is that handsome husband of yours refusing to come out and play again?"

"Helen, with all due respect, please don't ask questions about my affairs with Myron. Besides, I would think with you always being so busy, you wouldn't really have time to care about how we are doing, anyway." The elevator doors opened, and Shelby stepped off, saying, "Good night, Helen."

*   *   *   *   *

Shelby returned home to find Augusta in the kitchen chopping up onions and carrots to toss in a stew she had going on the stove.

"Hi Augusta," she yelled as she ran to Augusta's room to see if all her furniture had been delivered and set up as it should be, and it had. Augusta's room was beautiful. She had even made the bed up using the lavender sheets and white bedspread she'd chosen for her bed. She then rushed to the kitchen and threw her arms around Augusta who was drying her hands on her apron after tossing the onions and carrots in the stew.

"I absolutely love it, Augusta, don't you? You did a great job making up your bed and arranging things! That stew smells heavenly. Thank you so much for all you've done today, Augusta!"

"Well, miss, I have to do something to earn my stay here. I figured making sure I had hot meals ready for you, clean clothes, and a clean house is the least I can do."

Shelby motioned for Augusta to have a seat at the kitchen table, then she sat down beside her. Taking both of Augusta's hands in hers, she said, "Augusta, I want you to listen to me very carefully because what I'm about to say to you is very important and I want you to repeat it back to me exactly as I say it to you, okay?" Augusta put her head down. "No, no, look up! You look up. Always hold your head high and be proud of who and what you are, no matter what anyone else says to you or about you. Do you hear me?"

Augusta held her head up as Shelby asked and said, "Yes, miss."

"Stop calling me *miss*. Shelby, please call me Shelby."

"Okay, miss, I mean Shelby."

Shelby laughed and said, "That's all right. With practice, you will get used to it. Now repeat after me, enthusiastically!"

"Enthusiastically?" Augusta said. "This must be something big."

"Now speak with confidence and excitement!"

"All right, I will try."

With her head held high, in a clear, strong voice, and a smile as big as a baseball field on her face, Shelby said, "I am a wonderful, strong, classy, and smart woman who deserves to be treated with love and respect!"

Shelby and Augusta stared at each other. Shelby waiting for Augusta to repeat after her. Augusta, uncertain as to what to say. The bigger Shelby's smile grew, the bigger Augusta tried to smile but said nothing. "Augusta, now it's your turn to say what I just said."

Augusta stood up from her chair, placed her hands on her tiny hips, held her head high, and said, "My name is Augusta Rose Matthews, daughter of Holland and Mary Rose Bishop. I am a stunning, strong, sophisticated woman, and I *will* be treated with love and respect!" She then looked at Shelby and said, "Now that's the way it should be done. Please turn that stew off and bring me a bowl to my bed. I'm tired and my feet hurt."

Shelby stared at Augusta as she walked to her room, her mouth hanging open, then walked over to the china cabinet, pulled out a bowl, filled it with stew, and placed it on a tray along with the cornbread Augusta had cooling on the stove. Pouring a glass of iced tea from the fridge and placing it on the tray, she thought how confident Augusta was in herself. "Good for you, Augusta. You sure told me," Shelby said to herself. Picking up the tray, she headed to

Augusta's bedroom, saying out loud, "Now that's what I call a fast learner."

After Shelby finished her second big bowl of stew, because it was so good she just had to have another, she said to herself, "The woman can cook. I think I will keep her." Turning in the direction of the ringing of her cell phone, she ran to the living room to fish it out of her purse. Noticing it was Dr. Rosenbloom's number, she quickly answered, "Dr. Rosenbloom, hi! I want you to know I just finished the best bowl of stew this side of heaven! Augusta made it!"

"Hello, Shelby. I wish I could say the same. I know it's late but I got the results of Augusta's blood tests back. I had the tests expedited given the information you shared with me concerning Augusta's background. Thought you might be anxious to learn what they are."

"Yes, yes, certainly. Thank you, Doctor, I am!"

"Well, all of her blood work came back fine. Cholesterol is good. Sugar count is good. No indication of any diseases."

"Oh, that's great, *yes*! Oh, thank you so much!"

"Shelby, there's more," Dr. Rosenbloom said softly. Shelby didn't like the sound of his voice.

"No bad news today, please. My day has been great. Please no bad news!"

There was a long pause before Dr. Rosenbloom said, "Shelby, while examining Augusta's left breast, I discovered a small lump."

"Oh, dear God, no!"

"Now, now, I don't want you getting upset, so take a deep breath and calm yourself."

"Okay, okay, I'm calm," she said while placing her hand over her stomach in an effort to stop the flood of emotion and fear that threatened to overtake her. She was angry, angry that something was already threatening to take Augusta away from her when she barely had her. Angry that the minute she dared to relax, something would happen to throw her off balance. Determination to fight the cancer if it proved to be that drowned the anger and pushed her mind into attack mode for Augusta. She put the same hand she'd used to cover her stomach on her hip and spoke with resolve when she said, "It's not taking her away from me, Dr. Rosenbloom, it's not! So what is our next step?"

"What's not, Shelby? What are you talking about?"

"Cancer, that's what it is, isn't it?"

"We don't know that yet. We need to have it biopsied to determine what exactly we are dealing with. I need you to bring her in Monday morning. I had my assistant Claudia schedule you a ten-thirty appointment for Monday." Shelby put her hand over her mouth. She was so shaken she felt she was going to be sick.

"Okay, sure, we will be there. Thank you, Doctor." Shelby then quickly hung up the call as if the faster she hung it up, the quicker everything she had just been told about the lump in Augusta's breast would be erased like a dream.

Shelby walked to Augusta's room and peeped in. Augusta was sleeping soundly, snuggled under her brand-new matching comforter and bedspread she had picked out herself. She said she chose the color lavender because it matched her pink lipstick, the one she took from Shelby's bathroom and now claimed as her own. Shelby walked softly over to her and picked up her dinner tray from her small bedside table. Turning quickly to leave the room, she stopped suddenly. Closing her eyes, she said a silent prayer, asking God to please help her and Augusta to get through what Dr. Rosenbloom had just told her about the lump in Augusta's breast and to please let her keep Augusta.

CHAPTER THIRTEEN

SHELBY WOKE WITH A START, her heart racing. She'd slept very little during the night, her thoughts consumed with the possibility of Augusta having breast cancer. What should have been a morning for them to go shopping for Augusta a second time had sadly turned into a morning of going to the doctor to have the lump in her breast biopsied. Life, she thought to herself, you never know when it's going to take a turn for the worse, no matter how hard you strive to be healthy and happy. Life always throws you a curve ball just when you dare to think all is well. Reaching in her bag and pulling out her cell phone, she sent Helen a text, letting her know she would not make it in at all due to an emergency.

"Wake up in there. You are sleeping way too long. It is almost eight and I am ready to do me shopping, so get a move on! I've got pancakes on the stove and bacon in the oven, so get on out here, girlie," Augusta said in a huff.

"Coming, just let me focus for a minute." Shelby stumbled out of her bedroom while tying her bathrobe together and walking to the room's spacious attached bathroom. She surveyed her reflection in the mirror over the sink. With a heavy sigh, she immediately turned on the cold water and splashed it on her face.

"What's keeping you?" Augusta shouted impatiently.

"Coming, Augusta, on my way out now. Good morning," Shelby said while pulling out a chair to have a seat at the table.

"Are you feeling all right this morning?" Augusta asked while looking Shelby over before setting a cup of coffee in front of her.

"Yes, of course, I'm fine. Why do you ask?"

"You don't look all that fine. You look like you been scared to death by the sight of a skunk. Hair a mess, eyes red, skin all puffy. Maybe we better stay in today," Augusta said while filling both their plates with bacon, pancakes, and sliced fruit.

"No, I'm all right, just need to get some food in me. Yum, this looks and smells so good, can't wait to dig in!"

Augusta sat down opposite Shelby and stared straight at her before saying, "I haven't known you that long, Shelby Malloy, but I can tell when something is bothering you. Yes, ma'am, I certainly can. Now spill it." Shelby played with her bacon, pushing it back and forth on her plate with her fork. "What is wrong? Is the bacon too crisp for you this morning?"

"No, Augusta, it's delicious, perfect! Thank you!" Shelby sat up straight in her seat, tossed her fork in her plate, and wiped her mouth with a napkin. "Augusta, we have to go back to see Dr. Rosenbloom today."

"Why? What for? I don't like that doctor. I don't care how good he looks." Augusta thought to herself for a second about what she had just said about the doctor's looks. "You think he could develop any interest in an old woman like me?" Augusta asked with a smile.

"Absolutely! You're beautiful! Any man your age would be happy to have you. Well, you will get some more eye candy today because we have an appointment to meet with him this morning."

"He pokes and prods too much. Plus, he asks too many questions. I answer one. He asks me two more. I answer those two, and he ask me four more. Nope, not going back," Augusta said with determination.

"We have to go!"

"What about me shopping? I want to go shopping. I was looking forward to it, you promised me. I didn't want to go and make you spend money, but you were the one who insisted and now I can't go."

"Oh, we are still going. I am taking the entire day off now, just so I can get to spend the day with you and get in our shopping!"

"Oh, thank you, thank you! I got to find me something that matches my pink lipstick, some clothes that match it."

"Augusta, Dr. Rosenbloom found a small lump in your left breast. It has to be biopsied." Augusta didn't respond right away. Instead, she took a bite of her bacon, calmly wiped her mouth with her napkin, then stood up and walked to the window over the kitchen sink and stared out at the start of a new day.

"Augusta, did you hear me?"

"I'm not deaf. I heard every word you said. I'm an old woman, Shelby. My best days behind me now. My body hurts most days whether I stand or sit. My hair has turned gray. My movements slow. All this is an indication that I'm nearing my end. What will be will be," Augusta said while still staring out the window. Shelby slammed her fist down on the table so hard she almost broke a nail.

"Enough! Stop that! You are not going anywhere, not if I have anything to do with it! Now get dressed and let's get to that doctor's office, get this over with, move forward with our life! We've got shopping to do for you again, as if we haven't shopped enough for you already, Ms. Augusta!"

* * * * *

Claudia had Augusta and Shelby wait in Dr. Rosenbloom's office as soon as they arrived, per his instructions. As soon as he walked in, he reached down and hugged Augusta's tiny frame, then took Shelby's hands in his, patted the back of one of them before asking, "How are you, my dear?"

Shelby forced a smile and said, "I'm fine. I hope you are." Dr. Rosenbloom smiled and took a seat behind his desk to explain all that would be involved with performing the biopsy. When he was finished, neither Shelby nor Augusta said anything. They both just sat there, Shelby praying for strength in her heart to deal with the situation, and Augusta staring straight ahead.

An hour later, Augusta and Shelby left the doctor's office and stepped out into a sunny day. Shelby thought to herself, *Thank goodness that part is over*, then realized that now the wait for the biopsy results would be even more worrisome than learning about the lump itself. Determined not to let it ruin their day together, Shelby said cheerfully, "Hey you, let's go shopping!" She kissed Augusta on the cheek, and the two of them walked toward her car to head to the nearest mall.

CHAPTER FOURTEEN

SHELBY PUT THE FINISHING TOUCHES on a letter Helen asked her to type up and send to a prospective client, logged off her computer, and hurried to Helen's office to drop it off so she could head home. It was dark and cold out. She wanted to get home before it got too late.

After dropping the letter off, she headed for the elevators, but before she could push the button, her cell phone rang. She started to ignore it, but thinking it might be Dr. Rosenbloom calling with Augusta's biopsy results, she answered it. First, she stared at the number for a second in an effort to recognize who was calling, but the number was unfamiliar to her. "Hello," she said cautiously.

"Good evening, Shelby." Myron's voice came over the phone crystal clear, too clear.

"Well, to what do I owe this pleasure, and how did you get my number?"

"Remember, you called me a bit ago, wanting to talk on a Saturday or Sunday, so that's how I got your number. It showed on my caller ID. Also, I remember being a little rude to you. I apologize for that. I still love you, Shelby. I feel very bad about being so rude to you that day."

"What is it now, Myron? Did you lose your job again? What?"

"I'm here waiting at the Port Kilmonth Hotel."

"Hotel, Myron?"

"If you are not here in the next hour, I'll know it's really over between us, and I will move on with my life, never bother you again. However, if you are knocking on door 832 in the next hour, I will know you really want to save our marriage."

"Myron, I…" He hung up.

Shelby stood there for about five minutes trying to decide what to do. She tried dialing the number he'd just called from right back, but no answer. She thought about Paula, tapped her name under the speed dial list, and after three rings, Paula picked up.

"Hey you, I was just about to call to see if you wanted to go out for drinks."

"Not tonight, Paula. I have a big decision to make and I need your help. Myron just called and invited me to meet him at the Port Kilmonth Hotel, Rm. 832, to discuss our marriage."

"Don't go, Shelby. Don't do it, just go home!"

"Paula, I want my marriage to work and—" Shelby couldn't finish her sentence before Paula yelled at her across the phone.

"Have you lost your ever-loving mind? Think, Shelby, why a hotel? Why, instead of somewhere public, in the open where there are other people around?"

"I still love him, Paula."

"All the more reason not to go. Love will make you do and say crazy things, you know that. So why would you go there knowing how things are between you and Myron?" Suspicion and anger overtook Shelby.

"It just burns you up, doesn't it?"

"What, what are you talking about?"

"You know perfectly well what I'm talking about. It kills you that Myron wants to be with me tonight and not you, doesn't it? How did you know he'd lost his job before I did, Paula, how?"

"Shelby! Please! For the love of sanity, listen to me! Please don't go! Shelby… Shelby, do you hear me? Just tell me where you are and I'll come get you. We can discuss this calmly and rationally. Please just walk away from this, please!"

"Walking away from Myron is not the problem, it would be like eating ice cream to walk away, so easy and so sweet. But feeling I did not do all I could to save my marriage would be a bitter pill to swallow. This is his last chance," after having said this Shelby hung up on Paula.

Paula immediately dialed her back, and after what seemed an eternity, Shelby finally picked up. "Leave me alone, Paula, just leave me alone. I'm going to try and save my marriage."

"Shelby, he is engaged to some other woman, Haverty! Remember her? Why would you want to meet to discuss anything with a man who hasn't even divorced you and is considering marrying someone else. Why? Why ask for my advice and then not listen to me?"

"Because I thought I could count on you to help me Paula."

"I am trying to help you but you refuse to listen to me because it's not what you want to hear." Shelby hung up on Paula a second time.

Paula raced to her laptop and googled the address for the Port Kilmonth Hotel. Once she had it, she ran out the door and jumped into her truck. Traffic was thick. She wove in and out of cars, trucks, bikes, and people. She made it through three yellow traffic lights only to be stopped at a red light that took so long to change she feared it was broken. She sat there, her mind racing, then took a quick glance behind her. Noticing there were no cars, she backed up, and when she felt it was safe, she veered off to the right in another direction she was familiar with to the hotel address. The speed limit for the road she was on was forty-five miles an hour. She was doing eighty. She glanced in her mirrors every once in a while to make sure there were no cops around. Once she saw that there were none, she took her speed up to eighty-five, cutting in front of the car ahead of her that seemed to be about to fall apart. She almost lost control of her truck by breaking in front of the car, but she somehow managed to keep the truck steady while the driver in the car she had just cut off laid on their horn angrily.

Paula finally entered the parking lot of the hotel about an hour and thirty minutes later, cursing the traffic. She quickly backed into a spot, parked, and almost fell down in her haste to get out and run. She ran as fast as she could toward the entrance of the hotel while commending herself for being in terrific shape and proving faithful to her early morning jogs, as her speed picked up. She burst through the door and ran up to the reception desk. She was out of breath but was able to get the numbers 832 out.

"Eight three two, room 832! My boyfriend is in there and he is sick. I need to get to him and fast, may I please have a key to that room?" The front desk agent pulled out her book that listed the names and rooms of all their guests.

"What is your boyfriend's name, ma'am?"

"Myron, Myron Malloy," Paula said out of breath.

After checking her guests list the front desk agent said, "I'm sorry ma'am, but your boyfriend must be feeling better. He just checked out."

"What? Was there anyone with him?"

"I couldn't tell you. I don't know what he looks like."

"Paula, what are you doing here?" Paula turned in the direction of Shelby's voice. She froze, unable to speak or move. Shelby's right eye was swollen shut and the cut above it was made more obvious by the makeup she'd used to try and conceal it. Her bottom lip was slit and trembled as she tried to speak.

Shelby's dress was bloody and ripped at the sleeve, revealing a cut that looked to need about eight stitches. She tried to make it to Paula but fell before she could get to her. The front desk agent snatched up the phone and dialed 911. Paula stood there immobilized, unable to speak, to comprehend what Shelby must have gone through in that hotel room before she was able to get out of there. Rage and devastation paralyzed her entire body, her mind. As much as she wanted to rush to Shelby, she couldn't move.

When she was finally able to find her voice, she said to herself, "I'll kill you, Myron, so help me, I'll kill you, if it's the last thing I do."

*   *   *   *   *

Myron climbed in his car, locked the doors, and fastened his seatbelt. Before starting the engine, he pulled out his cell phone and sent Ricky a text message that said, "Remember the day you threw me to the ground in front of Shelby and I told you you'd regret it?" Ricky's text response came in less than five minutes.

"What have you done, man? Where is Shelby? Is she all right?"

Myron responded "LOL," slowly put his cell phone in his jacket pocket, started the engine, and drove off.

CHAPTER FIFTEEN

PAULA SAT IN THE EMERGENCY room waiting area eager for some news from the doctor on staff that night who was caring for Shelby. She was so tired she could hardly think straight. Her head hurt and she needed a good stiff drink. She'd begged the nurses to let her stay in the room assigned to Shelby in emergency, but they told her that Shelby needed stitches and other medical care, examinations that prevented her from being able to stay with Shelby. After a few rounds of debate with the nurses, security being called in, and Paula being warned that she either remove herself from the room or be removed from the hospital, she finally gave in, left the room, and tried to make herself comfortable on one of the seats in the waiting area.

Shelby had not come around since she'd passed out at the hotel. This bothered Paula greatly and made her almost explode with anger towards Myron. "Thank goodness I can't get to Myron, because I would truly wind up in prison tonight and strutting an orange jumpsuit, which would be punishment enough for taking his stinking life." Paula had called Helen earlier, giving her as brief and as vague an explanation as possible concerning Shelby. She let her know that she would not be in. She'd be with Shelby. Finally, the doctor appeared. Paula jumped up and rushed to him before he could get to her.

"How is she? Is she all right? Has she come around?" Dr., Isen held up his hands in an effort to calm Paula and stop her flood of questions.

"She has finally come around," the doctor said with sympathy for Shelby and Paula. "However, she had to have several stitches, and because she experienced some mild trauma to the head, we are keeping her overnight for observation."

"Of course, Doctor. May I see her now, please?"

"Give it about thirty minutes. She is being taken up to her room, room 702. You may go up to see her then, but please remember what she has gone through tonight and limit your talking and questions. Rest is the best cure for her tonight. I will check in on her before I leave. Good night. Oh, Paula, Shelby gave me her home number and asked me to tell you to please call someone named Augusta and let her know she is all right and will be home as soon as possible."

"Sure, I will. Good night, Doctor, and thank you again."

Dr. Isen gave Paula a reassuring smile and said, "You are welcome. You get some rest too, Paula. You look like you could use it."

"Yes, Doctor, thank you."

What a cutie, and he remembered my name, Paula thought to herself as Dr. Isen walked away. *Wonder if he is married.* Her thoughts of Dr. Isen were quickly erased by the vision of Shelby's bruised and swollen eye along with her other injuries.

Shelby turned toward the door when Paula walked into her hospital room. She then turned away out of shame and hurt. Paula walked over to her bed, bent down, and kissed Shelby on the forehead. She sat in a chair in the corner near Shelby's bed, allowing her head to rest against the back of the chair. Paula relaxed and said, "I'm hungry. Sure wish I had some potato chips." They both laughed, and Shelby soon drifted off to sleep.

Paula pulled out the slip of paper Dr. Isen gave her with Shelby's home number on it, although she didn't need it. She knew it by heart. She ran Augusta's name over and over in her mind trying to figure out who she was. She didn't remember Shelby saying anything about a relative coming to visit her. She gave up trying to figure out or remember who she was and quietly walked out of Shelby's room to make the call.

The phone didn't have a chance to finish ringing before Augusta picked it up. "Hello, hello, who is this? Shelby, is that you? Where are you? I've been worried sick!"

"Hello, this is Paula, a friend of Shelby's. I take it I'm speaking to Augusta?"

"Yes, you are, and where is my Shelby? Is she all right?"

"Yes, ma'am, she is. She asked me to give you a call and let you know that she will be home sometime tomorrow. She has to have something taken care of." Augusta did not respond. "Ma'am, are you there?"

"Yes, I'm here. Why didn't she call me herself to tell me this? Where is my Shelby? I'm no fool. I know something is wrong. Shelby is never this late getting in." Paula swore under her breath.

"Trust me, she is fine. We will see you tomorrow."

"I don't care about seeing you tomorrow. I want to see Shelby, and trust me, you'd better deliver her in one piece, lady!" Augusta hung up the phone, leaving Paula stunned and even more determined to find out who she was.

As promised, Dr. Isen came in to check on Shelby before leaving. It was eleven o'clock the next morning, and both Shelby and Paula were more than ready to leave the hospital. Police officers had come in earlier to question Shelby about her incident, what happened and who attacked her. To Paula's disappointment and anger, Shelby had refused to answer their questions. The only thing left to do was to help Shelby get dressed and take her home.

Augusta was sitting on the side of her bed when Shelby and Paula came in. As soon as she heard the front door open, she jumped up and ran to the living room.

"Oh, my goodness, what happened to you, Shelby!" Augusta said, scurrying up to them. "Why are you so banged up? What do you know about this, lady?" Augusta asked, turning her attention to Paula. "You had better answer right, 'cause if you don't, I have got a frying pan in the kitchen with your name written all over it."

"Listen, old woman, it was a long night and I don't feel like going to jail, so back off!"

"Old woman! Who do you think you are talking to, you half pint of a person."

"Half pint? Look who is talking," Paula said while putting her hands on her hips and staring Augusta down.

"Please stop it, you two," Shelby said while trying to make it to her bedroom.

"I'm so sorry, Shelby. Here, I'll help you." Paula took Shelby by the hand and gently led her to her bed so she could sit down and remove her clothes. She then went in the bathroom to start the shower for her. Augusta rolled her eyes at Paula, but for Shelby's sake, she went to the kitchen to make her hot tea and some lunch without another word, realizing that to argue about the situation with Paula was useless. However, she had already made up in her mind that as soon as the opportunity presented itself, she was going to question her again.

After Shelby had taken a painkiller that evening and drifted off to sleep, Augusta approached Paula. "What is going on? What happened to her?"

"Listen, I have no idea who you are, and I apologize for my show of disrespect to you. However, I think it best Shelby tells you herself when she is feeling better," Paula said while rubbing the back of her neck to alleviate some of the stress that was causing it to knot up. Augusta turned without a word, walked to her room, and slammed the door. Paula went in the bathroom and showered. After grabbing spare blankets and pillows from the closet, she tiptoed into Shelby's room, pulled a clean night gown from the drawer, slid it on, then curled up under the covers on the family room sofa and fell asleep.

CHAPTER SIXTEEN

PAULA SPRUNG UP WHEN SHE heard heavy banging on Shelby's door. Her thoughts shot directly to Myron as she ran to the kitchen to find a weapon, any weapon to defend Shelby against another attack from Myron. Augusta came running out of her room, asking, "What! Who is that banging on the door like that?" as she rushed to open it.

"Augusta! No!" Paula screamed as she raced back in the room. "Don't open that door. It's Myron, Shelby's husband!" Augusta stopped in her tracks. Meanwhile the banging on the door became louder and more persistent.

"Shelby's husband? Shelby is married? To who?"

"Myron, the man who beat her up last night!"

"Her husband beat the crap out of her like that?"

"Augusta, please! Call 911 now, right now!"

"Nine one one, I don't need no 911. Let him in," she said as she turned and ran back in her room returning with her hands in her pocket. "Let him in, Paula. Let the bastard in!"

"No, Augusta," Paula said as she raced to her purse to get her phone to call 911 herself. Before she could complete the call, she heard Augusta opening the front door.

Paula quickly turned around to see Augusta standing back from the door and pointing a gun right at Ricky's head.

"Augusta, no, stop! That is not Myron. I was mistaken! Please put the gun away. What in the world are you doing with a gun?"

Ricky walked in the room slowly, holding both hands in the air. "Augusta, put that thing away," Paula said cautiously, not wanting to say or do anything to set Augusta off. She knew that hurt mixed with anger was a dangerous combination, and all you want to do is rid yourself of those feelings at whatever expense. "Augusta," Paula said, speaking to her as if she were a child. "Please, Augusta, put it away before someone gets hurt. This is Ricky, not Myron, okay? I thought it was Myron coming after Shelby again, but I was wrong, thank goodness! Put the gun away now, please."

Augusta stood her ground and kept the gun pointed at Ricky while asking, "You the one who hurt me Shelby?"

"No, ma'am," Ricky said nervously. "It wasn't me! I swear, it wasn't me! I would never hurt Shelby." Ricky tried to make a connection with Augusta, hoping it would relax her into putting the gun away. "You must be Augusta. I've heard a lot about you," he said while flashing his sexy smile.

"Really, well, I've heard nothing about you. I am going to put the gun down, but I will pick it back up if I have to, and trust me, I will blow you from here clear to the North Pole if you so much as blink! Do you hear me?"

"Yes, ma'am, I hear you."

"My eyes may be growing dim and footsteps slowing down, but my hands are steady after years of practicing at a firing range, and I mean I will lay your soul to rest tonight if I have to."

Augusta slowly lowered the gun, stepping aside to let Ricky walk past her. She then turned and walked back in her room, closing the door softly behind her. "Just because I'm behind this door, don't think I am sleeping because I'm not and will be back out there before you can say help, if I have to," Augusta yelled from behind her bedroom door.

"What's going on?" Paula and Ricky turned to see Shelby standing in the room with a look of confusion on her face.

"Shelby, did Myron do this to you?" Ricky could not believe what he was seeing. Shelby's eye was still very swollen, to the point of almost distorting her face, and taking in her other bruises and cuts made Ricky ill. "Did he?" Ricky demanded a second time. He was so mad he yelled the words at her. Shelby jumped.

"Don't yell at her, Ricky. Give her time to answer. She has been through enough in the last day or so," Paula said.

Ricky put both hands on his head and paced from one end of the room to the other. He was devastated. Not knowing what else to do, he turned to a wall, and before he knew it, he'd put his fist through it. Shelby and Paula gasped and covered their mouth as they witnessed him do it. Augusta came out of her room at the sound of the noise. She looked at Ricky, then Paula, and then at Shelby before saying, "I hope and pray me and this Myron person never cross paths because I might forget I'm a lady." She then turned and walked back in her room, softly closing the door behind her.

Shelby walked over and sat down on the loveseat, curling her legs up under her as she said, "All right, let's just all calm down so we can discuss this quietly and like adults." Paula looked at her and rolled her eyes in frustration, but did as she was asked and went to sit down beside her. Ricky kept standing and staring into space as if he was in some kind of a trance, oblivious to the fact that he had just put a hole in the wall. "Ricky, please sit down," Shelby asked softly while making a mental note to call and make an appointment to have her wall repaired. "Augusta, will you please come out here?" Shelby called to her. Augusta didn't answer. The door to her room remained closed without any indication of Augusta coming out.

"Shelby, what are you doing?"

"What am I doing? What do you mean what am I doing, Paula?"

"You are sitting there looking like sh—"

"Don't say it, Paula, don't you dare say it. You know how I feel about that kind of language!" Paula turned on Shelby angrily.

"Well, then tell me, please! What type of language do you like and understand? What? Is it Greek, Latin, Portuguese? Because you obviously don't understand English! I begged you in English, Shelby! Plain, clear, unmistakable English not to go to that hotel to meet Myron, and what did you do? You went anyway! You know what, I know what language I should have used, how about this, *duh!*"

"I was trying to save my marriage, Paula. Can't you understand that?"

"Marriage, really! What marriage? Shelby, Myron is engaged to someone else, for god's sake!"

"Shut up! Both of you, just shut up," Ricky shouted and stormed toward the front door to leave.

"Ricky, stop, please! Where are you going?" Ricky froze and turned to answer Shelby with a coldness and darkness in his eyes she'd never seen before. Not Ricky, not happy-go-lucky Ricky.

He put his hands in his pockets and let out a heavy sigh before saying, "Shelby, look, I'm really sorry about your wall. I will pay to have it fixed."

"It's okay, Ricky, I understand. I've already got it covered, but I still want to know where you are going."

"I'm going to do something I should have done a long time ago, Shelby, something I should have done a long time ago!"

"Well, hell, let me come with you. I'll help you kill him!"

"Paula, stop that! Nobody is killing anyone. Violence is not the answer. Never has been and never will be. You can't fight a violent person with violence," Shelby said.

"Well, then, how do we fight him? How else?" Ricky said, walking up to Shelby and looking her right in the eyes.

"Ricky, I don't have the answer to that right now, but I know violence is not the answer. Usually, someone gets hurt and most likely it's the innocent ones who will suffer the most." Ricky laughed and looked up at the ceiling.

"When I walked in and saw your eyes and lips all cut and swollen, Shelby, so help me, I was ready to die. I didn't care anything about living, I didn't care if I lived to see another day, I just wanted Myron six feet under. So help me, Shelby, I don't care anymore. What good is my life if I'm constantly running, looking over my shoulder, constantly wondering if my next meal is going to be my last. Baby, that ain't living, so I got nothing to lose if I put that miserable SOB in the ground." Silence hung in the air as they each fought to hold their hurt, anger, and frustration at bay.

"I'll tell you how to fight a violent person," Augusta said as she walked into the room.

"Augusta," Shelby said, trying to figure out how she'd walked in the room without being noticed.

"After you've taken legal steps to protect yourself and reasoning with the person fails, you wait and you wait and you wait. But while you are waiting, you plan your defense and prepare yourself for the worst, because one of you during the next attack, whoever initiates it, might die. The next time you're with them and they are all calm and joyful, just when they think all is well and they are in a good mood, you haul off and smack the hell out of them."

"What?" Paula said.

"Just smack the hell out of them!"

"Augusta, that makes no sense," Shelby said. Augusta ignored her and kept talking.

"When they ask you, in this case we are referring to Myron of course, why you did that? You simply ask them how it feels being smacked around without just cause. At first, they will be stunned because they are not expecting you to initiate the attack. Then you call them what they are, an abuser and attacker. This will anger them to the point of coming after you, and when they do, you scream as loud as you can, pull out your weapon you have been holding onto the entire time, and lay their soul to rest. So invite Myron over for dinner one evening. Whenever you're ready, I'll be ready. Just do it."

"What do you mean you will be ready?" Shelby asked.

"What I mean is, I will be right here to help you if you need it, that's all I'm saying." Ricky looked at Augusta and tried to figure out if she was truly serious, because if so, he was all for it.

"Works for me," Paula said.

"It will never work. Myron will never come here for dinner, not now, not after what he has done. He will know it's a setup. No, it will never work and I could not live with myself knowing I set a plan in motion to take someone's life. No, no way. I am not that person, that animal who would just take another person's life."

"I have a plan," Paula said while getting up off the loveseat and walking to the middle of the room and folding her hands over her chest. "Trust me, it will work."

"Paula, I will be no part of a plan to injure Myron in any way."

"Fine, I will never touch a hair on his head, and you will not learn of what happened until after it's over, maybe? Augusta, may I have a word with you alone, please?"

"Can't say I'm too crazy about you, but all right." Augusta followed Paula into the kitchen to hear what she had to say.

CHAPTER SEVENTEEN

AUGUSTA KNOCKED ON MYRON'S DOOR for the fifth time, determined to stay there until he came to the door. Paula waited for her in her truck out of view, knowing Myron would recognize her truck, but glad he had never met Augusta and, according to her earlier conversation with Haverty, nor Haverty's mother. Just when Augusta was about to knock again, Myron opened the door. Myron took one look at Augusta and said, "Sorry, ma'am, you must have the wrong door."

"Oh no, sir," Augusta said quickly. "I am sure this is the right place."

"Myron, come on, babe. Dinner is getting cold and I'm hungry," Haverty called to him from the kitchen.

"Coming, babe. Listen, ma'am, what's up? Who are you looking for?"

"Please, sir, just a few minutes of your time. You see the lady that just called to you, I saw her when she went into this house. She is my daughter and I'm trying to surprise her with these pictures I'm sure she will love. Been following her around all day, waiting for just the right time to surprise her. You see, I know she would never expect me to show up at someone else's place," Augusta said with a big grin on her face. Myron still had his doubts about Augusta just showing up at his front door. Still, Augusta was able to convince him to let her in. "Okay, now I need your help. May I please use your coffee table to spread these pictures out while I ask you to go get her and bring her in the room? Just give me five minutes and I will be ready."

Myron did as Augusta asked, feeling good about being a part of what he thought was a surprise for Haverty. When he left the room, Augusta cleared all the things off the coffee table and then covered it with wedding pictures of Myron and Shelby, as well as a few pictures Shelby allowed Paula to take of her swollen eye and split lip. "I'm ready, you can come in now."

Myron walked in the room behind Haverty while covering her eyes, Haverty was giggling and trying to figure out what was going on. He uncovered her eyes and shouted "surprise!" excitedly before he realized the pictures were of him and Shelby. By the time he noticed their wedding pictures and the ones of Shelby all bruised and battered, Haverty had already seen them.

Haverty stopped giggling. Myron stood in shock. "Myron, is this some kind of a joke?" Haverty said, swinging around to face him. "Are you married, and who is this lady? Myron, what is going on?" Myron couldn't answer. He was too busy trying to gather himself and figure out what was going on himself. "I asked you a question. Are you married?"

"Who the hell are you, old woman, and how did you get my wedding pictures?"

"Then you are married!" Haverty shouted at him and smacked him so hard he was speechless for a second.

"Baby, wait, wait wait wait. I don't know this woman. I've never seen her before in my life! Get out of my house before I throw you out," Myron roared at Augusta.

"Oh, my goodness, sir, I am so sorry," Augusta said, pretending she was just as surprised and confused as he was.

Haverty angrily picked up the picture of Shelby with the swollen eye and took a closer look at it, still not recognizing Shelby as the one who had bought a townhouse from her in Green Oak. She was too stunned by the sight of her swollen eye and split lip. She slowly laid the picture down before saying, "Get out of my sight, Myron. Get out of my sight! Not only are you married, but a wife abuser as well. You did this to the woman in this picture, your wife?" Myron stood there not knowing what to say, searching for an excuse, afraid that whatever he said, Haverty would be able to see right through his attempted deception. "What happened to this woman's face?"

"I have never seen the woman in that picture before in my life!"

"Oh, and you just happened to be posing in a wedding picture with her as the man she just married? Plus, idiot, you just admitted to these being your wedding pictures. Myron, do you think I'm a fool, and what kind of fool are you, to believe I would accept the lie you just gave me? I never want to see you again. If you come anywhere near me or my home, I'll have my brothers hunt you down and beat the crap out of you, just as you did to the poor woman in this picture. She is your wife, Myron, your wife! How could you do this to her?" Haverty said while picking up the picture and shaking it in Myron's face. "How?"

Haverty helped Augusta pick up her pictures and put them back in the envelope. Just when they had put the last picture back in the envelope, Myron went to grab Augusta, but Augusta was too quick and pulled her gun from her coat pocket. Aiming it right at Myron's face, she said, "Make my day! Back up, or so help me, I will put a hole in you that will go through you and the wall behind you!" Haverty turned and grabbed her purse, then ran to the front door and flung it open, waiting for Augusta to get to it. She shouted at Myron, "You miserable lowlife!"

Augusta said before turning to leave, "You don't know me, but I know you and where you live. You know people, well, so do I. Touch my Shelby again and me and my people will help you end your miserable life." With that, she and Haverty turned and ran out the door, slamming it behind them.

Once outside, Augusta quickly apologized for ruining Haverty's evening, then warned her to stay away from Myron if she didn't want to wind up like the woman in the pictures.

"Oh, believe me, I'm done with Myron. I never want to see him again!"

"Good, take care," Augusta said while running to jump in Paula's truck.

"Wait, who are you?" Haverty called after her. Augusta jumped in the truck and slammed the door. Before Paula sped off, she answered Haverty by saying, "A woman from the streets with a lot of sense. See ya!"

Once Paula and Augusta pulled up in front of Shelby's house and made sure they had not been followed by Myron, they burst into laughter and cheers for their success in pulling off Paula's plan so well. "How on earth did you know Haverty would be at Myron's place around this time?" Augusta asked Paula while still laughing.

"Oh, I just paid Haverty a visit this morning and coaxed her into a little friendly conversation. Once she thought I was interested in buying a house, she was willing to tell me anything I wanted to know, including her plans for the evening."

"You do good work," Augusta said while putting the pictures of Myron and Shelby back in her bag.

"But, oh, Augusta, I'm not done with our boy Myron yet. As a matter of fact, I'm just getting started. He is going to pay dearly for what he did to our girl."

"Good, there was no reason for him to beat up on my Shelby like that, no matter how stupid she was for going to that hotel that night."

"Remember, Augusta, Shelby must never know what we did today, promise?"

"Promise," Augusta said. The two of them said good night while Augusta got out to go in the house. Paula then drove off heading for home.

CHAPTER EIGHTEEN

IT WAS A SATURDAY EVENING, two weeks after Myron's attack on Shelby. Rain fell in a soft mist outside, and Shelby was finishing up a conversation with Ricky who had called to see how she was doing. Ricky still could not believe Shelby had taken Augusta, a homeless person, in her own home off the streets. She was still trying to convince him that she had and did not regret doing so at all when they hung up.

"What's for dinner?" Shelby yelled in the kitchen to Augusta.

"Come see for yourself."

"Okay, I will." Shelby walked in the kitchen and let out a scream, jumping up and down and clapping her hands like a child at the sight of her favorite meal of baked fish, asparagus, and mashed potatoes. "Augusta, you truly are the best, thank you so much!"

"You are very welcome. Now sit down and eat your dinner before it gets cold," Augusta said while untying her apron to sit down and join Shelby for dinner.

After they finished eating, Augusta pulled out a small black suede box and handed it to Shelby.

"What's this?"

"Open it," Augusta said with a sheepish grin. Shelby carefully opened the little black box tied with a pink ribbon. *Seems she has fallen in love with the color pink since she took my pink lipstick*, Shelby thought to herself.

Inside the box was a shiny, silver dime. A small hole had been pierced in the top of it to allow for a beautiful silver chain to fit through it so Shelby could wear it around her neck as a necklace. "Oh, Augusta, it is absolutely beautiful, but why?"

"Today is our anniversary. I did not forget. A dime brought us together, the day I asked you for a dime to feed my Mittens and you gave me enough money to feed me and my cat. I baked you a cake too," Augusta said, jumping up from the table and going to the refrigerator to pull out an upside-down pineapple cake with "Happy Anniversary to Me and Shelby" written on it.

Shelby couldn't hold back the tears. In between sobs, she managed to say, "I don't have anything to give you."

"You have given me plenty," Augusta said. "A nice home to live in, healthy food to eat, medical care, a clean, warm bed to sleep in at night, and a family… me and you. You saved me life. Yes, ma'am, you saved me life," Augusta said while wiping away her own tears.

After they both blew their nose and hugged, Shelby said, "I invited Ricky to have dinner with you, me, and Paula tomorrow night. Is that all right with you?"

"Sure, I suppose you want me to do the cooking?"

"Well, you are the better cook."

"I will make something real special for you and your man."

"He is not my man. We are just friends."

"Sure, you are. I saw the way you were looking at that man when he was here the other day. Nothing wrong with that. I would look at him like that too, if I were younger," Augusta said with a wink.

Sunday came with a streak of sunlight filtering into Shelby's bedroom. For the first time in weeks, she was really happy for so many reasons. First of all, Augusta's biopsy had come back showing no trace of breast cancer. The swelling in her eye and face had gone down, and she looked like herself again, and knowing Ricky would be coming to dinner that night painted a smile on her face for the rest of the morning while she cleaned, decorated, and rearranged furniture in preparation for her dinner that night.

At six o'clock, she heard a knock on the door. Still in a very good mood and with the aroma of Augusta's dinner penetrating her nostrils, she opened it.

"Hello you!" she said to Paula. "Don't you look fabulous," Shelby complimented her. Paula sashayed into the room wearing a fitted black dress that boasted a slim V-cut in the back that went all the way down and rested just above her butt. The dress was stunning, and Paula certainly wore it well, Shelby had to admit. It showed off her every curve, falling just below the knee to introduce her shapely legs made more so by the slim black stilettos she was wearing. A small pair of diamond earrings, the only jewelry she wore, complimented her short black haircut. "What a beautiful, crazy woman you are," Shelby said while stepping to the side to let her finish sashaying into the room.

"Don't hate, darling. You're pretty too, just not as pretty as I am," Paula said jokingly. Paula stopped and stared at Shelby before saying, "What is that you are wearing? A jean dress and flats, are you out of your mind? Where is your sexy? A jean dress Shelby, you are hosting a dinner not a boredom party.

"Paula, I invited Ricky to dinner, not on a date."

"I told her not to wear that old rag," Augusta said while walking into the room. "She didn't even bother to put on any lipstick."

"That's okay, Augusta, 'cause you are wearing enough for all three of us," Paula said and went to pour herself a glass of wine. A few minutes later, she was back and saying, "Hurry up, Shelby. Please run upstairs, pull off that touch-me-not dress, and trash it. I will stall for you until you come down if Ricky shows up before you get back."

"Forget it, Paula. I'm rocking my jean dress tonight." Paula and Augusta looked at each other and shook their head.

Shortly after Paula arrived, there was another knock on the door, and Shelby opened it to see a glowing Agacia standing in front of her, holding Ricky's hand. Her beautiful brown skin was highlighted by the high-collared, ruffled white blouse that showed just a hint of cleavage, with which she wore a straight red skirt that flared at the hem and accented her red, white, and black stilettos perfectly. Her black mane of hair was pulled back from her face in a classy ponytail, showing off her deep dimples.

"Hey, Shel," Ricky said while giving her a hug and a kiss on the cheek. "You remember Agacia, don't you?"

"Of course, I do. Good to see you, Agacia. Please, the two of you come on in. Make yourself comfortable while I go check on dinner."

"I'll come with you," Paula said after a quick hello to Ricky and Agacia.

Augusta too followed them into the kitchen. "That woman put the B in beautiful and the S in sexy, Shelby, and what do you choose to wear tonight? You are standing there in Grandma's finest. You are hopeless, hopeless!" Paula said while putting one hand on her hips and tapping her fingertips on the kitchen island out of frustration.

"Bet you wish you had curled your hair now," Augusta chimed in.

"Look, you two, leave me alone. Tonight is about a nice dinner with friends. Ricky has been in hiding for a long time, and I'm happy he came out tonight to have dinner with us. So let's go in, sit down, and enjoy ourselves."

Just as they were finishing up dinner, Ricky asked everyone to give him their attention for just a few minutes. He turned to Agacia, took her hand, and said, while still looking in her eyes, "This is my Agacia, my soon-to-be wife. We just got engaged last night." Upon hearing this, Paula picked up the half bottle of wine that was sitting on the table, turned it up to her mouth, and drank from it.

"Paula," Shelby scolded her. Augusta, who was sitting right beside Shelby, nudged her and said, "You still enjoying yourself?" Shelby tried to put on a big smile in spite of the pain that was slowly overtaking the joy she had felt earlier in the day. Somehow, she was able to say, "Congratulations, you two!"

CHAPTER NINETEEN

"AUGUSTA," SHELBY CALLED AS SHE walked in from an evening jog and started pulling off her running shoes. There was no response from Augusta, so Shelby tried again, "Gussie, where are you? Want to go out for dinner?" Still no answer, so Shelby started walking through the house, opening doors and peeping in. "Oh, I know where she is—the kitchen of course! I hope she hasn't started cooking yet. I don't smell anything." Walking hurriedly to the kitchen and confident that's where Augusta was, Shelby called again, "Gussie!"

Puzzled, Shelby walked back to the living room, pulled out her cell phone and called Paula. "What's up?" Paula answered while trying to balance the phone between her ear and shoulder so she could continue to polish her toenails.

"Did you stop by this evening, and if so, was Augusta here?"

"Nope, I've been in since I got home from work. Is she not there? You didn't see her when you came in after work?"

"No, and that's a little strange 'cause she is usually in the kitchen cooking dinner around this time. I wanted to take her out to dinner tonight, but I can't find her."

"Well, don't worry. She probably just took a walk or something. Call me back if she doesn't show up."

"All right," Shelby said absentmindedly, beginning to do just as Paula told her not to, worry.

Shelby felt chilled, which made her think about what Paula said about the possibility of Augusta taking a walk. Glancing at the time on her cell phone, six fifty, and it being cool out, she doubted very seriously that Augusta had taken a walk under those circumstances. Fifteen minutes passed, then twenty. Finally, an hour had come and gone. Shelby had almost finished a whole pack of chocolate chip cookies while waiting and staring at the door, hoping Augusta would walk through it any second.

In an effort to calm her nerves, Shelby tried to think on the fact that she always made sure Augusta had at least twenty dollars in her pocket and she knew her way around the city. She was a pro at riding the train, and the station was only a few short blocks away. Still, it was getting later and later and darker and darker. Finally, she'd had enough and decided to go look for her. She thought about calling Paula, but before she could pick up the phone to dial her number, Paula was calling her.

"See, told you there was no need to worry. Where is she, sleeping?" Paula started in without saying hello.

"No, she is still not here yet, and frankly, I'm getting worried. Going out to look for her."

Paula paused before saying, "Hey, Shel, Myron doesn't know where you live, does he?"

"No, why? I would never give him my new address. What is it, Paula?"

"Nothing. I don't know why that question popped in my head. Listen, why don't you start looking for her around your neighborhood. I'll be there shortly and will help you look for her."

"Oh, Paula, will you please? Thank you so much." Shelby put her running shoes back on and pulled a jacket from the closet by the door to put on over her leggings and T-shirt. She considered driving but decided against it, thinking she would spot her more easily on foot. She decided to just take her house keys and cell phone. It was very dark out by now, and the temperature had dropped considerably since her run earlier. "Augusta! Gussie!" Shelby called as she walked from one end of her development to the other. A dog barked in the distance, causing Shelby to jump out of fear, but she kept calling for Augusta, thinking that maybe she had taken the train and was walking toward home.

After almost thirty minutes of walking and calling for Augusta with no sign of her still, panic tried to set in, but Shelby fought it and started running toward the subway station. She spotted Paula's truck and hailed it down. Paula immediately pulled over to stop beside her.

"Where were you?" Paula asked anxiously. "I went driving around your area looking for you and Augusta."

"I am so sorry," Shelby said out of breath from running. "I forgot. I forgot you said you were coming. Paula, where the hell is she? What if something has happened to her? I'm calling the police!"

"Shelby, calm down! Remember, Augusta's not a child. I'm sure she can take care of herself."

"And that's supposed to make me feel better? Well, it doesn't, so stop talking like that."

"All right, I'm sorry. Stay here. I'm going to park the truck, and we can go look for her together."

While Paula was parking her truck, Shelby tried to think of every possible place she could be. "Okay, let's go," Paula said while running over to join Shelby. Just as they started running to the subway station, Shelby yelled, "Stop, wait a minute. I think I know where she might be!"

"What?"

"The truck, get back in the truck. It's about thirty minutes from here, the park on Jefferson!"

"Jefferson," Paula said, turning up her nose. "That's where a bunch of homeless people hang out."

"Remember the little lady on the train that asked me for a dime that day?"

"Yeah, what about her?" Suddenly, what Shelby had just said hit Paula like a ton of bricks. "No, no way! Are you serious? Augusta is that lady that was on the train?"

"Yes. Paula, she is clean and free from any disease you could possibly think of. I had Dr. Rosenbloom check her from head to toe, run every blood test known to man."

"I can't believe it. Augusta is this beautiful, tiny person with large gray eyes and long, thick, curly gray hair. Nothing like the woman on the train that day."

"I know, right? Look, Paula, come on. We need to get in the truck and go, now!"

After parking the truck as close to the park as possible, Shelby and Paula got out and began to search the park for Augusta. Paula remembered to bring a flashlight, and for that, Shelby was grateful. "Augusta!" they both called while stepping over sleeping bodies, drunk bodies, smelly bodies, and heaven only knew what other kind of bodies.

Finally, they spotted her standing by a bench with a tray in her hands and slowly walked up to her. "Gussie, what are you doing?" Shelby asked as if she was speaking to a two-year-old.

"Hi, Shelby, Paula. What are you doing here?"

"Augusta, that's exactly the question we are asking you," Paula said, covering her nose in an effort to block out the smells resulting from bodies gone unwashed for days, maybe even years.

"These are my friends. I came to visit and I brought them this tray of brownies. Would you two like a brownie?" They both politely said no thank you. "This here is Gus," Augusta said, pointing to the sleeping man on the bench and saying, "Gus, wake up, have a brownie. It will make you feel better." Gus didn't answer.

"Gussie, he is asleep, sweetie. It's really late and we should be getting home."

"All right," Augusta said. She reached on her tray, took off two brownies, and placed them on the bench in front of Gus so he could see them when he woke up. "See you later, Gus. Sorry you were sleeping by the time I got to you, but don't you worry. Your brownies will be right here waiting for you when you wake up in the morning. Good night."

Paula was driving Shelby and Augusta home and still trying to figure out how Augusta and the lady from the train could possibly be the same person. Suddenly, Augusta said, "Gus gave me my gun. He gave it to me to protect myself when I was homeless. He said no woman should be living on the streets without something to protect herself. He took me to a firing range and everything, so I could learn how to shoot it. He is a real good friend, Gus is. Yes, ma'am, a real good friend."

"Augusta, is the gun registered?" Shelby wanted to know.

"Of course, I have the paperwork to prove it too. Gus made sure everything was done as it should be with that gun. He does things real proper. Yes, ma'am, real proper."

"So where did Gus get a gun and how was he able to afford to take you to a firing range? He lives on the street too, right?" Paula asked.

"Only when he chooses to. When he is so drunk he can't find his way back home, on those nights he just sleeps it off in the park, or on the first bench he makes it to. He and his son own a gun shop downtown, run by his son most of the time."

"I see," Paula said.

"Gus lost his wife a few years ago and hasn't been right since. He suffers from depression, says drinking helps dull the pain."

Chapter Twenty

SHELBY AND AUGUSTA WERE SITTING in the family room relaxing, feeling a little too relaxed perhaps because neither of them had moved since five that afternoon. "You know, we really need to go grocery shopping tonight. There is nothing in the house to eat. I guess since you are always cooking, I could make us some sandwiches and a cup of soup for dinner." Augusta said nothing, just kept biting on her apple. Shelby stole a glance at her out of the corner of her eye. She looked peaceful and relaxed, sitting on the loveseat with her hair pinned up and a pink bow tied around her head. Whatever would Augusta do, Shelby thought to herself, if the color pink one day became obsolete.

Augusta seemed to be enjoying her apple and was leafing through a magazine. "Hey, soup and sandwiches tonight?" Shelby asked.

"Soup and sandwiches is a lazy man's dinner," Augusta answered while trying to figure out something she had just discovered in her magazine.

"Well, I am feeling pretty lazy right now," Shelby said as she let out a loud yawn and stretched. "Augusta?"

"I am trying to enjoy my magazine, but since you keep bugging me, I will just toss it to the side and give you my undivided attention, your royal highness," Augusta said sarcastically while tossing her magazine on the coffee table. Shelby laughed and ignored Augusta's sarcasm.

"Seriously, what was it like?"

"What?"

"Being homeless," Shelby said cautiously. Augusta looked at her for a second, then got up and walked to the kitchen to toss her apple core away. She stayed in there so long Shelby feared she would not return, in an effort to avoid answering her question, but she came back and sat down on the sofa beside her.

For a long time before saying anything, Augusta just gazed off into space. Shelby noticed that one of her eyes would twitch every so often, so she reached out and laid her hand on her back in case she was upset, while saying, "Augusta, I'm sorry I asked. We don't have to talk about it if you don't want to, I—"

"Try to imagine being cold, hungry, needing a bath, sick, and scared all at the same time," Augusta said still staring off into space. Shelby tried as hard as she could to imagine being in such a situation but couldn't. Every time she tried to, the very thought of it made her ill.

"I can't, I can't imagine it, Augusta," she said sadly.

"Exactly, because that is the way being homeless is, Shelby. You can't even imagine. People walk by you. All they see is a homeless person—dirty, smelling, and lying on the street. Most of them don't even take the time to say a greeting to you, let alone offer you a clean sandwich or a dollar or two for a cup of coffee when it's cold and biting out. That is what hurts more than anything, being ignored and left to die without no one offering to help you. In the mornings, people hurry past you all dressed up, with their heads held high, trying to figure out how to climb the corporate ladder and gain the prestige they so desperately need to validate their elevated opinion of themselves. In the evenings, they rush past you, hurrying to their homes and families to tell them about their day, to eat dinner, not once thinking about the homeless person they passed on the street and didn't even stop to offer them a piece of bread for the night."

Shelby just listened and rubbed her back consolingly. She didn't know what else to do. She thought about all the times she had passed a homeless person on the street and, like Augusta said, looked right at them and didn't even say hello. She closed her eyes and mentally said "I'm sorry" to all the homeless people she had ever walked by and never even took the time to say a greeting to. She vowed to never do it again.

"I used to be a schoolteacher at an all-girls private school, making good money. I had everything, sitting on top of the world, so I thought, until one day I was called in and told their funds were running out and they could no longer afford to pay me what I was used to and were letting me go. I offered to do the same job for less money, but they just didn't have the money."

"What did you do?"

"I started looking for work, but no one would hire me. Why, I don't know. I had plenty of experience, over ten years.

I can only assume it was because of my age. Unfortunately, today, youth, not experience in most cases, is what a lot of employers look at when they are considering a person for a certain position. I searched for work for years, unsuccessfully, using up all my savings and finally winding up on the street," Augusta said, letting out a heavy sigh.

"Your daughter, you said you had a daughter. Why didn't you turn to her?"

"I did, oh boy, what a huge mistake that was. Kelly, that is my daughter's name. Well, she is one of those folks who love the prestige, the money, the material things that go along with it and won't let nothing stand in her way of getting exactly what she wants. Well, my baby is cute but not very bright." Shelby slowly shook her head and continued to listen.

"One day she met a doctor who promised her the world and gave it to her in exchange for someone to clean his house, cook his food, and keep him warm in bed with no attachments. She lives with him. They let me stay with them for a while, but with the passing of time and me still not being able to find work and having nothing to contribute to the household funds, he told Kelly I had to go to a shelter. At first, Kelly fought him, but then he told her that she could go too if she didn't like it. The day she came to me and said, 'Mama, a shelter is not so bad' was the day I packed what few clothes I had, left, and have lived on the streets ever since. I have not seen or spoken to my daughter since that day."

"Oh, Augusta, I'm so sorry, but you have a home now."

Chapter Twenty-One

"THE MOVIE WE JUST SAW, thumbs up or down?" Shelby asked Paula and Augusta as they walked to her car after leaving the movie theater. Augusta gave it a thumbs-up and Paula gave it a thumbs-down. Shelby laughed as she said, "Can't you two ever agree on anything?"

Paula and Augusta said in unison, "No!"

"Are we stopping for something to eat? I'm hungry," Paula said while rubbing her stomach.

"I know what, why don't we all go back to my place and I will treat you guys to pizza and wings?" Shelby suggested.

"Works for me," Paula said.

"Me too," Augusta agreed.

Shelby pulled into her reserved parking space in front of her townhouse. "Wonder who those two men are standing in front of your house. Hope they are not robbers dressed in suits."

"Paula, you never cease to amaze me with some of the things that come out of your mouth."

"Oh, Augusta, I feel the same way about you, but I just don't say anything. Must be the immense love I feel for you."

"Stop it you two," Shelby said as she got out of the car and approached the two gentlemen while Augusta and Paula stayed behind watching and listening out of curiosity.

"Good evening, this is my house. Are you looking for me?"

"Who are you?" the taller of the two asked.

"My name is Shelby. Can I help you with something?"

"Shelby Malloy?" the taller of the two again spoke up.

Shelby thought to herself, *If he is here to rob me, well, at least he is not bad looking.* She observed his nice build and very defined facial features crowned with an attractive bald head that moved slightly when he smiled. Extending his hand to Shelby, he said, "I'm Detective Maye, and this is my partner, Detective Harris." Detective Harris didn't smile or offer his hand to Shelby for a handshake. He just nodded his head in acknowledgment of her, which immediately put her on edge. Detective Harris was slightly shorter than Detective Maye, with thinning gray hair and a body that boasted its unfamiliarity with a gym.

"Detectives! What?" Shelby heard Paula say in the background.

She then turned and said, "Paula, please take Augusta inside while I speak with the detectives."

"I am not going anywhere, staying right here. What y'all want with my Shelby? She ain't done nothing. What you want with her?"

"Augusta, please! Go inside with Paula. I'll be in shortly."

"Come on, sweetie. I will make you some tea," Paula said while gently guiding Augusta toward the front door.

Augusta looked at Paula and said, "This must be bad. You are calling me sweetie and offering to make me tea."

"What's going on? Why are you here?" Shelby asked anxiously. "Is something wrong? Did someone try to break in my house?"

Detective Maye stepped forward and said, "Do you know a Myron Malloy?"

"Yes, he is my husband."

"He is dead. He was found in his home with a gunshot wound to the head." Shelby tried to clear her mind, tried to make some sense of what she had just been told. She walked to the steps leading to her house to have a seat on them and staggered in the process, Detective Maye put his hand out to catch her.

"When?"

"He was found last night by an ex-girlfriend, Haverty Copetti."

"Why am I just being told if you learned of his death last night?"

"We didn't know he was married until we spoke with his mother a few hours ago in an effort to get some more information on him. She gave us your name and some information on you. That's how we were able to find you."

"Look, Myron and I were not together, haven't been for a while now. He was actually engaged to Haverty."

"Oh, so you two were divorced? I thought you said he was your husband," Detective Harris interjected.

"Not officially, but we were getting ready to start the process."

Detective Harris cleared his throat before saying, "Let me get this straight. You and Myron Malloy were still married yet he was engaged to someone else?"

"Yes, sir."

"What you are telling me is that you and your late husband were having marital problems and you knew about his being engaged to someone else?"

"What I am telling you is, I was married to Myron, yes, but we were not together. His being engaged to Haverty was not a concern of mine. As I mentioned earlier, Myron and I were getting ready to start divorce proceedings. I can't say that I still had strong feelings for him, Detective."

"Not strong feelings, but you still had some feelings for your husband is what I'm hearing. Sometimes all it takes is a little spark to start a fire," Detective Harris said.

"I didn't kill my husband, Detective, if that's what you're getting at."

Detective Maye turned to Detective Harris and said, "Listen, it's late and I am sure Ms. Malloy is probably anxious to get in to be with her friends. Would you mind us coming in and asking you just a few more questions? We will try to make this as quick as possible. The phone number for someone by the name of Ricky, no last name, was found in his cell phone as one of the last people he spoke to before his death. We haven't been able to catch up with him."

Shelby tried to remain calm but knew she was doing a lousy job of it. "Sure, come on in," she said before getting up and turning to lead them into the house.

Once inside, she noticed Paula and Augusta sitting at the kitchen table, both turning in the direction of Shelby and the detectives as they walked in. Augusta immediately got up and walked over to Shelby and asked if she was all right while Paula stayed at the kitchen table and sipped on the glass of wine she'd poured for herself.

"I'm okay, Gussie, thank you. Will you and Paula excuse us for a little while? You can go to the Family Room if you will please." Detective Maye waited until they had left before he started asking about Ricky.

"Ms. Malloy, do you know anyone by the name of Ricky? If so, do you know if he would have any reason to kill your husband?" Shelby hesitated, not knowing what to say. She didn't want to point a finger at Ricky, but she knew she had to tell the truth. She had to.

She thought for a moment before saying, "I'm sorry, but I don't know a Ricky." There, the lie was out there before she knew it.

Detective Maye looked at her, straightened his tie, and said, "Are you sure? You don't know Ricky?" Detective Harris spoke up and said, "Is that a fact? His mother said the two of you worked together."

"I know Ricky. Shelby you know Ricky. Remember he was the one who was always borrowing money from everyone, remember?" Paula said quickly. They all turned to see Paula standing in the room with her empty wine glass in her hand. Shelby pleaded with her with her eyes to please shut up and leave, but Paula stood her ground.

Shelby slowly turned to look at the detectives. She wanted to dig a hole in the floor, crawl in it, and never come out.

"Yes, I remember Ricky now. You are right, Paula. There was a Ricky who worked with us. I'm sorry, I am so sorry I—"

"It's okay, Shelby. May I call you Shelby?" Detective Maye said while motioning for Paula to leave the room.

"Yes, sir."

"I know this is really hard for you and you are under a lot of stress right now, having just been told your husband was found dead. We are going to leave now but we will be in touch. Just one more thing before we leave. Can you tell us something about who Augusta is?"

"Augusta is a very dear friend of mine who was homeless and is now living with me."

"And Paula?"

Shelby hesitated before saying, "Paula is my best friend."

"If you think of anything, anything at all you can tell me that might help bring the person who killed your husband to justice, please call me," he said as he reached in his shirt pocket and pulled out his card with his contact information on it. Shelby stared at the card for a second then took it.

Detective Maye said as he and Detective Harris turned to walk out the door, "Okay. Thank you for your time and I am very sorry for your loss." Paula walked back in the room as she heard the detectives leaving.

As soon as they closed the door behind them, Shelby turned to Paula and said, "Really! Paula, why? Why did you do that? You made me look like a liar in front of those detectives!"

"You were lying. I know it, you know it, and those detectives sure as hell knew it! Do you think with all their experience in their line of work, they don't know when they are being lied to, Shelby?"

"I said what I had to, to protect Ricky!"

"And I said what I had to, to protect you! Eventually, that grand lie you were trying to tell would have come back to haunt you. One of us had to think, use common sense, and it looked like it had to be me, so I did!"

"Shelby, I love you and I think the world of you, but to lie to those detectives was the worst mistake you could have made tonight," Augusta said. Paula and Shelby turned to see Augusta standing in the room with sad eyes and shaking her head. "Paula, up 'til now I didn't give you much credit for having good common sense, but tonight, you proved me wrong and I want to thank you. Thank you for being a true friend. Only a true friend would have spoken up and said what you did, even if they knew it might cost them the friendship," Augusta said and walked out of the room.

Shelby sat at her desk, her mind a jumble of whys and what-ifs. She couldn't get a thing done. She tried to finish one of the many tasks that were quickly piling up, but couldn't because she just couldn't concentrate.

When Helen asked her why she even bothered to come in, all she could say was "I don't know." The funeral services had been set for the coming Saturday, and all Myron's family had allowed her to take part in as far as the preparations was the picking out of his clothes. Why, she didn't know. It was clear they all hated her and blamed her for everything that had gone wrong in Myron's life since they married.

"Shelby, go home. Go home and rest. Don't come back here until you are ready. Your job is safe. I assure you of that." She was so lost in thought she did not notice Helen until she spoke.

"Thanks, Helen. I didn't get to finish—"

"I know, no worries, go home," Helen said then walked over and gave her a big hug before saying good night.

"Hey!" Paula said, as she rushed up to catch Shelby before she got on the elevator.

"What is it, Paula?"

"I went by your desk, but Helen told me you had just left. I just wanted to know if you needed me to do anything, maybe bring by some dinner or something later tonight? Pick up your dry cleaning, anything! Just name it!" "No, thanks, I think you've done enough, don't you?"

"Please don't shut me out, Shelby. I'm not the enemy."

"Yeah, and how would I know that? For all I know, you could have killed Myron. Heaven knows you hated him enough."

"You are right. I despised him and what he did to you, but I didn't kill him, wanted to, but didn't."

"Unbelievable!"

"What is, the fact that I'm honest, the fact that I call a spade a spade?" Paula said sharply.

"Myron was my husband, Paula, so at least respect the fact that I might, I just might be grieving a little." Paula threw up her hands and walked away, then stopped and whirled around to face Shelby.

"Hey, Shel, when you need me, I'm here. Believe it or not, everything I do and have done as far as you're concerned has been for your benefit. Later!"

"Don't call me, Paula, don't text, don't come by my house. Do you hear me? I mean it!"

"I know you do, but *you* know I never listen to you."

"B—"

"Hey, hey! You don't like that kind of language, remember? Yeah, I may be what you started to say I am, but one of us has to be. Might as well be me. I'm not going anywhere Shelby, I'm here, so I guess you are just going to have to deal with me."

"Now that creates a problem Paula, you see, I don't want you here anymore."

"A problem for you Shel, not me. Like I said, I'm here. Later!"

CHAPTER TWENTY-TWO

SHELBY STOOD IN FRONT OF the mirror, eyeing herself in the black dress she had decided to wear to Myron's funeral. She smoothed it out over her stomach area and tried to pull it down a little lower past her knees. "You bought me this dress years ago, Myron, for our second wedding anniversary. Who would have thought I would be trying it on today to wear to your funeral soon," Shelby said softly to herself.

"Shelby," Augusta called from the living room.

"Yeah," Shelby said without turning away from her reflection in the mirror.

"The detective is out here to see you. Can you come out here, please?" Shelby stood and thought for a second, *What could he want now? I've answered his questions over and over again. This is really beginning to irritate me.* Snatching open the door to her bedroom, she walked swiftly to the living room.

"Detective Maye, I just got in and I'm very tired. Do you guys make it a habit of just popping up whenever you feel like it, without warning?" Detective Maye made no effort to conceal his pleasure in seeing Shelby in the black dress. She was so mad she had forgotten she was wearing it. "Detective, is there something I can help you with? I thought I had answered all your questions already."

"If he could stop gawking at you in that dress, he might be able to remember why he came here tonight," Augusta said and walked back to the kitchen to check on dinner. Ignoring Augusta's comment, he walked over to the sofa and, before doing so, asked Shelby if it was all right with her if he had a seat.

"What is it, Detective?" By this time, Shelby's patience had worn thin.

"We found an interesting piece of evidence at the crime scene of your husband, lying next to his body. At first, we didn't give it too much attention, but now think it might prove helpful in solving this case and worth mentioning to you."

Shelby tried to brace herself for the detective's answer before she asked, "Really, what did you find?"

"A broken heel belonging to a pair of women's stiletto shoes." Shelby licked her lips and sat down on the loveseat opposite the detective.

"You said Haverty discovered Myron's body… Perhaps the heel belongs to her?"

"We've checked with her already."

"And of course, she said it didn't belong to her."

"That's correct. Shelby, is there anything else you can tell me that might help us in this investigation? Talk to me. It's just you and I now."

"Talk to you, I have nothing else to tell. I've told you all I know, what I know."

"Are you romantically involved with this Ricky you were asked about from the start?"

"What kind of question is that? How dare you insinuate that I or Ricky had anything to do with Myron's death!" Detective Maye leaned forward, rested his arms on his knees, and paused for a second.

"Okay, Shelby, if you think of anything else, you still have my card right?"

"Yes, if I think of anything else, I'll be sure to call you."

"Goodbye, Shelby."

"Goodbye, Detective."

Standing with his hands on the door knob, Detective Maye turned and said, "Oh, Shelby, one more thing."

"Yes?"

"A pair of stilettos would go nicely with that dress." He then slowly opened the door and walked out.

"Don't let him get to you, Shelby," Augusta said as she walked into the room and sat down beside her. "That's what they do. They get paid a lot of money to work people's nerves. Problem is, they work the wrong people's nerves before they get to the nerves of the ones they should have worked on in the beginning."

"Augusta, I didn't kill Myron. Lord knows I had plenty of reasons to. So help me, I wanted to, so many times. But I didn't do it. I could never take another person's life."

"Child, when you live the type of life Myron lived, treat people the way he did, you give a lot of people reason to kill you. Myron got what was coming to him. It was just a matter of time. That night he took a bullet to the head was when his time ran out."

Cars, trucks, cabs, even a few limousines lined the streets outside the Bethany Memorial Temple where Myron's body was laid out in a black-and-silver casket, dressed in a black pinstripe suit with a white shirt and red tie. Clothes Shelby had carefully picked out for him at his mother's request. She said only a wife would know best how to adorn her husband, even if they were not together.

At first, Shelby felt her request to be a strange one, since Connie had so politely in the same breath told her she was not expected to sit with the family. Later, she realized that Connie was simply saying that even though she and Myron were estranged, she would still show her at least some respect as still being his wife.

Connie did not make it a secret to all who would listen that she cared little for Shelby and always felt that Myron married beneath him. Realizing she could have fought Connie every step of the way and won, because they were still legally married at his death, she would have been the one in charge of Myron's entire funeral arrangements, but she didn't. Her message to his family was that she didn't care what they did. They could no longer hurt her.

Shelby took a seat in the back and waited for the family to march in. She had decided that she would then walk up to view Myron's body, greet, and give her condolences to the family, then leave. Time passed slowly as people filed in greeting and hugging each other. How sad, Shelby thought to herself, that it took a funeral to bring out the warmth in an otherwise-cold person, a person who would not hug you if their life depended on it under a different circumstance.

Finally, the family marched in. Connie clung to the arm of Myron's brother, Nate, who could pass for Myron's twin had he been a little taller. Following them was Myron's sister, Victoria, an elegant woman with short, wavy chestnut brown hair and large expressive eyes. Her five-foot-five slender frame was clad in a long black dress that flowed from her body in waves with her every move. Suddenly, for some inexplicable reason, she stopped and looked in Shelby's direction. Removing her sunglasses, she stared at Shelby for a second before she was encouraged to keep moving by the people behind her, most of whom Shelby didn't recognize.

The more the minister talked and praised Myron, the angrier Shelby became. Angry because the Myron she knew was nothing like the one he described. Angry for all the abuse she took from him for years before finally packing her bags and leaving, and angry because he was still her husband no matter what, because their divorce was never finalized before he was killed.

It was time, she decided, to go view Myron's body then take her leave. She stood up quickly but sat right back down because her knees shook, and she was certain her legs were about to give way. No Augusta, no Paula, equaled no emotional support for her. Both had decided Myron just wasn't worth their time and energy, so why bother even pretending to care by being at his funeral, knowing they could care less about him or his family?

"You can do this," she said to herself. "Just get up, keep your eyes focused straight ahead, and walk to the casket." Somehow, before she knew it, she was standing over Myron's dead body. The memories came rushing to mind—the happy ones, the sad ones, and the ugly ones. She placed one of her hands over his hands that had been positioned to rest on his stomach. Wiping away a tear, she said, "Rest in peace, Myron, goodbye."

Rushing to get out of the temple, she collided with Connie who was returning from the bathroom. They both looked at each other, silently communicating the suffocating pain they each battled at that moment. Shelby couldn't begin to imagine the pain of a mother who had just lost her son.

"I'm so sorry, Connie." Shelby embraced her, held her tight, and said, "I'll be thinking of you and your family." Connie pulled away from Shelby, rolled her eyes at her, and continued on her way.

CHAPTER TWENTY-THREE

SNOW FELL LIGHTLY AS SHELBY stood at the kitchen window that evening. The large tree on the street behind her house looked beautiful, as the street lamp cast a soft glow on its snow-covered leaves. Shelby couldn't eat, couldn't think straight, couldn't sleep. Visions of Myron's body laid out in his casket kept forcing their way to the front of her mind and causing her so much anxiety she felt she would actually have a nervous breakdown.

Paula called after she returned home to see if she was all right and needed anything. She told her she was fine, more out of an effort to quickly end the conversation than anything else. Augusta cooked a delicious dinner, but after taking just a few spoonfuls, she just did not want anymore and picked at the food. She apologized to Augusta for not being able to eat it and excused herself from the table.

"Gussie, I'm going for a walk. I won't be long." Augusta was in her room applying pink nail polish to her toes. Shelby had bought her all different shades of pink nail polish for her to just have fun with.

"All right, wrap up good. It's late and it's cold out. I'll have a bowl of soup waiting for you when you get back."

"Okay, thank you."

Buttoning up her jacket and pulling her hood down over her head, she headed to the kitchen to grab a flashlight and her cell phone before descending down the steps leading to her backyard. Turning on the flashlight, she started to walk as fast as she could, where to, she didn't know. All she knew was hopefully, the faster she walked, the quicker her head would clear.

Just as she rounded the corner, she was knocked to the ground with a force so hard the flashlight flew out her hands, spilling its contents all over the ground! Before she could get herself together and get up, the person came at her again. She let out a scream and rolled quickly to the side to avoid them jumping on her and pinning her down! She searched wildly while still on the ground for something to defend herself with. Before she knew it, she was kicked hard in the ribs. Crying out in pain, yet determined to survive her attack, she grabbed a big piece of broken glass, and when her assailant came at her again, she jabbed the glass in their leg as hard as she could, then kicked them with all the strength she could find. The attacker grabbed their leg and tried to remove the glass, but it was jammed so deeply beneath the skin they could not pull it out. Taking advantage of their injury, Shelby got up while holding her injured ribs and ran as fast as she could, though her ribs were killing her. She kept moving as best as she could. Once she got to the gas station near her house, she stopped to see if they had followed her. When she saw that she was in the clear, she pulled out her cell phone and called Paula to come get her.

Sitting on the bed in the emergency room after being examined, bandaged, and given painkillers, Shelby gently pulled on her jacket, and with Paula's help, she slid off the bed slowly so her feet would touch the floor. "I mean really, Shel! Can you not stay out of this place?" Paula said jokingly. "I wish that cute Dr. Isen was on staff tonight."

"Paula, please, will you take your mind out of the gutter long enough to help me make it to the car?"

"Thank goodness your ribs were not broken."

"Seriously, they sure hurt like they are, though."

"So, I guess you needed me sooner than you thought, huh? You know all you have to do is call and I'm there. I'm not a fair-weather friend, I'm a 24/7 friend free of charge. Told you I'd be here when you needed me," Paula said with a smirk.

Shelby rolled her eyes at her and said, "Yeah, whatever."

"You know your life wouldn't be sane without me."

"No, my life is insane because of you but I appreciate you anyway. Thank you for coming to get me Paula."

"Oh, Shel, really, and you're welcome."

*　　*　　*　　*　　*

Paula turned the key in the door when they reached Shelby's place, and Augusta swung it open from the opposite side.

"Girl, I tell you the truth, you are always somewhere getting beat up. Do I have to go with you every time you leave the house? Come on in here and get into some warm pajamas. I got them and a cup of soup waiting for you."

"What about me?" Paula said, pretending to pout.

"Move out my way, Paula," Augusta said, gesturing for her to move to the side. "I don't love you that much, but I do appreciate you calling me from the hospital tonight to let me know what was going on with Shelby."

"Yes, you do love me and you know it," Paula said teasingly.

Once they had gotten Shelby settled, fed, and in bed, Paula and Augusta started in with the questions. "What happened to you? You left here saying you were going for a walk. Did someone try to rob you?"

"I don't know what happened. I was just walking, and all of a sudden, this person came out of nowhere and knocked me to the ground, then kept coming at me."

"I think you need to let the detectives know what happened tonight, Shelby."

"Paula, why? I mean, I'm sure it was just some crazy person with nothing better to do with their time than prey on innocent people."

"Paula is right, Shelby. Someone just killed your husband. We have no idea who or why. I don't mean to scare you, but if a person is evil enough, they won't stop at just killing the person they wanted, but they may come after their family too."

"Gussie, I know you said you don't mean to scare me but you are."

"Just get some rest tonight. We will talk about it more tomorrow. But you have to let the detectives know what happened to you tonight," Paula said and hugged her before saying good night.

Once Augusta let Paula out and locked the door behind her, she went back in Shelby's room and stood looking at her. "Shelby, listen to me. Tonight was no coincidence. Somebody is after you, and I think it is, for whatever reason, the same person who killed Myron. I will talk to Gus tomorrow about getting you a gun. I think it's best we both have one here in the house, just in case."

"Augusta! No! I don't need a gun! I don't like having those things around!"

"One of those things, as you put it, if used wisely and properly, can serve as a protection. Get some sleep for now. I will be sleeping on the sofa by the door tonight. Everything is going to be just fine. Yes, ma'am, trust me. It's going to be all right."

For close to an hour, Shelby laid there just looking up at the ceiling. Sleep would not come. Now, in addition to having to deal with Myron's death, she had to at least consider the possibility that the same person who killed Myron might be after her now. But why? she wondered. She knew very little about any of his friends. When they were still together and his friends would come around, she would leave the room. It was just something about the people Myron chose to call friends. Money was always at the height of their conversations followed by what woman they had successfully been able to get in bed.

Ricky, where was he? Shelby had been trying to reach him for days. Every time she called, his phone went straight to voice mail. No matter the time of day she tried to reach him, there was no answer. *Well, he is engaged now,* she thought to herself. *Maybe Agacia keeps him tied up all the time.* This thought just added to her depression and anxiety. She tried to turn over on the side that was not injured, but it even hurt to do that, to move. "When are those painkillers going to kick in, for heaven's sake?" Finally, she dozed off to sleep, thinking about Ricky and wondering where he was.

"Augusta! Augusta! Help me, please help me! No! No! I didn't do anything. I know nothing about it! Get away from me, leave me alone! Augusta!" Augusta came running into the room where Shelby was tossing and turning, fighting her pillow, and calling Augusta's name over and over again.

"Shelby, Shelby, wake up," Augusta said while trying to pull the pillow out of her hands. Shelby continued to scream so loud Augusta stopped for a second and covered her ears. "Shelby!"

"Oh my god, oh my god, Augusta! They were here. They got in the room, in the house! Where were you, where—"

"Calm down, calm down. There is no one here, Shel, no one but you and I. You were dreaming. Here, lay down, lay back down," Augusta said while gently pushing her back down on the bed so she would relax. Taking her pillow, Augusta smoothed it out then propped it up under her head along with the extra pillow that had fallen to the floor as a result of Shelby struggling around in the bed. She then ran to the kitchen and made a cup of hot tea and brought it back to her, gently lifting her head to take a few sips. "Go back to sleep now, baby, go back to sleep. It was all just a bad dream. I'm here, I'm here. Go back to sleep."

The next morning all was quiet and peaceful. It almost felt as if yesterday and last night had never happened, until a mental picture of Myron's dead body all dressed up came to mind. What was the point of caring how a person looked once they were dead? *I mean they are dead,* she thought to herself. *Oh my gosh, Shelby, either you are losing your mind, or you need some more sleep because you are not making any sense.*

She reached over and picked up her cell phone off the table beside her bed. While dialing Ricky's number, she said a silent prayer that he would pick up this time, and on the fifth ring, he did.

"Hello."

"Ricky, hi! Where have you been? I've been trying to reach you for days!"

"I already know, so I have been laying low. My cell has been ringing off the hook, but I needed some time to think, to figure things out."

"Figure things out? Ricky, what are you saying? Do you know something about who killed Myron?"

"All I know is that he is dead and I need to lay low for a few days. Shelby, those people Myron was dealing with ain't playing. He owed them a lot of money, and he obviously didn't pay it back, so they took him out!"

"Are you sure they killed him? You and I both know Myron made enemies wherever he went, one of the things he did best."

"Shelby, you really need to listen to me. You be careful, be very careful. Those guys are still after their money and will stop at nothing to get it. Maybe they didn't kill him, hell, I don't know! But I do know you need to be careful, very careful!"

"Ricky, how did you know Myron was dead?"

"Shelby, did you hear what I just said," Ricky said angrily.

"I heard you, Ricky, but I still need to know how you knew Myron was dead."

Ricky let out a heavy sigh. "I had someone watching him."

"What, why?"

"I had to know where he was at every second, Shelby. It was either he got me or I got him. One of us had to go. But I swear to you, I didn't kill him or have anything to do with it. Before I knew it, the person I had keeping an eye on that scum was calling and telling me I could finally chill because they'd read in the paper about Myron's murder, and he also told me where to look in the paper to find the article. Sure enough, the article was about Myron and his being killed."

"Ricky, I was attacked last night, by who, I don't know. This is scary because Augusta seems to think that whoever killed Myron might be after me now."

"NO! No, no, no! I really hope she is wrong. Are you all right?"

"Yeah, a little banged up and sore but I'm okay."

"Thank God," Ricky said and exhaled heavily.

"Ricky, I need to see you, to talk. Can I meet you somewhere?"

"Like I said, I am trying to lay low and you should too for a few days."

"I will agree to do that only if you will agree to meet me at the 601 Café this coming Saturday at twelve thirty. Please, Rick, I really need to talk to you face-to-face." It took a real long time for Ricky to answer but finally he agreed to meet her.

CHAPTER TWENTY-FOUR

"WHY YOU RUSHING DOWN YOUR breakfast like you've lost your mind? It's a Saturday morning. Slow down and eat proper before you choke to death."

"I know, Augusta, but I have got a lot to do before my afternoon appointment, and it's already eleven and I still need to shower and do my hair."

"Where are you off to? What appointment? Are you sick? Going to see a doctor maybe? Is there something you're not telling me?" Augusta asked with concern.

"No, it's nothing like that! I just can't be late for this meeting that's all!"

"Meeting or appointment, which is it?"

"Gussie, don't you worry your pretty little head about it. I will be back before dinner." Shelby jumped up from the table, rushed over, kissed Augusta on the head, and dashed to the shower.

It was pouring rain as Shelby searched for a parking space as close to the 601 Café as possible. As usual, rain or shine, the area was bustling with weekend shoppers and people just out to enjoy their Saturday afternoon. There were a few very nice stores that lined the street, along with a movie theater and some really nice eating spots on the same side of the street as the 601, as it was sometimes called.

Shelby loved the café with its painted black walls, pictures of actors and actresses of old decorating the walls, along with guitars and other musical instruments. When you walked in the door, an antique sage green sofa and a hall tree welcomed you to the nostalgic atmosphere. The café was softly lit by large silver floor lamps and small silver table lamps that sat in the center of each table.

After finally finding a parking space, Shelby jumped out of her car, put up her umbrella, and ran in the front door of the café, only to be greeted by a mob of people waiting to be seated. She was glad she had called ahead and reserved a booth for herself and Ricky who she searched for among the crowd. Finally, she spotted him standing against a wall and sipping on a drink. "Hello," she said as she approached him, then gave him a big hug and kiss on the cheek. "Man! I've missed you, Rick, so good to see you. Come on, I have a booth reserved for us. Ricky tossed his empty cup in the trash and followed Shelby up to the front to give their reservation name. "Hi, reservation for two, under the name Shelby Malloy please."

"Sure, follow me ma'am," the hostess said with a smile.

Shelby and Ricky slid into their reserved booth opposite each other. Ricky stared at her as if he were a doctor, looking for signs of any illnesses. "What?" Shelby said, wondering why he was looking at her the way he was.

"You look tired, Shel. You sure you're all right? I haven't been able to stop thinking about what you told me, that you were attacked." Before Shelby could answer, Detective

Maye slid in the booth beside her and Detective Harris slid in beside Ricky. Ricky's expression showed confusion, question marks decorated his face. "What is this, Shel? What's going on? Who are these guys?" Shelby was shocked and confused as to why they were there.

"Detective Maye? What are you doing here?" Shelby asked anxiously.

"Detective? Come on, Shelby. You have got to be kidding me," Ricky said angrily. "Why would you do this to me? I know this has something to do with Myron's murder!"

"Ricky, I didn't know they would be here, I don't understand!" Shelby turned to Detective Maye, she was furious! "What are you guys doing here? I have had just about enough of your surprised pop ups!"

"So this is Ricky," Detective Harris said with a slight smile.

"What is this? Why are you here? How did you know I would be here? Have you been following me?" Shelby shouted at the detectives, causing people sitting nearby to turn and stare in their direction. No one said anything. Ricky just stared at Shelby, searching for an excuse and feeling she'd betrayed him. Shelby turned to Ricky. "Ricky, I had no idea they would be here. Please believe me! You have got to believe me! I would never do this to you! Never! I just wanted to talk, that's all. They followed me, Ricky, they did!"

"I guess an apology would be nice since what you are saying is true. Yes, we followed you, Shelby. But I'm not here to address your anger and pacify your friend's feeling of betrayal. I am here because I want and need answers. A man is dead, Shelby, your husband, and the last person to have contact with him prior to his murder is this man, the one sitting right in front of you, Ricky," Detective Maye said.

"Ricky didn't kill Myron," Shelby shouted while banging her fist on the table.

Ricky took a sip of his water that had been placed on the table and said, "It's okay, Shel, it's okay. Listen, I will go with you, tell you anything you need to know, just leave her out of it."

"You sound like a smart man, Ricky," Detective Harris said.

"No! If you take Ricky, you have to take me too!"

"Shelby, it's all right," Ricky said while reaching over and touching her hand to calm her. "I will be in touch."

"Ricky! No! Please, Detective Maye, you have got to listen to me. Ricky didn't do it!"

"Gentlemen, shall we go?" Ricky said while standing, buttoning his sports jacket, then walking out of the café with Detective Maye in front of him and Detective Harris following him.

Shelby sat there not knowing what to do. When the waitress came to take her order, she ignored her. Finally, she got up and walked out of the café. She was devastated beyond description. She stood on the sidewalk in the pouring rain, searching her purse for her cell phone. When she finally found it, her hands were shaking so much it took her a good two minutes before she was able to successfully dial Paula's number while keeping her phone from getting wet.

When Paula answered, she was so distraught she couldn't form any words. All she could do was cry into the phone.

How she got home, Shelby honestly did not know. She couldn't even remember if she was able to drive herself or if she had told Paula where she was so she could come get her. All she knew was when she woke up on her sofa at home, Paula and Augusta were sitting on the loveseat in front of her talking softly. All of a sudden, they all jumped because of the loud banging on the front door. Paula rushed over and put her arms around Shelby while Augusta ran to her bedroom, came back, and calmly asked Paula to open the door.

Paula couldn't get the door opened wide enough before Agacia rushed in, almost knocking her down. "Friend! Some friend! Ricky is in jail tonight because of you!"

"Agacia," Shelby said while trying to get up off the sofa. "I didn't know they would be there. I didn't know. I'm telling you the truth!"

"Liar, you are a got—"

"Hold on, Agacia. You will not come into this house with that kind of language and hurling accusations."

"Shut up, old woman!"

"That is enough, Agacia," Shelby said while glaring at her. "You can accuse me of whatever you want, believe of me what you want, but you will *not* speak to Augusta that way!"

Augusta walked over to Agacia and said, "Didn't your mother teach you any manners? Do you need me to knock some into ya? This old woman will dust the floor with you."

Agacia ignored her, while never taking her eyes off Shelby and putting her hands on her hips. "You call yourself a friend! No friend would have done what you did to Ricky today! You handed him over to the detectives!" Agacia took a step closer to Shelby. Paula stood up and blocked her way to Shelby.

"Back off, Agacia!" Agacia didn't move. Paula then stepped right in her face and said, "I may be shorter than you and smaller than you, but so help me, if you don't back up, I will beat the sugar, honey, iced tea out of you, and trust me, it won't be sweet."

Agacia rolled her eyes at Paula and turned to walk toward the door to leave, but before she left, she turned around to face them again and said, "You people, you think you are better than me because of the color of my skin and the texture of my hair is different than yours. You talk about my people because we come to this country and bring our families with us, seeking a better more prosperous way of life. They live ten people in a house at a time, you say. What you say is true and you know why we do this? Well, I will tell you why. It's because we care about each other and we are true friends. That is what a true friend does, help each other, not betray each other. We stand up for and by each other. We would never betray a friend. *Never!*"

Paula started to respond to Agacia, but realizing how hurt Agacia was, Shelby told Paula not to say anything, to let Agacia have her say. "For two years, two years," Agacia said while holding up two fingers. "For two years, I lived next door to a woman of a different race. Every day, I would speak to her, and every time I did, she would ignore me.

But that is okay, I said to myself and I kept speaking to her even though she never spoke back."

Agacia stopped and thought to herself, reflecting on what she was saying before she continued. "One day, I heard she had lost her job, so what do I do? When I would go to the grocery store, I would put a loaf of bread in my cart for me and my boys and a loaf of bread in my cart for this woman and her children. A pack of chicken in my cart for me and my family and a pack of chicken for her and her family. I would take it to her, but she would turn me away. I went on like this with her for close to a month. Finally, my sons they say, 'Mommy, why do you keep trying to help this lady? She don't even speak to us.' I say to Diego and Joshua, keep quiet. We do not treat people the way they treat us, but the way we want to be treated. This is the right way. My boys just shook their heads and walked away from me. Do you know what I did instead of letting hatred grow in my heart for this woman? Every night I would pray for her, and finally, one day when I spoke to her, she spoke back." "Agacia, I am sorry, I am so sorry those detectives showed up today."

"I will not let hatred grow in my heart for you, Shelby, but I will instead pray for you, pray hard. I was more of a friend to my neighbor who wanted nothing to do with me than you were to Ricky today, because I tried to help her even though she hated me. I don't feel you tried to help Ricky today." Agacia then turned and walked out the door, closing it softly behind her.

CHAPTER TWENTY-FIVE

SHELBY SAT AT HER DESK. She had to help Ricky, but how? What could she do? There was no need of trying to talk to Paula, because if truth be told, Paula just didn't seem to want to discuss the entire matter at all. Augusta told her to stop worrying over it so, that the truth would eventually come out—it always did. Still, she could not just sit back and do nothing to help Ricky. She thought about Alex Manson whom she'd researched. He was an excellent attorney and had never lost a case. However, she also knew that neither she nor Ricky could ever afford him and that he was not a pro bono attorney. Before she knew it, she had picked up the phone to dial his extension but quickly put it back down, realizing Helen would kill her if she even suspected she was thinking of turning to Alex Manson to help Ricky. She knew firm policy did not allow employees to seek the help of the attorneys without going through the proper channels.

When she mentioned that Ricky was being questioned and held for the murder of Myron, Helen just shook her head and changed the subject. There was no indication on her part that she was the least bit upset over the death of

Myron or Ricky being held in connection with his death. Shelby found this to be cold and odd. Well, that was Helen for you, cold and odd, she thought to herself.

"Hey," Paula interrupted her thoughts. "Did you get my text? Let's go grab lunch. It's after one already."

"I'm not hungry, Paula. Thanks, but you go ahead without me."

"Shelby, for heaven's sakes! Stop worrying over Ricky. He is a big boy. He got himself in this mess. Now he just has to get himself out of it."

"You think he did it, don't you? Well, I am telling you he didn't, Paula. Ricky did not kill Myron!"

Helen walked in just in time to hear Shelby telling Paula that Ricky didn't kill Myron. "Well, if it isn't the two ladies of the firm."

"Ladies of the firm?" Paula said, looking at Helen as if she'd lost her mind. "You make us sound like unmentionables, Helen. That's something you would know about, not us," Paula said and walked out of the room.

Helen stared at Paula before saying, "If that short makeshift of a woman isn't careful, she will be getting up off the floor. She always has something smart to say."

"You started it, Helen."

"Whatever! Listen, I overheard you two talking about Ricky. Shelby, you have got to let this go. It's consuming you and your work. You were supposed to have information to me by noon on an interviewee. Where is it? This isn't like you."

"I'm sorry, I just... I'll get on it right now, I'm very sorry. I'm not taking lunch today. I will have it in your office in twenty-five minutes, I promise you, Helen!" Helen looked at Shelby. She could see her misery. She liked Shelby and knew she was a hard and good worker. That she couldn't overlook.

"Come to my office, please."

"When, now?" Shelby asked. She was confused and a little afraid she was about to be fired.

"Yes, now, please."

Helen sat down behind her desk then requested that her calls be held. Shelby sat in the chair opposite Helen's desk with her head down, staring at her fingers and trying to figure out how she would pay her mortgage if she was fired today.

"Shelby, look at me, please," Helen said sympathetically. Shelby looked at her, bracing herself for the worst. "You can't save the world. It's in too much of a mess, and getting worse by the minute. You have too much on your plate. You've taken in this homeless woman off the street, you are trying to figure out a way to help Ricky, and you just lost your husband."

"How do you know about Augusta?"

"Paula told me."

"Of course, I should have known."

"You have got to scrape something off your plate, and it has to be Ricky." Shelby didn't say anything. She just put her head back down and stared at her hands. "Did you hear what I just said to you?"

"I heard you, Helen," Shelby said while still holding her head down.

"So what are you going to do?"

Shelby looked straight at Helen and said, "I'm going to Alex Manson to see if he would be willing to help me get Ricky out of jail."

"You are going to do what?" Helen said as if she thought she'd heard Shelby wrong.

"I'm going to Alex Manson."

Helen got up from her desk, walked around to stand in front of Shelby, folded her arms, leaned against her desk, and said, "You do that and so help me, you're out of here. You know the firm's policy pertaining to such matters."

"Are you threatening me, Helen?"

"No, I am promising you."

"Well then, I want to thank you for all you've done for me, Helen. I admire and respect you, appreciate you giving me this job, but as of right now, I resign from my position here at Cordial. I will have my written resignation on your desk before close of business today." Helen couldn't believe what she was hearing.

"Are you crazy, Shelby? You must be! You are going to jeopardize your job for Ricky. Why?"

"Because he is a friend and he needs help. Alex Manson is my only hope of getting Ricky the help he desperately needs." The two of them stared at each other, neither of them willing to back down. "Excuse me, Helen, I still need to get you that information you asked for on the interviewee you are expecting." Without another word, Shelby walked quietly out of the room.

* * * * *

"What in the world were you thinking? Your job, Shel! What the hell! How are you going to pay for this place, your bills, your car note?"

"I don't know. I still have some money left from what my parents left me, Paula. I'll manage." Paula paced back and forth, almost wearing a hole in the carpet of Shelby's bedroom floor. Augusta sat in a chair opposite Shelby's bed and said nothing.

"You can't go to Alex Manson, Shelby! Tomorrow morning, get dressed, and go see Helen, apologize to her. Tell her you made a huge mistake and you're sorry!"

"I can't do that, Paula."

"Why not? You took Augusta in off the street. Well, if you don't do something, you both will be living on the street unless you come live with me."

"I ain't coming to live with you. I don't even like you," Augusta said smartly.

Paula looked at her and said, "You love me and you know you do."

"I am sticking by my decision, Paula. I made a very bad decision once, and that was to marry Myron. My life has been miserable ever since. Well, this is a good decision, to try and help someone who I know is innocent the best way I know how and hopefully make their life a little better."

*   *   *   *   *

Paula walked into Helen's office without knocking and sat down in the same chair Shelby had sat in the day before and glared at Helen. "What do you want? Oh, let me guess.

You heard about Shelby," Helen said while continuing to compose a letter she was working on.

"You fired her? Simply because she wanted to do what she could to help Ricky?"

"I didn't fire her. She quit."

"After you threatened to fire her, same thing to me. I know the story, Helen. Shelby shared it with me. She shares everything with me. My father helped start this firm, Helen. He may be eighty-six years old, but you and I both know that he still has a lot of power and a lot of say when it comes to this firm. So I just have five words for you, respectfully, of course."

"Oh, of course," Helen said sarcastically.

"GIVE. SHELBY. HER. JOB. BACK."

"And if I don't?"

"I like you, Helen, but I love Shelby. So think about that? Oh, and Helen, I heard you are a fair person when it comes to matters such as this. Here is your chance to prove it."

"You don't scare me Paula! I don't like your tone, it's unprofessional and unwarranted. I don't care if your father laid every brick in this building with his bare hands, you will not disrespect my position at this firm."

"I am not trying to scare you Helen, just treating you the same way you treated Shelby yesterday."

"What do you mean?"

"You left her no choice but to quit! Firm policy is firm policy, I respect that no matter what. But you could have at least given her some suggestions or alternatives as to what else she might try to do to get Ricky some help. You gave her nothing! Well. Today you are on the receiving end of a similar situation. How does that feel, Helen?" For the first time, Helen looked up at Paula since she'd walked into her office, but said nothing. "I thought so," Paula said.

"It was Shelby's decision to resign, Paula. That was her choice not mine."

"We are all faced with decisions in life, Helen, but those decisions are based on circumstances and knowledge mainly. There are times when we make bad decisions that haunt us for the rest of our life, based on our poor judgement and selfish desires. Then there are times when we are forced to make a decision based on circumstance and having no choice in the matter. Shelby was forced to resign yesterday because of circumstance, and you left her no other choice. It was either leave Cordial, then seek Alex Manson's help for Ricky or stay here and hate herself for the rest of her life for not taking what she felt, was her only chance, of getting Ricky the help he needs." Paula stood up, glared at Helen, and said, "You know Helen, I do respect your position here at the firm. All I'm asking is that you cut Shelby a little slack, please? She has been through a lot." Paula then turned and walked swiftly out of Helen's office shaking her head.

*   *   *   *   *

Shelby lay across her bed and tried to figure out how things had gotten so out of control. Myron dead, Ricky in jail, and she out of a job. *Helen was right. I should not have said I was going to Alex Manson without following the rules.*

But following rules, paperwork, and approvals take too long, she reasoned to herself. *Ricky needs help and he needs it now.* Even from the grave, Myron still had a way of making her life a living hell, she thought to herself. She thought about Detective Maye, who she hadn't reached out to since he'd arrested Ricky because she was too hurt and angry to do so. They'd followed her that day, wanting to trap Ricky and knowing she would lead them right to him. No, she wasn't calling him. She'd handle things her way.

Shelby's cell phone rang. She ignored it as she didn't feel like talking to anyone. It stopped after eight rings then started up again. She got up and walked over to the table where she'd left it and noticed it was Paula calling. "I'm in no mood to be scolded, so don't start," she answered.

"Oh, stop with the pity party. You did this to yourself, you know."

"Well, that may be true but still."

"Let's have lunch tomorrow."

"Where? I'm not coming down to the office to meet you. I no longer work there, remember?"

"Yes, you do. I had a talk with Helen. It's all been straightened out, a simple misunderstanding, that's all."

"Paula, you have got to stop fighting my battles for me!"

"See you at work tomorrow."

"No, I haven't heard from Helen and won't disrespect her by showing up for work tomorrow without talking to her first."

"Oh, she will be calling you before the night is over, believe me," Paula said and hung up. Just as Paula said,

Helen called two hours later and asked if she was okay, then asked her to be at work thirty minutes early tomorrow morning because they had a lot to do and hung up.

*   *   *   *   *

Shelby arrived at her desk thirty minutes early, just as Helen had asked. She'd put a little extra care in her appearance. She needed the reassurance. She wanted to start the day off with an apology to Helen, realizing she had overstepped her bounds by deciding to take matters in her own hands and go directly to Alex Manson. Her desk phone rang. It was Helen asking her to come to her office. Shelby pulled out her compact, touched up her lipstick, checked her hair, then got up, and smoothed away an imaginary wrinkle in her skirt before walking swiftly to Helen's office. She'd already prepared herself to eat humble pie by apologizing to Helen when she first walked in the office.

When Shelby reached Helen's office door, she heard voices—Helen's and that of someone else she did not recognize. Not wanting to interrupt a private conversation, she knocked softly on the door before going in.

"Good morning, Shelby," Alex Manson said as he stood while she walked in and reached out his hand to shake hers. "How are you this morning?"

Shelby was surprised to the point of being speechless, but Helen helped her to recover by saying, "Shelby, Mr. Manson just said good morning to you. It would be rude not to reply, don't you think?" Helen then excused herself, saying she had to check on something in another office and that they were welcome to use her office as long as they needed to.

"Good morning, Mr. Manson. I'm sorry, it's just that I…"

"No need to apologize, Shelby. It's early. We are both still trying to wake up. Here, please, come sit down," he said while motioning for her to sit in the extra guest chair beside his. He then turned his chair around so he would be facing her.

"So Helen tells me you'd like to talk to me about a friend of yours who has been arrested for the death of your husband. I believe she said his name is Ricky, correct?" Shelby couldn't believe what she was hearing. Helen had actually paved the way for her, taken the appropriate steps for her to meet with Alex Manson. She now felt even worse about the way she'd acted toward Helen concerning the entire matter.

"Yes sir, I…"

"Please call me Alex."

"Oh, yes, I'm sorry. Alex, my friend Ricky is being held for the murder of my husband Myron, a crime I know he did not commit."

Alex shifted in his seat and cleared his throat before asking, "How do you know Ricky didn't kill your husband?"

"I just know he didn't. He would never do such a thing."

"How well do you know this Ricky? What's his last name?"

"Clay, Ricky Clay."

"Why would he even be considered as a suspect in the death of your husband?"

"Because on the night my husband was found dead, the detectives said his phone showed that Ricky was the last one or one of the last people he communicated with."

"Do you know what the conversation was about?"

"No, I don't really." Alex Manson was quiet for a few seconds, pondering over what Shelby had just told him.

"There must have been something that was mentioned in their conversation that gave the detectives reason to question Ricky and eventually hold him for the death of your husband. Otherwise, they would have no reason or right to hold him. I take it, it was a text message?"

"Yes, that's my understanding."

"You mentioned detectives. Do you have the names and phone numbers for the detectives who are investigating the death of your husband?"

"Yes, the information is in my purse at my desk. I can run and get it for you now, if you want."

"No. No, that won't be necessary. I have a few things to finish up this morning, but I will stop by your desk to pick the information up this afternoon. Is that okay with you?"

"Yes, of course, I'll have it ready for you. Thank you so much!"

"You're very welcome, Shelby. Have a good day and I will see you this afternoon."

"Okay, thanks again and you have a good day too."

After Alex left, Shelby waited for Helen to return to her office so she could apologize. When Helen walked in the door with a cup of coffee, Shelby almost made her spill it on herself by jumping up to apologize to her. Helen quickly stepped back and winced in pain. "Helen, are you all right?"

"Yes, sure, I'm okay, it's my leg. I injured it a while back and it still gives me problems." Shelby looked down to see a medium-size cut in Helen's leg where stitches once were. Her mind flashed back to the night she was attacked and how she had fought off her attacker by jabbing a piece of glass in their leg.

"Shelby, are you okay? Is there something more you need? Did everything go all right with your meeting with Alex?"

"Oh yes, yes, it did. Helen, I just want to apologize to you for the way I acted when I told you I was going to Alex Manson on my own. I'm so sorry. I was way out of line."

"Don't mention it, Shelby. I had no right to speak to you the way I did, so I guess you could say we are even," Helen said with a smile and went to sit behind her desk. Shelby stared at her for a second, a million questions in her mind wanting to bubble forth, but she kept them there, right in her mind for the time being. "Shelby, is there something else you need?"

"No, thanks again, Helen, for everything. Have a good morning."

"Thank you, Shelby. You too."

Chapter Twenty-Six

THE SUNSET CAST A WARM golden glow over the Hampton Shopping Center as shoppers scurried from store to store. It was an unseasonably warm late afternoon, and people took advantage of the beautiful weather to do some last-minute grocery shopping, clothes shopping, or household shopping, as whatever was needed could be found at the Hampton Center. Shelby and Paula walked to the hot dog stand located right in the heart of the shopping center that offered hot dogs and half smokes with just about any topping you chose, be it cheese or chili and any other topping imaginable. Augusta needed fresh mushrooms for the dinner she was making tonight for herself, Paula, and Shelby. After finishing their hot dog and tea, they walked the short distance to the McGuire Grocery Store.

"Weekend grocery shopping is overrated, if you ask me," Paula said as she grabbed a shopping cart and the two of them headed into the store.

"Weekend, weekday, take your pick, Paula?"

"I say hire a maid and let her do the shopping for you, then any day of the week would be fine with me."

"Such is the life of the rich and famous, my dear friend, not for me. Besides, I like picking my own tomatoes and greens," Shelby said with a smile.

"You would, Ms. Picky. I could care less who picked my food just so it's clean and ready for me to eat when I want it."

"I like the jeans you're rocking today, a few more rips in them than the ripped jeans you normally wear."

"I know, hot, right? I love them, and what's more, I got them on sale."

"Paula, since when have you ever cared about or bought anything on sale?"

"Since the day I walked into the store and saw these hot little numbers on sale. Would have picked you up a pair, but you and your conservative self would have just stuck them in the back of your closet and left them there."

Just as Paula and Shelby finished loading the last of their groceries in the back of Paula's truck, Paula happened to look up in time to see a car barreling straight at them.

"Shelby! Look out!" Paula screamed and pushed Shelby out of harm's way, just in time. Both of them fell to the ground, Shelby first, then Paula right on top of her. Paula jumped up, ran to her truck, started it up, and went after the car that tried to run into them. The car was about to turn the corner, but Paula sped up and was able to catch up to it. Once she got close enough to the back of it, she rammed her truck into its rear. The car swerved, almost tipping over, but was able to stay upright. Paula accelerated and rammed into the back of the car again, then quickly pulled around to the side of it to try and see who was driving, but couldn't because the windows were tinted. This angered her even more, so she then side-swiped the car, hitting it as hard as she could without endangering herself, causing it to swerve uncontrollably. The sound of police sirens sounded behind her. Not wanting to have to deal with the police, Paula sped off, leaving the driver of the car to deal with the questions from the police.

Once Paula reached a safe distance from the car and the police, she reached in her glove compartment, pulled out her spare cell phone, and called Shelby. "Shelby!"

"Paula! Where are you! Are you all right?"

"Yes, I'm fine, furious but fine. What about you, you okay?"

"Yeah! What was that all about? What is going on?" Shelby asked frantically.

"I don't know, but you need to get in touch with that detective tonight and let him know what happened to us this afternoon. Shelby, this is really serious. Whoever was driving that car meant to kill us without hesitation."

"I know, I know! I will call him as soon as we get back to the house."

"Good! I will be there in about twenty minutes to get you, on my way now."

"All right."

*   *   *   *   *

While Paula and Augusta busied themselves putting away the groceries, Shelby tried to reach Detective Maye. She dialed his number repeatedly, but each time there was no answer. Finally, she gave up and left him a lengthy message. "Gussie, I'm not very hungry right now. Can we do the spaghetti another night, please?" Shelby asked.

"Nope, we are having our dinner just as we planned, tonight. No crazy maniac is going to ruin our evening. Now you two go sit in the family room and relax. I will call you when it's ready." Paula and Shelby walked slowly out of the kitchen and into the family room. Paula was still so angry she couldn't see straight. Someone had tried to run them over and in a crowded shopping center. The person had to be crazy! Shelby kept checking her cell phone for a call from Detective Maye, which made no sense since it hadn't rung at all the entire evening.

Now more than ever she was seriously considering asking Augusta to get her a gun from Gus. Things were starting to get out of control, there was no need to second guess the fact that someone was after her, someone wanted her to join Myron. A gun seemed to be one of her best means of protection now. She'd battled with the idea of keeping one just for her safety after her last attack, but the other side of her was totally against it. Guns injure and kill, but they also save and protect. *What to do?* she thought to herself.

"Where is he?"

"Who?"

"Detective Maye, I've called him a million times."

"Text him."

"No, texting is too personal."

"Really, Shelby? Someone just tried to kill us and you're worrying about texting him being too personal? Give me the phone. I'll text him," Paula said while reaching for the phone, but Shelby pulled it back out of her reach.

"You girls listen to me. From what you tell me happened in that shopping center tonight, you need to be really careful. You are obviously being watched. Someone is angry, and an angry person is a dangerous person."

"Augusta, I don't know what's going on. Why would someone want to kill me or Paula?"

"Well, you, I don't know. Paula is a different story," Augusta said, trying to bring some humor to the conversation.

"Ha-ha," Paula said and rolled her eyes at Augusta. Shelby's cell phone rang, and she jumped up from the table to get it, thinking it was Detective Maye calling her back.

"Hello, Shelby," Alex Manson said.

"Alex, hello."

"Alex Manson?" Paula mouthed to her. Shelby nodded her head yes.

"I hope I'm not disturbing you."

"Oh, no, we were just sitting here talking."

"We… do you have guests?"

"Paula is here along with Augusta, my adoptive mother as of right now," Shelby said with a smile.

"I see, well, good news. I spoke with Detective Maye earlier today regarding your friend Ricky. Seems he was released days ago, not enough evidence to hold him."

"Really, that is wonderful news. I am so happy!"

"I thought you would be!"

"Thank you so much for your help. I really appreciate it!"

"Sure, Shelby, anytime. Good night."

"Good night," Shelby said and danced across the floor to her seat, singing over and over, "Ricky is free. Ricky is free!"

Augusta and Paula sat staring at Shelby until they all turned to the knocking on the front door. Shelby stopped in her tracks. Augusta was the first to get up while saying, "Hold on a minute."

"Augusta, what are you doing? Don't you go get that gun. Has it come to this? Every time we hear a knock at the door, we think we are in danger?" Shelby asked while throwing her hands up in the air.

"Yeah, because after today, I'm convinced that we are. Go get it, Augusta," Paula said.

"Yes, can I help you?" Shelby asked as she peeped through the small hole in the door to see who was outside.

"Shelby, it's Detective Maye, and I have my partner with me, Detective Harris. I got your message. I came as soon as I heard it. May we come in?"

"Yes, of course," Shelby said as she hurriedly took the locks off the door and let them in.

"Detective Maye, Harris," Shelby greeted each of them respectively as they walked in past her. Detective Harris was his usual cold-shouldered self and only nodded his head in acknowledgment of Shelby who could have cared less. As far as she was concerned, he could just turn around and walk right back out her door. "I have been trying to reach you over and over again. I didn't realize you were so hard to get."

"We do have other cases, ma'am," Detective Harris said.

"Shelby, my name is Shelby. I thought I made that clear when we first met? Oh, but I'm sorry, you must have forgotten it while planning how you'd follow me to trap Ricky."

"All right, let's all calm down. I know this has been a very difficult evening for you, and I'm sorry, Shelby, but believe me, we really are here to help."

"I'm sure *you* are, Detective Maye," Shelby said while disregarding Detective Harris intentionally.

Paula and Augusta exchanged glances. They knew Shelby could get angry, but they had never seen her like this before.

"First of all, Shelby, the next time something like what happened to you and your friend today happens again, call the police immediately, the first chance you get. You can get them a lot quicker than you can get us."

"Thank you. I'm sorry, Detective Maye. I honestly didn't think about that. I was too, too…"

"I understand. So why don't you start from the beginning and tell us what happened," Detective Maye said while taking a seat on the loveseat. Detective Harris remained standing.

"Well, it was just as in the message I left you. Paula and I had just loaded the last bag of groceries in the back of her truck, when all of a sudden, I heard Paula scream my name. I looked up just in time to see this car coming straight at us before Paula pushed me out of the way and fell on top of me. Paula then jumped up and went after the car in her truck."

Detective Harris looked at Paula and asked, "Did you get a look at the car, the color, license plate?"

"No, I'm sorry, I didn't. I was too busy chasing it."

"That was a very dangerous thing to do, Paula," Detective Harris said, making it a point to direct his conversation towards Paula.

"Maybe, but at the time, I was too angry to think about that. I just wanted to get my hands on the person who almost killed me and Shelby."

"You mean to tell me you couldn't hold it together long enough to pull out a scrap of paper and a pen to at least write down the color of the car once Paula took off after it?" Augusta asked while shaking her head.

"Augusta, no, it all happened so fast, I didn't think—"

"It's all right, Shelby. It's okay. I understand. Excuse us for a minute," Detective Maye said as he walked over to Detective Harris and whispered something in his ear. Then he walked back over and stood before Shelby and said, "You haven't given us a lot to go on tonight. Tonight, before you go to bed, sit down and make a list of everything you can think of associated with what happened today. Everything prior to, during, and after the incident and I will call to discuss it with you tomorrow. Paula, you sure there is nothing you can give us as far as the color, make, and model of the car?" Detective Maye asked.

"No, I'm sorry, nothing."

"Shelby, try to get some rest tonight. You too, Paula. I will call you tomorrow to see how you did with the list. For now, keep your doors locked and your eyes opened. Call the police first if anything unusual happens tonight, then us," Detective Maye said as he walked toward the door to leave.

"Thank you. I will do as you asked and look forward to speaking with you tomorrow," Shelby said disappointedly.

Detective Maye noticed her disappointment and fear. "What is it, Shelby? What's bothering you?"

"I don't know. It just seems like with all that's happened over the last week or so, and now this, you guys should be able to tell me something by now."

"I understand your frustration, Shelby, but believe me, we are working very hard to solve your husband's murder. And to find out if these latest incidents are related to his murder. We will find the person who did it. We always do. It's just a matter of time."

"Thank you, Detective Maye. I will talk to you tomorrow. Good night."

"Good night, Shelby, Paula, and…"

"Augusta, me name is Augusta, you handsome devil, you."

"Augusta!" Shelby said, unable to believe Augusta had just said what she did to Detective Maye's face.

"Well, he is," Augusta said.

"Oh, my goodness, Augusta," Shelby said and let them out.

Paula just laughed and said, "You go, Augusta! I'm sleeping over tonight. It's too late to head home now. Plus, my truck is about to fall apart after ramming it into that car so many times."

"Of course, Paula. You know you are always welcome to stay here any time you'd like."

"No, she's not," Augusta said while setting the table for dinner.

"Gussie, now, now, that's no way to treat our Paula, apologize."

"Nope."

"Well, all right, I guess I will just have to keep my little surprise I have for you tomorrow," Paula said teasingly.

"Surprise, for me?"

"Oh, now you want to be nice to me."

"Oh, all right, I'm sorry. Now what's me surprise?"

"Gussie, you taught school. Why do you keep saying *me* instead of *my* when referring to something that belongs to you? I thought we talked about that and you were going to try and work on it," Shelby said.

"I don't know, old age I guess. When you get to be my age, you just talk and hope any sound at all comes out of your mouth, be it wrong or right." Shelby and Paula laughed. "Now, what's me surprise?"

"I was going to wait until tomorrow, but with all that's happened this evening, I think we could all use some cheering up. So I can show you better than I can tell you," Paula said while walking to her purse and pulling her wallet out. She motioned for Augusta to come over before saying, "Remember that day you asked Shelby for money so you could feed your cat? Well, Shel told me it died and so…" Paula said as she took a picture of a beautiful white-and-gray kitten out of her wallet. "She is all yours. I bought her from a family that lives in my neighborhood. The mother gave birth to a litter of beautiful kittens and her owners had me come over to see them. I immediately thought about you."

"For me, really?"

"Yes, I pick her up tomorrow. The owners wanted her to stay with the mother for one more night before passing her on."

"I don't know what to say," Augusta said.

"Thank you would be nice," Shelby said. Augusta then walked over and gave Paula a big hug.

"What are you going to name her?" Paula asked.

"I have the perfect name for her," Augusta said.

"What?" Shelby asked.

"Gracey, her name is going to be Gracey," Augusta said while taking the picture away from Paula and pressing it against her chest. She then said "come on, let's eat dinner, it's ready."

CHAPTER TWENTY-SEVEN

JUST AS DETECTIVE MAYE HAD promised, he called Shelby the next day for the list of what she could remember about what happened the previous day. Shelby reluctantly read him what she had, which was basically nothing. She was so ashamed of herself for falling apart and not being more observant. Detective Maye thanked her and reassured her that every bit of information she could pull together for them, no matter how small, would be very helpful. "While I have you on the phone, I want to mention this one thing. I hear you had to let my friend Ricky go because you didn't have enough evidence to hold him." Silence hung in the air between them.

"Shelby, listen, I'm sorry we had to catch up with Ricky by following you. But keep in mind, a man is dead. That man was your husband. We are after his killer. That's our first priority in this line of work."

"I understand. I just felt a little betrayed is all."

"We had no intention of betraying you."

"I know."

"This is a lonely and cold business sometimes. We make a lot of enemies."

"I'm sure you do, but somebody has to do it right? I appreciate all you are doing to solve Myron's murder. And find out if the latest incidents I've been experiencing are related to his murder in any way."

"Shelby, what happened between you and your late husband?"

"Is this off the record or what, Detective?"

"I'm not trying to trap you, Shelby, if that's what you are asking."

"Myron and I had a lot of problems, Detective Maye. Don't get me wrong. I had my faults too. It just seemed no matter what I did, I could never please him. If he complained that I'd gained too much weight, I'd lose weight. When I would lose the weight, he would complain that I was too small. At first, the abuse was verbal, then it became physical. Still, I tried to hang in there, tried to hold on to my marriage. The first time Myron struck me, I was honestly stupid enough to believe I'd said or done something to warrant it. Then it seemed the least little thing I said or did that irritated him, he would just haul off and hit me, as hard as he could."

"Why didn't you leave the first time it happened? Why did you stay with him?"

"I loved my husband. I honestly thought I was the one making him miserable, making him treat me the way he did."

"Just before your husband was killed, he lured you to a hotel, then he beat you. Is that correct?" Shelby didn't say anything. "Is that true, Shelby?"

"Yes, sir, it is."

"Tell me what happened that night, Shelby." Shelby was reluctant to say anything to Detective Maye or anyone else about that night, but she also knew she had to get it off her mind or it would eventually destroy her.

"He called me, told me where he was and if I wanted our marriage to work, then I should meet him there. So I went. I really thought he wanted to work things out."

"So you went to his room, and what happened next?"

"As soon as I walked in the door, he knocked me to the floor and started calling me all kinds of names, accusing me of having an affair with Ricky. I pleaded with him. I begged. I tried to explain to him that nothing was going on with Ricky and me, but he wouldn't listen. He just kept hitting me harder and harder."

Shelby stopped talking in an effort to keep her composure. "Are you all right, Shelby? You don't have to go on if you're uncomfortable with sharing this information with me."

"When I was finally able to somehow get up off the floor, he tried to tear my clothes off me. That's when I started to fight back."

"What made you decide to fight back then, Shelby?"

"Fear."

"Fear?"

"Yes, fear. The fear that he was going to try and rape me." Shelby paused again. Detective Maye waited. "There was just no way I was going to let him have his way with me sexually after he had smacked and kicked and punched me almost senseless. I felt, for him to do that to me, after beating me so severely, would have been the ultimate show of disrespect for me as a person and as a woman. I just couldn't allow him to do that to me without putting up a fight." Shelby's voice broke, but she continued. "There was no way I was going to let him use my body for his sick pleasure after he had treated me like an animal. No way."

Detective Maye let out a heavy sigh before saying, "Shelby, I want to ask you something. You don't have to answer me if you don't want to, okay?"

"Okay."

"At that moment, that very moment, when you were driven to fight Myron back, did you at any time feel that you could kill him? That given the chance, you could take his life?" An eternity seemed to pass before Shelby answered.

"No, sir."

"No?"

"The more we fought, the harder I prayed that I would just make it out of that room alive. Every bone in my body hurt, from my head to my toes. I honestly thought my life was going to end in that hotel room that night. I didn't think about hurting him, seeking revenge on him in any way, killing him. Detective Maye, I just wanted to make it out of that room alive, that's all."

Detective Maye sighed heavily before saying, "You know Shelby, so many women have had the same experience, not necessarily in a hotel room. Maybe it was in a house, apartment, maybe even just walking along a street. But sadly, they are no longer here. You are one of the fortunate few who lived to share what happened to you in that hotel room. I can't tell you how sorry I am you had to go through that."

"How did you know this had happened? About the night Myron invited me to the hotel?"

"It was a part of a conversation between him and Ricky we discovered in his phone, a text message conversation between them."

"Did Ricky threaten to kill Myron in that conversation?"

"Yes, he did."

*   *   *   *   *

Augusta sat at the kitchen island that was covered with food. Bread started the long line of the food train, followed by mustard, mayonnaise, ham, turkey, cheese, tomatoes, cookies, chips, and ended with bottled water.

"Gussie, what is all this?" Shelby asked as she walked in the room, picked up a slice of cheese, and ate it.

"Don't bother me. I'm busy, and if you're hungry, you have to get your own lunch today. This food is for my friends, and I have to hurry to the park to feed them before they all fall asleep or are too drunk to eat it. I'm referring to Gus, of course, on the drunk part."

"Sweetie, how many people are you trying to feed? You must have enough food here to feed an army."

"Enough to feed as many as possible. Some of them haven't eaten in days and are on their last leg," Augusta said while jumping up from the island and scurrying to the refrigerator to pull out more turkey.

"Hey, Paula and I are coming with you. We can help you feed them." Shelby ran out of the room, got her cell phone, and called Paula, telling her to meet them at her house and what they were going to do.

*   *   *   *   *

When they got to the park that afternoon, it was about five thirty, and homeless people were everywhere. Paula backed her truck up as close to the park as possible so the homeless could get to it easily. They got out the truck then Paula and Shelby started opening the bags of sandwiches, chips, cookies, and bottled water while Augusta hurried over and tried to gather as many people as possible and lead them to the truck to get food. The line formed quickly, and before they knew it, they were handing out food to the homeless that included men, women, and children of all ages. Shelby couldn't believe it. She'd never considered the fact that there were children, even babies that were homeless. Her heart broke as she surveyed the crowd forming in front of them.

"Paula, there is no way we are going to be able to feed all these people today. What are we going to do?"

"Simple, women and children get food first," Paula said as if it should have been the most obvious thing in the world to Shelby.

Shelby turned to take more sandwiches out of the bag. When she turned back around to hand them out, a woman that looked like she was knocking on death's door was standing in front of her. The woman's hair looked to be dark brown or just dirty, Shelby couldn't tell. Her about five-foot-three frame Shelby figured, carried maybe a hundred pounds, if that. She clung to the hand of a little girl that looked to be about six years old with blond hair pulled back in a ponytail and secured with a rubber band. The child's face was dirty and her nose ran. It was cold out, and the mother wore only a sweater to cover herself while the child wore a coat that looked to be about three sizes too big for her, no socks, and lace-up shoes minus the laces.

Shelby forced a smile and handed the mother and daughter a sandwich along with tissues for the child to wipe her nose with. Paula added chips and cookies, and Augusta handed them water.

"Hi Mattie, how you doing today? Krystal, you are growing up nicely—yes, ma'am, nicely. You look just like your mother. You are such a pretty little thing," Augusta said. The little girl said nothing and moved closer to her mother. Shelby wasn't surprised Augusta knew their names; after all, these were her friends. The woman and little girl took their food, thanked them, and rushed off to grab a bench to sit on and eat.

Shelby watched them. As Krystal finished her sandwich, her mother took her own sandwich from its bag and handed it to her. The child quickly finished that one too. Instead of reaching for her chips next, Krystal ate her cookies, then her chips, and drank all her water. Mattie then took her pack of cookies and handed them to Krystal who ate them all except one before turning to her mother and offering her the last one, but her mother refused it and encouraged Krystal to eat it. The child stared up at her mother and tried a second time to give her the cookie, and again, her mother refused it, then took the cookie from

Krystal's hand and stuck it in the child's mouth. Mattie then took the last bag of chips, ate a few, then gave the rest to Krystal who crumpled them up and tossed them to the pigeons that had gathered in front of them. When the food was all gone, Mattie walked over and picked up a blanket someone had left on the ground, took it back to the bench, and wrapped it around her and her daughter, as they huddled close together.

"Paula, will you please hand out the rest of the sandwiches? I will be right back."

"Where are you going?" Shelby didn't answer. She walked around to the passenger side of Paula's truck where her purse lay tucked under the seat, picked it up, pulled out her wallet, and took out a fifty-dollar bill and walked over to sit on the bench beside Mattie and Krystal. Krystal inched closer to her mother and laid her head on her shoulder.

"Hi, Mattie, Krystal! My name is Shelby, and I am a good friend of Augusta." They both stared at Shelby but did not respond. Shelby tried again. "Did you like your sandwich? Gussie made it. Gussie makes everything taste so good, even a sandwich," Shelby said with a chuckle.

"Krystal, do you have a favorite color?" Shelby asked, still trying to reach the child, her mother, one, or both of them. Krystal didn't answer but instead looked up at her mother who nodded to her that it was okay to talk to Shelby.

"Yes, ma'am, it's yellow. I like yellow."

"Really, so do I. But my most favorite color of all is orange. I love the color orange." Krystal gave way to a slow smile. "Hey, if you could choose one toy right now that you would just love to have, what would it be?"

"I don't know. I don't have any toys."

"But if you could have a toy, what toy would it be?" Krystal thought for a moment.

"A dollhouse, a dollhouse with lots of pretty furniture and people in it, and…"

"What is it, Krystal? What would you like to say? It's okay," Shelby said, trying to encourage the child to speak freely.

"I would like to have a really big dollhouse for my mommy and me to live in, with a kitchen, and beds, and pretty furniture in it like the one my friend Kayla at school has. She has a really big house. She shows me pictures of it sometimes. A house with a kitchen for Mommy to cook in would make her happy. She loves to cook and makes the best fried chicken and mashed potatoes ever!" Shelby looked at Mattie who was staring off into space, then back to her child.

Paula walked up and, sensing Shelby's sadness, softly said, "Shel, it's getting late. We have run out of food, and Gussie is tired. Can we go now, please?" Shelby looked at Mattie again, hoping she would look at her, tell her what happened, why they no longer had a home. But Mattie continued to stare off into space. "Shel?"

"All right, Paula. Do you have a pen and something to write on?" Paula reached in her bag and handed Shelby a small scrap of paper and a pen then walked back to join Augusta. Shelby scribbled her address on it, then walked over to Mattie and handed it to her along with the fifty-dollar bill.

"Mattie, I would like to have a party for Krystal at my house this Saturday. That's my address I've given you. Will you please allow her to come and you with her?" Mattie stared at the paper and the fifty-dollar bill, then slowly looked up at Shelby and nodded yes. "Thank you, Mattie, thank you so much! See you this Saturday at two."

"You are a nice lady, Ms. Shelby. Maybe you and my mommy can be friends. I think she would like that, it would be fun."

"I would like that very much, Krystal. Good night. See you Saturday."

Before Shelby returned to join Paula and Augusta, Paula turned to Augusta and said, "I've been thinking about what the detective said as far as Haverty being the one to find Myron's dead body, Shelby told me this."

"Yeah, what is your point?"

"Well, didn't you tell me she said to you she was not going to have anything to do with him anymore that day you showed her the pictures?"

"Yes, she sure did."

"Then what was she doing at Myron's home the night he was killed? Strange?"

Augusta looked at Paula thoughtfully and said, "You're right. It is strange." After this neither of them said anything more about the matter.

"I don't know how these people do it. It's cold as I don't know what out here today," Paula said while pulling her thick scarf tighter around her neck.

"They will be heading to the shelter soon, but for now, they just needed to get out of there for a while and breathe in some fresh air," Augusta said as they all piled into Paula's truck to head home.

When Shelby and Augusta returned home, they showered and had their dinner. Shelby couldn't stop thinking about the homeless people she'd help feed today. She sometimes would leave a little of her food on her plate not wanting to eat it all because it made her feel she'd eaten too much. However, that night, she ate every single bit of her food while thinking the food she might throw away would have been eaten by a homeless person today.

*   *   *   *   *

It was a busy week at work, and Shelby was stressed beyond belief, partly due to it being so chaotic in the office and partly due to her being exhausted. Every night after work, she and Paula would rush out to the party store to purchase decorations for Krystal's upcoming party. Almost everything they bought was yellow. Finally, she grew sick of yellow and started throwing in some pinks, which was at Augusta's suggestion of course. Tonight, after work, she and Paula would go on the hunt for a dollhouse, not just any dollhouse but the perfect dollhouse for Krystal.

"Where to, boss?" Paula asked as she steered her new truck expertly on the road. "What store next?"

"Okay, so the last store we tried did not even have a dollhouse. What a waste of time, dang it," Shelby said out of frustration.

"Yeah, but that salesman was fine as you know what!"

"Paula, what in the world! Will you please focus, bring it back, focus! Oh, I meant to tell you, I love this new truck, meant to say something when we were at the park to feed the homeless, but I was so overtaken by the number of homeless people there needing to be fed, I forgot to mention it."

Shelby's mind drifted to Krystal, what a precious little person she was, and she'd made up her mind that she was not going to spare any expense to make sure she had a party that she would never forget.

"Thank you. I traded the other one in after it got so banged up by me ramming into that car that tried to run us over." Shelby did not respond. She was still lost in thought over Krystal's party. "Hey! Where are you?"

"Sorry, Paula, I was just thinking about some things, is all."

"You all right?"

"Sure, fine."

"Guess what I did," Paula said excitedly.

"Oh boy, dare I ask," Shelby said laughingly.

"Well, I didn't get laid. That's for sure."

"Is that all you ever think about?"

"No, I think about getting married, children, the whole nine, but where are all the good men on this earth? It's as if they've all vanished. Oh, where are we going?"

"Well, since we are close to the mall, let's go in and see what we can find."

"Okay," Paula said and pulled into a parking space after turning in to the mall."

"I hired a pony ride for the children this Saturday!"

"How awesome is that!" Shelby said and gave her a high five as they walked to the mall entrance.

Just as Shelby reached for the door to open it, someone pushed her from behind so hard she fell through the door hands first, which she used to break her fall. Paula saw her just as she looked up from closing her handbag. She ran over to her and helped her up.

"What! What happened?"

"I don't know. I went to open the door, and before I knew it, I was on the floor," Shelby said while dusting her clothes off.

"Did you trip? I mean, Shelby, you just don't fall without stumbling or something."

"Paula, I don't know. I'm telling you I don't know exactly what happened. Honestly, I think I was shoved into the door," she said angrily.

"What!"

"Paula, please, let's just go look for Krystal's dollhouse and call it a night," Shelby said frustratedly. Paula tried to walk and look at Shelby at the same time, causing her to almost bump into two people. "Will you please stop staring at me and watch where you're going? I'm fine. Now let's just go get the dollhouse."

*　　*　　*　　*　　*

"I am so tired but look at this dollhouse, Augusta! Paula and I searched the world over, but we found the perfect one. What do you think?"

"It's beautiful," Augusta said with a big smile on her face and clapping her hands together. "Krystal is going to love it!"

"You really think so?" Shelby asked while standing back with her hands on her hips and inspecting the dollhouse one more time before putting it away.

"Oh, I know so, thank you, Shelby. Thank you so much, honey, for taking the time to do this for Krystal. She and her mom have been through a lot."

"You think she will like the color?"

The dollhouse was huge and bright yellow, with red shutters and a red door. The windows were large enough for you to see in, and just as Krystal had requested, there were several rooms in it, two levels. Living room and kitchen on the lower level and bedrooms upstairs. There was tiny furniture and tiny people in it, just as Krystal had asked for.

"She will love the color. It's yellow, her favorite color."

"Great, that's why I chose this particular one. It's massive and Krystal's favorite color, yellow."

*   *   *   *   *

Saturday morning came in bright and sunny. *A great day for Krystal's party*, Shelby thought to herself as she laced up her running shoes. She and Paula had agreed to meet for a run around nine, and it was now eight-fifty. Shelby finished lacing up her shoes and started stretching and was almost done when she heard Paula running up to her, saying good morning.

"Hey, you are looking great, kiddo. Did you take off a few?" Paula asked while looking Shelby over.

"Stress, one sure way to take off the pounds if you are like me and don't eat when something is bothering you."

"What's up? What is bothering you?" Paula asked while stretching and warming up for the run too.

"That night at the mall when I fell through the door. I know I didn't just fall, Paula. I was pushed. Had whoever pushed me done so a little harder, I would have hit that hard floor head first, and that could have been the end of me."

"Shel, you have got to talk to that detective. This is crazy and scary. But I asked you the same night it happened if you stumbled or what, and you said you weren't sure how you fell."

"That's because I didn't want to get distracted by it. We still had to find Krystal's dollhouse." Paula stood with her hands on her hips and nodded in agreement.

"Well, let's get our run started. It will be time for the party before we know it, and there is still lots to be done."

"All right then, let's get this party started. I'm going to run your buns into the ground, girlfriend," Paula said.

"Shoot your best shot! Go!" Shelby said and took off running. Paula soon caught up to her, and the two of them jogged and talked for a mile before Paula noticed they were being followed.

"Shel?"

"Yeah?" Shelby said while trying to keep up with Paula and breathe too. She had to admit to herself that Paula was the better runner.

"I want you to listen to me. We are being followed."

"What?" Shelby said while starting to turn around to see who was behind them.

"No, no, no, don't look back. Just keep running as if you don't even know they are there."

"Paula!"

"Trust me on this one, okay? I have an idea. We need to split up, run in opposite directions, in order for it to work."

"Oh my god, Paula, what in the world?"

"When I say run, you take off running as fast and as hard as you can, and I am going to run in the opposite direction. Nine times out of ten, they are going to follow you. Just keep running as fast as you can and control your breathing, Shel, control it, because that's what's going to keep you going. Ready, go!"

Shelby did just as Paula suggested and took off running as fast as she could while trying to remember to control her breathing. Just as Paula said, the person following them was thrown off and a little confused but quickly pulled it together and took off after Shelby. Paula ran as fast as she could in the opposite direction, stopped suddenly, and searched for a weapon, something like a large, thick stick. Finally, she found one that wasn't exactly what she wanted, but it would have to do, she thought to herself. Grabbing the stick, she took off running, pushing short gulps of air through her lips in an effort to prevent herself from getting tired too quickly. She raced back in the direction of where she'd left Shelby. Feeling herself getting overheated, she somehow managed to pull her sweatshirt off and toss it to the ground, enabling her to run faster in her tank and sweats.

Before she knew it, she was in pursuit of the person chasing Shelby. When she had gotten close enough to them, she yelled, "Hey" as loud as she could, and when the person turned around, she hit them as hard as she could with the stick. They grabbed their shoulder and staggered. Just then, Shelby rushed on them and kicked them as hard as she could, causing her own self to fall to the ground. Paula went after them again with the stick, but the person recovered and ran off, leaving Paula and Shelby panting and coughing hard in an effort to catch their breath.

"Are you okay?" Paula asked Shelby as she walked over, gave her a hand, and pulled her off the ground.

"What the hell!" Paula said out of breath. "Who was that?"

"I don't know," Shelby said while bending over and placing her hands on her knees in an effort to catch her breath. "I couldn't see their face. It was covered with some type of crazy mask. I do know this: I think it's time I take Augusta up on that gun she offered me."

Mattie and Krystal arrived on time for the party. Shelby and Paula invited about six other little girls of their coworkers since neither of them had children of their own. When they returned home after their run that morning, they found that Augusta had finished decorating the family room with yellow and pink streamers as well as hung up the large balloons Shelby and Paula had blown up the night before. In the kitchen, Augusta busied herself with putting out the pizza, chips, chicken tenders, and salad she, Paula, and Shelby had also prepared the night before.

"Hey, you," Shelby said as she walked in the kitchen and gave Augusta a bear hug. "Go, get off your feet. I'll finish up here." Augusta turned around to face Shelby, concern written all over her face.

"What happened out there this morning? When you and Paula walked in here this morning, you both looked like you'd seen a ghost."

"It's nothing. Everything is fine," Shelby said, faking a smile.

"Don't tell me everything is fine. I may be old but I'm not stupid. Something happened this morning while you and Paula were out for that run."

"Gussie, listen to me, please. This is Krystal's party, and I am not about to spoil it with concerns for myself. I've contacted Detective Maye. I'll be talking with him after the party over the phone, but for now, let's just give this little girl the party of her life." Shelby picked up the tray of hot dogs, turned, and walked back to the family room where the children sat playing games and eating chocolate chip cookies.

"Hey, guys, who wants hot dogs!" Shelby yelled.

"I do!" they all said excitedly.

"Just don't eat too many. There is more food in the kitchen, including salad."

"Salad?" one of the little girls said and turned up her nose.

"Yes, salad," Paula said with a smile.

After the children finished eating, Shelby walked to the center of the room and called for the girls' attention.

"Girls, girls! I want you to all listen up for a minute. I am going to turn off all the lights for a second, and when I give Ms. Paula the signal, she is going to bring on a surprise. Okay, ready? Turning off the lights now, Paula will you do the honors, please?" Shelby said while signaling her. Just then, Paula flipped a switch on the dollhouse and it lit up. The girls went crazy, screaming and jumping up and down!

"It's beautiful!" Krystal said.

An hour after the girls finished playing with the dollhouse, Paula and Shelby ushered them outside to take turns riding the pony Paula rented for them. After the party ended, the last slice of pizza was eaten, and the parents of the other six little girls had picked them up, Shelby called Krystal over.

"Krystal, sweetie, do you like your dollhouse?"

"My dollhouse? It's mine, really?"

"It sure is!"

"Oh, thank you, thank you so much, Ms. Shelby!"

"You are very welcome. Oh, please, thank Ms. Paula and Ms. Augusta too. I could not have done all this without them."

Krystal obeyed and thanked them all over and over again. Mattie walked over to Shelby and, with tears in her eyes, hugged her and said, "Thank you, thank you so much, Shelby, for making my little girl's dream come true."

CHAPTER TWENTY-EIGHT

SHELBY SAT IN HER BED, propped up by several cushiony pillows, with her cell phone in her hand. She was waiting on the call from Detective Maye. After leaving him a message as to what time she would be able to talk to him after Krystal's party, she showered and jumped in bed to rest before his call. He was late, she thought to herself, but that was fine because she was so tired she feared she'd fall asleep while they were talking, so she was glad to be able to just relax a bit before he called.

When her cell phone rang, she jumped, having dozed off to sleep. The phone had somehow gotten lost in the covers while she was sleeping. She searched desperately for it while scolding herself for not simply laying it on her nightstand where she could easily reach it when he called. Finally, she found it buried under a pillow.

"Hello?"

"Shelby, Detective Maye here. How are you? I'm sorry I'm late, crazy day. Two back-to-back murders to be investigated today. Seems the murders are related in some way. I've been a detective for a long time, but I still can't get use to looking at dead bodies. It just does something to me to see what's left of a person who only hours earlier was talking, walking, planning for their future or the next day, now lying dead as a result of a bullet or whatever it was that ended their life."

"Well, I have to say, Detective, I don't envy you your job. I don't think I could do it," Shelby said sadly.

"Shelby, tell me something. You mentioned when we talked earlier today about this morning's incident with you and Paula while out for a run, that she decided the two of you should split up and run in different directions when she learned you were being followed. Why?"

"I don't know. I can only assume that it was to throw whoever was following us off. She wasn't gone long, Detective. She was back soon and using a large stick to fight our follower off."

"Okay, okay," Detective Maye said and cleared his throat. Shelby shifted in the bed in an effort to get more comfortable and stay awake. *I should have just gotten up and sat in the chair when he called,* she said to herself.

"Shelby, how well do you know Paula?"

"What do you mean? We are best friends."

"I know, but on a scale of one to ten, how well would you say you know her? She and Ricky were both working at the firm when you started there, right?"

"Yes, that's right. What are you insinuating, that Paula had something to do with what happened this morning? She was with me, remember? She was being followed too. We were together on the run this morning. I told you all of this already!"

Detective Maye didn't respond right away. He knew he was upsetting Shelby, and that if the conversation turned in that direction, they would accomplish nothing in the way of finding out what really happened this morning. He decided to end the conversation on a positive note and soon. "Shelby, I have plenty of information to go on for now, according to what you told me this morning and just confirmed. We are on it, trust me! You try to get some rest. It's late. I'll be in touch. Be careful, Shelby. Good night."

"Good night, Detective," Shelby said disappointedly. She was really hoping he would be able to tell her something more positive, soothe her frayed nerves, erase it all by one simple word, but such was not the case. She was left to get through the night feeling just as confused and frightened about the situation as she was before they talked. Even worse, he had managed to plant the seed of doubt as to whether Paula's friendship was genuine.

*   *   *   *   *

A horrible day full of mistakes and disagreements added to Shelby's already-somber mood. Nothing was going right at work that day. She sent a letter to Helen to sign full of mistakes only to have Helen come storming out of her office to stare at her as if she had two heads.

"Really, Shelby, did you proof this or just type it and forget to proof it? Maybe you need some more time off. You could be still grieving, although I seriously doubt it. I don't know! You look horrible. When was the last time you took a trip to the hairdresser? You are losing weight like crazy. Are you eating? You know what! Forget it! I'll proof the letter and get it out myself. You make yourself a doctor's appointment because you are obviously not well, and for the sake of my sanity, go get your hair done. Maybe even buy a new lipstick."

Helen rushed off and returned a second later, slapping twenty-five dollars on Shelby's desk. "Take that money and buy yourself a lipstick, a rich color, red even. You'd wear that color nicely, and you'd look alive. You need some color." Shelby didn't say anything. She just ignored Helen, something she'd perfected in all her years of working with her, because she knew that deep down Helen meant well. She just didn't know, with all of her college education and her attempt at professionalism, how to express it. She just sat at her desk and stared at Helen. That was all she could manage to do. "Did you hear me?" Helen asked with concern. "Whatever! Where in the world is Paula! Maybe she can talk some sense into you," Helen said and walked off, throwing her hands in the air.

Shelby felt anxious and sad. She wanted, needed to talk to someone about the entire mess her life was in right now. But there was no one, no one at all. Thanks to Detective Maye, she didn't know if she could trust Paula or Ricky now.

Augusta, there was no way she was going to her. Augusta was getting on in age. She needed rest and relaxation so she could enjoy the rest of her life. She'd lived on the streets, fought to survive, known sleepless nights and hunger Shelby couldn't imagine, eating out of a trash can and finishing off someone else's drink. It was a wonder she was still alive and had managed to escape picking up some dreadful disease. No, she was not going to her. She had to find a way to get through this on her own.

"Hey!" Shelby looked up to see Paula standing in front of her with a sandwich and a cup of coffee.

"Hey, what's this? Did Helen send you?"

"Nope, I haven't seen Wonder Woman. I swear she thinks she can run this office on her own, but you and I both know she can't," Paula said while unwrapping the sandwich for Shelby.

"Thank you," Shelby said while taking the sandwich and coffee from Paula. She sat it down without even bothering to try and eat the sandwich or drink the coffee.

"Well, aren't you going to eat your lunch? You told me this morning you couldn't go out for lunch because you had too much work to do, so I brought lunch to you," Paula said with a smile. "Oh, and I found these little babies. Sure to bring a smile to your face," Paula said as she handed Shelby a small bag with a pair of gold studs in it.

"Thanks, Paula, they are very pretty," Shelby said sadly and closed the bag back up.

"What is wrong with you? I'm really trying here and you are not even cracking a smile. What's up?"

"Paula, I need to ask you something."

"Sure, you can ask me anything, you know that." Shelby took so long to say anything Paula began to get annoyed. "Shelby, what? Eat your sandwich because you look like you are about to pass out. Hold on a minute. I'm going to get you some water. I'll be right back." Paula ran from the room to get Shelby some water and was back with it in no time. "Here, Shel, drink up. You will feel better. Now talk to me. What is going on?"

"Were you ever involved with Myron, intimate with him?"

"What?"

"I didn't stutter, Paula. You heard me, so please, cut the act and answer the question, please."

Paula shifted and crossed her arms, staring Shelby right in the eyes. She said, "Yes, I was once, but it was long before I met you or knew he was married to you. He lied to me, the bastard! Shelby, Myron stopped by the office one day, I guess to see you, although I didn't know this at the time. I ran into him in the hallway. We greeted each other, laughed, and joked. He asked me out, and we dated for about a month, just long enough for me to realize he was not at all my type," Paula said nervously. Shelby got up from her desk and walked around to stand in Paula's face.

"You stand there and admit this to me like it is the most normal thing in the world for a supposedly best friend to date her friend's husband. You are impossible, you know that. You really are!"

"Again!" Paula said angrily. "You had just started working here. I'd seen you at a distance and had not even so much as greeted you, had no idea who you were. For all I knew, you were single and so was Myron. I knew no differently. He told me no differently!"

"You expect me to believe that bull, Paula," Shelby spat at her.

"Yes, because I have never given you any reason to doubt my word! I also expect you to trust me, Shelby."

"Trust you! You are kidding, right? Paula, how in the world am I supposed to be able to trust you ever again after what you just admitted to me regarding you and Myron? Trust you! Think about that word, Paula—*trust*! Then ask yourself if it's even reasonable for you to ask me to do so after what you just told me."

"When our friendship started to grow and I learned that you were married to Myron, I cut him off completely. I have done no wrong, Shelby. I've been a loyal friend to you. You know I would never do anything to hurt you. You know I wouldn't! Why are you questioning me like this? Shelby, please! I never meant for you to find out like this. I was going to tell you. I was... I'm sorry, I'm so very sorry. Please believe me," Paula said as her voice began to break.

"You cut the relationship off with Myron, really? So how did you know he'd lost his job, Paula? Why did he turn to you to ask me for a divorce?" Paula went to touch Shelby, but Shelby stepped back from her. "Don't touch me, Paula. Don't come anywhere near me!"

"When he came to me, he promised me, promised me," Paula said, gesturing with her hands to prove her point. "He promised me that he would leave you alone to live in peace. That's the only reason I allowed any communication between him and me. The only reason!"

Shelby turned from Paula to her desk and picked up her purse; she had to get out of Paula's presence before she did something she would later regret. Before leaving, she said to Paula, "Don't call me, don't text me, e-mail me, and by all means forget where I live." She then turned and walked quickly from the room. Paula stood there, a mixture of hurt and anger threatening to suffocate her. "Oh, and one other question," Shelby said. Paula looked up to see that Shelby had returned to the room and was standing in the doorway. Tears started to run down Paula's face, but she didn't try to wipe them away. She stared at Shelby, begging her with her eyes to believe her. "Ricky—have you ever slept with him?"

Paula's lips quivered as she answered, "Yes, I have."

"You say that like it's something to be proud of, Paula, something you should receive a trophy for." Paula held up a hand to silence Shelby.

"I say it like a woman who realizes she is human, prone to make mistakes and willing to admit it when she does. I never claimed to be a saint, Shelby, just your best friend. A best friend who has been loyal to you from day one of our friendship."

"You are a liar and a whore. Why am I not surprised? Remember saying if Ricky was just a little older you'd be with him? Well, that didn't stop you from sleeping with him, did it? So Myron and Ricky, who else have you slept with? Or should the question be who haven't you slept with, Paula? You make me sick," Shelby said through clenched teeth then turned and walked back out of the room. Paula started to go after her but knew it would not do any good.

"Oh my god! Why didn't I just tell her a long time ago!" Paula didn't know what to do. She felt disoriented. As if Shelby was still standing in the room with her, she said, "You forgot about your sandwich, Shel. It's all right. I will just wrap it up and put it in the fridge for you. You can have it for lunch tomorrow." She picked up the sandwich.

Her hands were shaking so much, and she was so upset she had to wrap the sandwich over and over again before she was finally able to wrap it correctly.

After Paula put the sandwich in the fridge and poured out the coffee, she went to the bathroom, blew her nose, and wiped her face with paper towels. Taking some eye drops from her makeup bag, she put two drops in each eye, then walked out of the building to her truck. She was devastated to the point of feeling faint. She couldn't figure out why Shelby would all of a sudden question her the way she did. She loved Shelby and worked hard to nurture their friendship. She'd told her the truth about her and Myron as well as Ricky. She could have lied to her, but she didn't, didn't want to. Shelby was her best friend, and no matter what happened, she was not going to lie to her.

It has always been hard for me to make friends, Paula thought to herself. *I finally find someone I can connect with, talk to, hang out with, and I'm about to lose her.* "I told her the truth," Paula said while banging her hands on the steering wheel after settling in her truck. Someone knocked on her window just as she started the engine. She looked up. The person fired two shots into her truck and ran off.

CHAPTER TWENTY-NINE

"GUSSIE, I'M HOME," SHELBY CALLED as she struggled out of her coat and hung it in the hall closet.

"Hi, wash up. I've got dinner on the table and I'm hungry. Where have you been? You're late."

"I'm sorry. I rode around for a while, rough day." Gracey came running in and stared up at Shelby as if she wanted to be picked up. Shelby reached down and patted her. "Not tonight, sweetie. I'm too tired." She then walked to the bathroom and washed up for dinner.

"This is delicious, Gussie. I love meatloaf!"

"Good, glad you like it. I made enough for Paula too. I will make her a plate and set it aside. She coming over later tonight? If not, you can take it to work for her tomorrow."

"Gussie," Shelby said while laying down her fork and wiping her mouth with a napkin. "Paula won't be coming over anymore. We are done. I want nothing else to do with her." Augusta picked up her glass of water and drank from it. She took a forkful of potatoes and put them in her mouth, chewing them slowly. She put the fork down, swallowed, and looked at Shelby.

"You can't get through this life alone, Shelby. A good friend is hard to find. Some people never find one. Paula is a good friend and she loves you. So whatever is wrong with the two you, you need to fix it."

"She slept with Myron long before he was killed, Gussie, and she never said a word to me about it. She also admitted that she has slept with Ricky too. She disgusts me. I never want to see her again!"

"She admitted all this to you, did she? Did she tell you why or how she came to sleep with Myron?"

"Yes, but I don't believe her. She must think I'm a fool to believe that bull she told me. I was so angry I called her a whore!" Augusta finished her food, got up, and took her plate to the sink and rinsed it off. Walking back to the table, Augusta wiped her hands on her apron and sat back down.

"How many men did you sleep with before you married Myron?"

"I don't know. I didn't sleep around. Maybe one or two, I don't know. Why?"

"Did that make you a whore?" Shelby stared at Augusta trying to figure out where she was going with what she'd just said.

"Gussie, what are you talking about?"

"You said Paula admitted to sleeping with two men, Myron and Ricky, two men, and you want to label her a whore. You said you may have slept with two men before marrying Myron, so I guess that makes you a whore too," Augusta said with a smile. Shelby rolled her eyes at Augusta before jumping up, rushing to the sink, and tossing her plate in it with a clatter.

"This is serious, Augusta. She slept with Myron!"

"You said she explained to you what happened and you didn't believe her. A woman who has busted her butt to please you as a friend, who practically worships the ground you walk on. Yet Myron, the man you were married to, who beat the crap out of you at every opportunity, calls and invites you to his hotel room, telling you this grand lie that he wants to discuss the two of you getting back together, you *believed*? We both know what happened as a result. He beat the crap out of you again, almost killing you! His bull you *believed*. Well, I don't know, Shelby, but I think I would have bought Paula's bull before I would have bought Myron's bull. Sounds like something is wrong with you, not Paula," Augusta said as she got up and walked in her room, closing the door behind her.

The next morning, Shelby got up and immediately thought about what Augusta said last night after she'd shared what had happened at work with Paula yesterday. What if Paula was telling her the truth? she asked herself. She didn't really have time to think about it. She had to get dressed and get to work.

After barely making it to work on time, Shelby walked to her desk and stuck her purse in the drawer before heading to the kitchen to grab a cup of coffee. She opened the fridge to get milk for her coffee. That was when she noticed the sandwich Paula had given her yesterday, wrapped up with her name on it. She picked it up and tossed it in the trash.

The kitchen was packed, which she thought odd. Usually, around this time, most people had already gotten their coffee and were at their desk working. She noticed people whispering and crying. There were several groups huddled together in conversation. Shelby didn't know what to think, but she couldn't stay in the kitchen any longer. She had work to do she reasoned. She quickly filled her coffee cup and rushed back to her desk to turn on her computer.

Shelby was about to start typing up a document Helen must have left her the night before when Helen walked up to her desk. Helen's eyes were red and swollen. She looked sick. She tried to speak, but each time she did, she had to stop and pull herself together. "Shelby, I need you to come in my office," Helen said and walked quickly away.

"Now?" Shelby called after her.

"Yes, right now," Helen said as she battled to keep her composure.

"Oh boy, what have I done now?" Shelby asked herself, then got up, and quickly followed Helen to her office. Before Shelby could sit down or say anything, Helen blurted it out.

"Paula is dead, Shelby. She was shot and killed last night. Ralf, one of our paralegals, found her slumped over the steering wheel of her truck in the garage when he left last night. He called 911, but it was too late. She was pronounced dead on the scene."

Shelby stared at Helen as if she'd never seen her before, then felt herself stagger. She knew Helen was still talking but she couldn't hear her. Was she going deaf? she wondered. She grabbed for something to keep her from hitting the floor. She knew she was falling but was powerless to stop herself. When she woke up, Augusta was standing over her, gently calling her name.

"Augusta, what are you doing here? Where am I?"

Augusta looked at Shelby, her heart breaking. "You are in the emergency room. That woman in your office called me, Helen. She said you had me in your employee file as your next of kin. You were given a mild sedative."

"Sedative, why?"

"When you were picked up at your office, they said you were yelling and screaming, so they had no choice but to give you something to calm you down." Then it came to her, Helen telling her that awful lie that Paula was dead—how dare she!

"Gussie, Helen... Helen... she lied to me. She told me Paula was dead! How could she say that? How could she? How cruel," Shelby said while trying to get out of the bed. Augusta gently pushed Shelby down on the bed and wiped back a stray hair.

"It's the truth, Shelby. Helen didn't lie. Paula is gone. Our girl is gone." Shelby closed her eyes and pounded her bed with her fist.

"No! Paula!" Shelby screamed. "Gussie, take me to her! Please take me to Paula. I don't believe you! I need to see her. I need to see her for myself! Why are you all lying to me? Is this some kind of a sick joke to pay me back for speaking to her the way I did? Well, it worked. Now stop it! Stop, please STOP!" Shelby kept trying to get out of the bed. She was causing such a commotion that the nurse came running in. She yelled for help from a second nurse after seeing Augusta's struggle to keep Shelby down wasn't working. Together the two nurses, with Augusta's help, were able to keep Shelby down and quiet her.

"Please leave me. I need to be alone," Shelby said out of breath from struggling with the nurses and Augusta.

"Shelby…"

"I said leave me!" Shelby screamed. "Just leave me! I want to die."

"No, sweetie, you don't want to do that," Augusta said.

"Yes, I do. Just leave me, Augusta."

*   *   *   *   *

Paula's beautiful smile and face stared at Shelby from her obituary as Shelby laid on the sofa in the psychiatrist's office, staring at it. Shelby thought about the loveseat in her own home where Paula had sat many a day eating a bag of potato chips. Her beautiful, wavy, thick hair that she wore short when she was alive was long in the picture and fell to her shoulders. Always the life of the party, Paula was posed with her hands in the air and one foot kicked out happily.

"Paula, I am so, so sorry. I miss you so much. I miss you. I am so sorry," Shelby said to herself as if she was the only one in the room.

"Shelby, Paula is resting now, and I'm sure she would have forgiven you had you been given the chance to apologize to her," the psychiatrist said. Shelby just looked at the doctor while she pressed Paula's obituary close to her chest and dabbed at her eyes with a tissue she'd given her.

"You get paid a lot of money to tell me what? What you just said! I'm supposed to find that consoling? Well, I don't, so try to come up with something a lot better!" Shelby stared at the doctor, waiting for her to come up with the magic words to make her pain instantly disappear.

The doctor looked at her and said, "Shelby, I wish I had a quick fix for what you're going through, but I don't. Death is hard. The unexpected death of someone we love is even harder. Our lifespan at best is seventy years, a little longer if we're fortunate. That's why it baffles me that so many people waste away their precious years of life worrying about things that are beyond their control instead of enjoying the day they have been given."

For a long time neither of them said anything. Shelby thought about what the doctor had just said. It was true, she had to admit. Even she worried too much about the future. But Paula wasn't like that. She lived her life to the fullest every single day. She loved life. She was full of it. Always going after what she wanted against the odds, trusting her own abilities instead of allowing others to limit them with their criticism. That's why it hurt so much that someone would just in an instant snatch life away from her without warning, without giving her a chance to fight for her life. Because she would have. That was Paula. A fighter.

"Shelby, are you still with me?"

"Yes, I was just thinking about what you said. How true it is. I appreciate all you're trying to do to help me deal with this crippling pain. I'm hurting so much I can hardly function. I feel like I'm about to have a nervous breakdown. Honestly, I think the only thing that is going to help me is the passing of time, if that. I just get so angry sometimes when I think about what happened to her and how I treated and talked to her the night she was killed. This is so scary, because Detective Maye thinks the same person who killed Myron, killed Paula. I'm afraid I might be next."

"Shelby, please try to release that fear and trust that the detectives will catch the person soon. I know it's hard but you have got to try. You also have to try to find a way to forgive yourself, that is the only way you will ever start to heal. Your anger, you have just got to use it to your advantage. You told me you like to run. Well, the next time you feel yourself getting angry, put on your running shoes and go for a run. Call me, if you'd like. If my schedule is free, I will run with you."

"Really, you'd do that for me?"

"Of course I would. I don't limit my treatment for my patients to this office. Whatever will help them heal faster or deal with the adversity they are facing is what I will do, if it's within the law and my ability to do so."

"Thank you, Doctor. You're an exceptional person."

"You're welcome, Shelby. So are you."

CHAPTER THIRTY

STANDING AT ONE OF THE large palladium windows in her living room, Shelby looked out at her neighborhood as the sun set, casting a gray hue on the evening. *What a lovely neighborhood, with its large trees and well-manicured lawns,* Shelby thought to herself. A dog barked somewhere in the distance, indicating movement of some sort in the area, although it seemed very quiet, very still outside.

Three months had passed since Paula was found dead in her truck and Shelby released from psychiatric care. Still her broken heart refused to mend. Honestly, Shelby felt that each day the wound seemed to gradually open a little more, breaking free of the bonds of psychotherapy she'd received that was supposed to mend it, help her cope with life, function on a daily basis without losing her mind. The hurt she thought would subside with the passing of time didn't. She continued to lose weight at a rapid pace, her diet consisted of a cracker here, an apple there, and water.

Her last words to Paula were recorded in her head, and every day, every single day they would play out when she least expected them to, causing her to stop what she was doing and cover her ears in an effort to drown them out. But it didn't help—nothing helped.

She thought about the sandwich Paula had bought her that day when she couldn't make it out for lunch, how she'd taken care to wrap it for her lunch the next day. The thought was almost unbearable. She'd learned a sad lesson too late, that you should be careful of what you say to people, how you speak to people even in the heat of anger. If your parting words were malicious and unwarranted, you may have to live with that regret for the rest of your life, because death will have paid them a visit, robbing you of the opportunity to say I'm sorry.

Augusta walked up behind Shelby and gently nudged her. Shelby turned around and put her arms around her, holding her so tightly Augusta thought she would suffocate. "I miss her so much Gussie. She was a part of me. She was more than my best friend. She was like a sister to me. There were times it seemed she was trying to tell me something. I wonder what it was. I guess I will never know."

"I think you do know. May not want to admit it, but you now know what Paula was trying to tell you." Shelby shook her head and slowly walked over to the middle of the room, mentally searching for answers as to why she was suffering so much. Why? What had she done so wrong to deserve all the pain she was having to endure? What? she wondered.

"Gussie, Stevie Wonder had a song out once called 'These Three Words.' It mentioned the importance of telling the ones in your life how much you love them because they can instantly be taken away. How true I've learned those words are."

"Shelby, listen to yourself child. You have got to come to grips with Paula's death. If you don't, it will mentally and physically destroy you. Look at you. You're skin and bones. It even looks like your hair is shedding. Worry and stress will do that to you. You are killing yourself. The person who killed Paula will have succeeded in killing you too without ever even touching you, if you keep this up."

"I can't help myself, Gussie. I've tried, Lord knows I've tried!" Augusta walked over to her and shook her by the shoulders so hard Shelby looked up at her, puzzled.

"Well, try harder! You can start by going in there and cleaning that room of yours. It looks so bad, for a minute there, I thought I was back living on the streets. Now get!" Shelby looked up at her and smiled sadly, then slowly walked to her room.

Sitting on the side of her bed, Shelby tried to think of what her mom, if she were still alive, would do if she were going through what she was right now. "Mom, what I wouldn't give to be able to talk to you right now," she said to herself.

She knew what her dad would say. He would say, "Shelby Malloy, life will be around the corner, and you will still be trying to catch up with it if you're not careful." Shelby smiled to herself as she thought of the facial expression of her father when he used to say that to her.

"You're right, Dad. Life is not going to wait for me to heal. It's going to keep right on going whether I like it or not."

Augusta knocked gently on her bedroom door, then walked in carrying a tray of crackers, cheese, a bottle of wine, and wine glasses.

"What is this, Gussie?"

"We are getting ready to have us a little celebration!"

"Yeah, what are we celebrating?"

"Life, Paula's life! We love her and we miss her, but we know that Paula was not one to sit around and mope. She'd do something to pick her spirits up." Shelby smiled because she knew what Augusta had just said about Paula was undeniably true, she remembered the day Paula talked her into going for a ride on a sled down the hill behind her house.

Augusta poured herself a glass of wine, then she poured Shelby a glass of wine before saying, "A toast to Paula. To the beautiful, strong, happy, and feisty woman that we knew her to be."

Augusta and Shelby raised their wine glasses up. "Until we meet again, Paula," Augusta said, then the two of them tapped their glasses together in a toast to Paula.

CHAPTER THIRTY-ONE

SHELBY AND AUGUSTA WALKED FROM bench to bench in the park handing out sandwiches, apples, and small containers of tea to the homeless who had gathered there that day. Shelby looked across the street at the police cruiser that sat in watch over her and wondered if she would ever be able to go anywhere again without them following her around.

"Shelby, Ms. Shelby!" Shelby turned to see Krystal running toward her. She sat down her container of sandwiches and held out her arms so Krystal could run into them. She then picked her up and planted a kiss on her forehead.

"Where is Mommy?"

"She is there." Krystal turned and pointed to her mom standing in the distance, watching her. Shelby raised her hand and waved at Mattie.

"My, look at you, curls and frills. You look beautiful, darling!" Krystal's long blond curls glistened in the sunlight as she stared at Shelby.

"Mommy found a job. We have an apartment now, and it's great! Mommy now has her own kitchen, and she cooks me the same meal every night. She cooks me whatever I ask for every night!"

"Yeah, and what do you ask for?"

"Fried chicken and mashed potatoes. It would be perfect if she would just not add the vegetables," Krystal said with a chuckle. "Guess what!"

"What?" Shelby said with a look of excitement on her face.

"Mommy and I found a special place in my room for the dollhouse you and Ms. Paula bought me and Mommy painted my room yellow to match the dollhouse."

Krystal jumped down from Shelby and looked around, searching for Augusta and Paula. She saw Augusta, but when she didn't see Paula, she asked, "Where is she?"

"Where is who, sweetie?"

"The short, tiny lady with the dark hair. She is so nice, just like you! Where is she?" Krystal asked anxiously. Shelby tried to ignore Krystal's question and change the subject.

"Hey, what are you guys doing here? Thought you have your own place to live now?"

"I know, but Mommy brought me to the park to play on the swings. That is the only thing wrong with our new apartment. It doesn't have swings." Shelby laughed and picked her container up in preparation to leave, hoping she would be able to before Krystal had a chance to ask for Paula again.

"Well, sweetie, I have to finish handing out my sandwiches."

"No wait, please! Where is the lady? You never said. Ms. Paula, where is she, please?"

Shelby looked down at Krystal and smiled before saying, "She is sleeping. Paula is sleeping, honey."

"Oh, she must be very tired. It's the afternoon, not even dark yet."

"Yes, Krystal, Paula was tired, very tired." Krystal looked up at Shelby.

"You look sad and skinny. Why?"

"I'm not sad, Krystal, just tired is all."

"Like Ms. Paula, you're tired like Ms. Paula was, and you are going to sleep too?"

Shelby stared at Krystal for a second before reaching down and kissing her on the forehead again and saying, "Hopefully, I will stay awake a lot longer before I go to sleep."

"Okay," Krystal said with a smile. "Come visit me and Mommy sometimes. We don't live far away. Mommy gave Ms. Augusta our address, so come see us soon and bring Ms. Paula with you. Okay, bye," Krystal said as she turned to run and catch up with her mom, then stopped, turned around and said, "I love you Ms. Shelby. Please tell Ms. Paula I love her too! Come see us soon." Krystal then turned and continued to run to catch up to her mother. Shelby smiled and waved at Krystal as she ran off.

When Shelby and Augusta returned home, they sat down at the kitchen table to have a glass of water. At the sound of the knock on the door, they put their glasses down and looked at each other, puzzled, because they were not expecting anyone.

"I'll get it," Shelby said and walked swiftly to the door, looked out the peephole, then opened it. Ricky stood before her. *My goodness*, she thought to herself, *if I felt I could trust him, I'd kiss him. He looks so good—sorry, Agacia.*

"For you," he said as he handed a large bouquet of flowers to her. "Agacia picked them out, so I thought I would bring them to you."

"Where is Agacia?"

"She's home. I told her I was going to see you, to see how you are doing."

Shelby took the flowers from him slowly and stepped aside for him to come in without uttering another word. Once he was inside, Shelby said, "The flowers are beautiful, Ricky, but I must say, I'm a little surprised to see you. I've been trying to reach you for days, what... ?"

"I know you have, I just…" Ricky stopped and shrugged his shoulders as if he didn't know what to say. "I can't believe she's gone—Paula, dead! It's unfathomable!"

Augusta walked over and took the flowers from Shelby who had sat down on the sofa and was just holding them as if she'd forgotten they were in her hands. "Hello, Ricky," Augusta said. "I'll put these in water and leave you two to talk. Nice to see you Ricky, I think?" Augusta said and left the room.

"Wow, Shel, there is a police car parked in front of your house. What is that about?"

"Detective Maye feels, at this point and after Paula was found dead, that I need police presence."

"So do they have any idea who killed Paula?"

"No, but they seem to think it's the same person who killed Myron."

"What is going on, Ricky, and please, I need to know the truth. Was there something going on between you and Paula? She told me the night she was killed that the two of you had slept together. Is that true?"

"Yes, but she was drunk. It happened last year after an office party. Paula was stoned, so I offered to take her home. Once we got in the car, she was all over me. I tried to get her off me, but after a while, I said to hell with it. I mean, Paula! What man in his right mind is going to say no to that!" Shelby smiled to herself.

"Paula was very beautiful, from head to toe," Shelby said and shook her head slowly. "Ricky, do you still owe those people money? You never really told me what happened, how you got in trouble with them, but I do know Myron had something to do with it." Ricky walked over and looked out the window.

"Myron. He told me all I needed to do was deliver a Fed-Ex to some people he knew and he'd pay me one hundred dollars. I was broke, Shelby. Needed the money, so I did it."

Ricky paused for a very long time, then he turned and walked back and sat down across from Shelby so that they were face-to-face. He wanted her to be able to look at him, to see he was telling her the truth before he continued. "When I got to the drop-off point, some run-down hotel I had never heard of before, this guy who goes by the name of Spect was waiting for me, he and his boy. I just wanted to drop off the Fed-Ex and get the hell out of there because I was starting to feel that something wasn't right. But Spect wouldn't let me leave until they had checked inside the

Fed-Ex envelope. When he opened the envelope, it was empty. He looked at me and said, 'Where is my ten thousand, man? Where is my money?' Shelby, I didn't know what to do, what to say. Then it hit me, Myron, that son of a—!"

"Ricky!"

"I'm sorry, Shel. He had set me up. He obviously owed those guys that amount of money for some reason but either didn't have it to pay them or didn't want to pay it. So he sent me to them with an empty envelope to make it seem like I had stolen their money! Before I knew it, I was fighting my way out of the room. How I got out of there alive, I will never know. It must have been my will to live because I knew if I didn't fight, they were going to kill me in there. When I was finally able to get out, I ran and I just kept running. When I stopped to hide behind this warehouse, I learned that I was bleeding, my nose, my arm, but I didn't care. I was alive and that was all that mattered to me."

Shelby couldn't believe what she was hearing, but considering who was behind it, Myron, it was totally possible. "I'm sorry, Ricky. I am so sorry I ever introduced you to Myron. This whole mess is my fault." Ricky got up and walked over to sit down beside Shelby. He pulled her to him and held her tight.

"No, Shelby, none of this is your fault. I honestly believe Myron was trouble from conception and you just, unfortunately, happened to fall in love with him, and he took advantage of that whenever the opportunity presented itself, and I was an opportunity."

Shelby pulled slowly away from Ricky and asked, "Are those guys still after you?"

"No, Agacia paid them off. She took what was left of her savings and paid them off. Myron had given me Spect's number so we could arrange a meeting point for me to drop off the Fed-Ex that day. When Agacia came to me and told me she had the money and she wanted to pay those guys off so they would finally be out of our life, I couldn't believe it! She told me she had the money, all of it, and asked me to call them and arrange a meeting place. Reluctantly, I did, and surprisingly, it went well." "Ricky, why didn't you just tell them Myron set you up, that he was the one who took their money, he owed them not you!"

"I'd tried explaining that to them several times, but they just would not listen. So, I arranged to meet them in a restaurant where I knew there would be lots of people. I gave them the envelope with the ten thousand in it. After Spect opened it and actually sat there and counted the money, which was easy because it was in large bills, he put it in his bag. Then he and his boy got up and walked out of the restaurant. I haven't seen or heard from them since."

"How long ago was this, Ricky?"

"It's been almost a month now. They used to call my cell day and night threatening to kill me, but as I said, it's been almost a month now, and I haven't heard a word from them. I am finally free to get on with my life."

"Agacia really loves you. She is special. Take care of her, Ricky, hold on to her. You don't find that kind of love too easily."

"Oh, believe you me, I know. That's why we are leaving at the end of the month for her hometown to get married. Well, I have got to get going. She is waiting for me to return home for dinner," Ricky said while slowly raising to his feet. "You deserved better, Shelby. I can't tell you how sorry I am you decided to marry that dude. You know my mother once told me that to love a person doesn't necessarily mean that you appreciate the person, recognize their value. I never really understood what she meant until you, your situation, being married to Myron. I honestly think he may have truly loved you once, but sadly, I don't think he ever developed an appreciation for what he had in you as a wife, as a person. You know what makes it even sadder, in the end, he lost out in so many ways, even before someone took his life."

Ricky hugged Shelby and said softly to her, "I love you, Shelby. Take care of yourself. I will be checking on you."

"I love you too, Ricky. All the best to you and Agacia."

"Shel, one more thing. All this time you were willing to help me, loan me money, yet you never asked me why I was always so broke. Never once—why?"

"Not my place to judge you, Ricky, just try to help you every once in a while if I can. Plus, it was rumored that your mother had several medical bills and they were starting to pile up."

"Yeah, it's been pretty rough. It's just me and my mom. Her health won't allow her to work. So I guess people were talking, huh?"

"People talk, Ricky. Sadly, some people need to consume their lives with the misfortunes of others just so they can feel better about themselves."

Ricky shook his head as if he was trying to clear his mind and said, "Sad but true. I'll check on you soon, Shel. Good night."

After Shelby showed Ricky out and locked the door behind him, Augusta walked back in the room. "You heard?" Shelby asked her.

"Every word. Shelby?"

"No, Augusta, please! I don't want to hear it. I blew my chance with Ricky a long time ago. He is getting ready to marry Agacia now, so let's just be happy for them. I'm going to bed. I'm not very hungry. Good night."

Augusta walked to the kitchen, sat at the table, closed her eyes, and started praying. "Lord, I don't claim to be no Christian, and I can't remember the last time I prayed but please hear my prayer. Please help my Shelby. I know she is a little stupid, but she is a good person. Yes, sir, a good person. She took me in off the streets, and cleaned me up. Then she let me live here in this beautiful house without charging me one red penny. She is an angel, my angel, and she has been through so much. Seems more than one person should have to bear. Lord, all I am asking you to do, please, if I may, is to stop the pain." Augusta opened her eyes, got up and turned off the kitchen lights and went to bed.

CHAPTER THIRTY-TWO

SHELBY TURNED OVER IN BED for what seemed like to her the umpteenth time. Although she'd taken a sleeping pill, the result of not being able to sleep well for the last few weeks, there she lay, wide awake. She kept telling herself that at six o'clock her alarm was going to go off whether she liked it or not.

The day she'd dreaded the most since Paula's death was finally here. The day she returned to work, returned to going out to lunch without Paula, without texting her, without hanging out with her. The day she returned to her desk, the place where she last saw Paula, dressed as always so fashionably yet tastefully. Her beautiful hair in place, not a stray strand anywhere on her small head, and her deep red lipstick complementing her flawless brown skin.

"Had I known, oh dear God, had I known that would be the last time I would ever see her alive, I would never have said all those horrible things to her! Help me, please help me, because honestly, I feel I'm about to lose my mind."

Just as Shelby knew it would, her alarm went off at six. What time she'd fallen asleep she didn't know. She believed it must have been around four or five o'clock. Why hadn't that sleeping pill worked, she wondered as she pushed back the covers with barely the strength to do so. Augusta knocked softly on her door before coming in with a tray of eggs, toast, bacon, and orange juice. "Gussie, I can't do it. I can't," she said, tears starting to roll down her face.

Augusta walked over to the dresser and sat the tray of food down. "Get up!"

"Augusta!"

"I said get up! Now you listen to me, Shelby Malloy. You've had months of laying around and crying and regretting! Are you hurting? You'd better believe you are! You've lost the best friend you ever had! But now it's time to get up. GET UP! I will be back in fifteen minutes, and when I return, I expect that tray of food to be eaten and those clothes I ironed for you over on the chair to be on your body, and for heaven's sake, flat iron your hair and put on some lipstick, a bright color because you are pale as I don't know what." Shelby looked at Augusta, trying to figure out what had gotten into her.

"Gussie, why are you talking to me this way? Why?"

Augusta walked over to where Shelby had managed to stand up, stood right in front of her and said, "I lived on the streets for years until you took me in. I went for days sometimes with nothing to eat but what I could find left in a trash can. There were times when I soiled my clothes because I was too ashamed to even go into a public place to use a bathroom. I looked and smelled so bad. One day I was so hungry I asked this man for one dollar, just one dollar so I could buy me a candy bar, something to put in my stomach so I could keep going, and you know what he did?" Shelby didn't say anything. She just waited for Augusta to continue. "He spat in my face, that's what he did. He looked right at me and spat in my face."

Shelby couldn't say anything. There were no words to describe how bad she felt for Augusta at that moment. All she could do was hug her. "I'm sorry, Gussie. I'm so horribly sorry."

Augusta pulled away from her and said, "I wiped his spit off my face, held my head up high, and kept walking and begging for money until finally someone gave me enough money to get me something to eat. You've got to wipe those tears off your face today, Shelby, and keep walking, just keep moving forward. Your heart may be breaking this morning but keep walking until you set foot in that office, hold your head up high, and greet everybody you see with a smile. Yes, ma'am, with a smile. Now eat and get dressed. I will have a hot dinner waiting for you when you get home tonight."

Somehow Shelby made it through the day. She had her moments, but every time she did, she would think about what Augusta said to her before leaving for work. Many of her coworkers stopped by her desk to tell her how sorry they were about Paula. Helen and Alex Manson took her out to lunch, and for the rest of the afternoon, Helen kept her so busy, she didn't have time to feel sad. Every time she finished one assignment, Helen had another one waiting for her. After a while, she realized Helen was trying to keep her mind off Paula by keeping her as busy as possible, which she silently thanked her for.

*   *   *   *   *

When Shelby returned home, as promised, Augusta had a delicious hot dinner waiting for her. They watched a movie after dinner, then Shelby showered and went to bed because Augusta insisted she do so while she clean up the kitchen.

The sound of Shelby's cell phone made her sit up in bed. She thought it was her alarm, but she then reasoned it couldn't be, not this soon. She picked it up and checked the number. She didn't recognize it, so she started to ignore it. Then for some reason she decided to answer it. "Hello," she said sleepily.

"Shelby, it's me, Agacia!" Shelby immediately thought about Ricky.

"Agacia, what! What is it? Is Ricky all right?"

"I don't know. I can't find him!"

"What? You can't find him!" Shelby checked the time on her phone. "Agacia, it's three thirty in the morning. What do you mean you can't find him?"

"I… I don't know. We had dinner. He said he was going for a walk afterward. That was around nine, and I haven't seen or heard from him since. Shelby, I'm downstairs, in front of your house! I've looked everywhere for him and still can't find him! Please, you've got to come help me look for him. I'm going crazy!"

"Okay, okay… I'm coming! Just wait right there while I throw something on!" Shelby jumped out of bed and ran to her dresser drawer, recklessly throwing clothes on to the floor until she found a pair of jeans and a sweatshirt. She ran to Augusta's room and woke her up, telling her briefly what was going on so she would know where she was, in case it took all night for her and Agacia to find Ricky and not return home until morning.

When Shelby ran down the steps to meet Agacia, she could see that she was terribly upset and nervous, very nervous.

"Agacia, where could he be? You tried his cell phone?" Agacia didn't say anything. She just stared at Shelby strangely. "Agacia!"

"I heard him. He called Ricky one day and threatened to kill him, that no good piece of trash of yours, Myron. When I was able to check Ricky's phone without him knowing it, I found Myron's number, called him, and got him to agree to meet me at his place. I told him who I was and that I had money for him, lots of it, so he agreed to let me come."

"Agacia, what are you saying? What the hell is going on? Where is Ricky?" Shelby shouted at her.

"Oh, don't you worry. Ricky is fine, and you know why? Because of me, I made sure of it. I had to kill Myron. I couldn't let him hurt Ricky."

"What the hell! You, you killed Myron! So that was the heel of one of your stiletto shoes that was found at the scene of Myron's murder?"

"Correct. From one woman to another, stilettos, after a while, will let you down one way or another," Agacia said with a wicked smile. "Now it's your turn. Of all the people I've killed, Myron and Paula, you are going to be the hardest, because I like you."

"Why, Agacia, why Paula? She had nothing to do with Myron."

"Paula possessed something you lack, Shelby, *guts*! She had fight in her. I would never have been able to kill her without one hell of a fight had I took the approach with her that I'm taking with you tonight. That's why I had to sneak up on her and kill her. Shame, she was a beauty, but she had to go. As long as she was alive, it would have been hard for me to get to you. I honestly believe she would have risked her own life to save yours. So now, here we are, face-to-face. You and me, Shelby."

"For some reason, I'm beginning to feel this has something to do with you thinking I'm after Ricky. Agacia, I know you and Ricky are about to be married. I respect that fact, and I would never try to do anything to come between you two. I'd be lying if I said I was never interested in him, but I gave up having any desire to be with him once I learned you two were a couple. I don't want Ricky."

"Maybe not, but he wants you."

"You're wrong, so help me, you're wrong!"

"Shut up! I'm not stupid, Shelby. I've seen the way he looks at you. I have to listen to him talk about you night after miserable night."

"I was so mistaken about you, Agacia. I really thought Ricky had found a treasure in you. You mentioned once how you had cared for a neighbor who wouldn't even speak to you, how you would never betray a friend but try to help them. Yet you stand here in front of me and admit that you killed two people. It's almost as if you're two different people."

For some odd reason, Agacia laughed and said, "Well, Shelby, you know what they say, 'love will make you do crazy things,' and I love Ricky, so I am doing what I have to, to keep him."

Shelby's mind raced. She was so angry she could kill Agacia, especially now knowing that she was the one who took Paula away from her, but she had to be calm, try to reason with her. "Are you that insecure?"

"I am not going to play the guessing game with you, Shelby, so whatever you are trying to say, just say it!"

"No man is worth you harming or killing another person for. If you think you killing me will secure your relationship with Ricky, you are relying on a false sense of security! You said you would not let hatred grow in your heart for me. What changed your mind? Ricky, a man, are you serious?"

Agacia laughed, then walked up to stand in Shelby's face before saying, "Do you honestly think I don't see past your pretense? Are you honestly trying to stand here and tell me you're not attracted to Ricky? 'A man,' you say. Wasn't it a man who beat you black and blue a few times, still you went running back to him time and time again? So, tell me, how are we different when it comes to trying to hold on to the man we want and love? What you put up with to keep Myron was crazy. I admit what I'm doing to keep Ricky is crazy, but at least I am willing to admit it."

"You know nothing about what happened between Myron and me, in our marriage, nothing!"

"Oh, I know plenty! Myron talked a lot on the night I killed him. When he learned you would be next, he told me if I let him live, he would help me kill you."

"Do you really believe Myron meant that, Agacia?"

"I think that is a question you should be asking yourself right now, Shelby. Do you believe he meant it?" Both women got quiet, anger and hurt ripping them apart. "Do you, Shelby? Do you believe Myron would have helped me kill you? I do."

"Believe what you want. Just don't let hatred and jealousy destroy you. You have taken two lives already. It's time to stop this, Agacia, right now!"

Agacia stared at Shelby for a second, then said, "I don't hate you, Shelby. As I said earlier, I like you, but I don't trust you when it comes to Ricky. Given the chance, you'd try to take him away from me. I can't give you that chance."

The wind picked up. Shelby shivered and backed away from Agacia. "Agacia, if Ricky loves you, truly loves you and I believe he does, I could never come between the two of you. Please! Listen to me! You are a beautiful and caring woman. You have a lot to offer any man." Agacia rolled her eyes at Shelby and looked at her as if she'd grown bored with her words.

"Let's just say Ricky was interested in me. Would you let that stop you from moving on with your life? Would you let it rob you of fulfilling your hopes and dreams, bettering yourself, finding happiness with someone else? Would you? Your boys, what about your boys, Agacia? They should be more important to you than any relationship with a man, and they need their mother, especially at their age—they need you! If you take my life tonight, you will be taking life away from your sons. They will lose their mother in so many ways, their thirst for life!"

"Shut up! I've heard enough of your pleading and foolish reasoning! Not another word about my boys! I'm their mother, not you! I know what is best for them! They need a man in their life, and Ricky is a good man. He is good for me and my boys!"

Shelby's patience had run out. The anger and hurt she'd tried to suppress after learning Agacia was the one who killed Paula got the best of her. "You are a weak woman! Where is your strength to live your life with or without a man? You were right. Paula had guts, something honestly you lack, not me, Agacia. Paula wasn't dependent on the love of a man to be happy and successful in life. She made her own way, found happiness in life itself. But you..." Shelby's voice broke. She tried not to cry, but she simply couldn't help herself. "You... you took that away from her, you miserable, sick individual!"

Agacia walked up to Shelby and smacked her so hard she stumbled backward. Shelby was shocked at this sudden move and quickly put her hand to her face. The blow hurt so bad her hand trembled from the pain. "See, I told you—no fight in you," Agacia said mockingly. Without realizing it, Shelby went at Agacia, knocking her to the ground. Agacia quickly recovered and kicked Shelby hard in the stomach just as she came at her again. Shelby fell to the ground. Agacia jumped up and pulled a gun from the pocket of her jacket.

Just then, Augusta fired a warning shot into the air. Agacia and Shelby turned to see her coming down the steps toward them, holding a gun in her hands and saying to Agacia, "From the day you laid foot in our house, I got a bad feeling about you. That's why when Shelby told me she was coming out to meet you, I went to her phone, looked up that detective's number, and called him. Then decided to come out here to see what was going on. I fired a warning shot, Agacia. The next one won't be a warning. Now put the gun away!"

"Old woman, if you know what's best for you, you'd better stay out of this or you will be next."

"Try me! I was able to reach the detectives. They will be here any second. Put the gun away, Agacia," Augusta demanded.

Headlights flickered as Detectives Maye and Harris sped toward them. Just as their car came to a screeching halt, Agacia aimed her gun at Shelby's head, but Augusta was quicker and fired a shot at Agacia, hitting her in the chest, causing her to collapse to the ground. Detective Maye and Detective Harris jumped out of their car and rushed over to Agacia. Detective Maye called 911 while Detective Harris checked her pulse. "It's too late, man. She's gone." Detective Maye slowly put his phone away and looked over at Shelby and Augusta. Augusta was still holding the gun in her hand while trying to calm Shelby. Detective Maye slowly shook his head and said, "This reminds me of something my father told me when I was a little boy and afraid of the night time."

"Yeah, what's that?" Detective Harris asked him.

Detective Maye let out a heavy sigh and said, "He told me, 'When the day gives way to night and danger is in sight, it is the one least expected who will make sure you are protected.'" He then looked into the distance and said, "Who would have ever thought, that an old homeless woman Shelby Malloy took in off the streets, would be the one to save her life."

Two Weeks Later

"Okay, I think we've got more than enough cupcakes here, little girl," Shelby said with a smile and a playful tug at Krystal's ear.

"No, please? Can I just put the icing on one more? There are a lot left. What are you going to do with them if we don't put icing on them and eat them?"

Shelby laughed and winked at Krystal. "We are going to share the leftover cupcakes with our friends in the park."

"Oh great, but they still need icing on them. They won't taste that good without the icing."

"Don't you worry, Gussie and I will take care of that. But you, my dear, have to get cleaned up. Mom will be here to pick you up in about an hour."

"Oh man, can't I stay over just one more night?"

"You said that Friday night, then last night. You know I love having you stay over, but you've got school tomorrow. Now scoot, so you will be ready when she gets here and she'll not have to wait!"

"Okay." Krystal jumped down from the kitchen island and ran to get her things together.

Augusta stuck her head in the kitchen and looked at Shelby as she finished off a cupcake. "Thank goodness you are finally eating something. It may be junk but at least you're eating."

"Well, it's good junk, how 'bout that?" Shelby said while licking her fingers.

"There is a Mr. Queria here to see you." Shelby froze.

"Paula's father?"

"I don't know. I've never met Paula's father."

"Is he in a wheelchair?"

"He is an elderly man, and yes, he is. There is a nurse with him." Shelby picked up the dish towel she and Krystal had been using to clean up behind themselves and wiped her hands with it. After brushing the cupcake crumbs off her shirt and patting her hair to make sure it didn't look too much of a mess, she said, "Thank you, Gussie," and walked to the living room.

"Hello, Mr. Queria, how nice to see you. I've been meaning to call…"

"No worries, Shelby. We are all still trying to adjust to life without my Paula. I don't know that I ever will, but life will go on. I am dealing with it as best I can and treasuring the memories of my little girl."

"I miss her so much—a text, just one text from her. What I wouldn't give for a 'hey, Shel, what's up? Let's go get drinks after work.'" Shelby paused, swallowed hard, then walked over, and sat down on the sofa.

"Shelby, this is my caregiver, Ms. Savoy." Shelby greeted the tall, neat woman with gray hair pulled back in a bun. She rested her hands on Mr. Queria's wheelchair as if it would roll away from her if she dared to move.

"Hello, nice to meet you," Shelby said. Ms. Savoy just nodded at her and patted Mr. Queria on the shoulder.

"Shelby, I'll get right to the point. Paula made you her beneficiary. Left everything to you. She knew of course I didn't need it, and she was an only child. She loved you very much, Shelby. Said you were the sister she never had. She left her home, which I paid off a week before her untimely death, her life savings, and her 401K fund. My daughter was very well off, Shelby. I made sure of that. Now it all belongs to you."

Shelby sat there and stared down at the floor. She wanted to run out the door and scream to the top of her lungs, throw something, punch something, curse someone out, *something*.

But all she could do was sit there and hurt.

"I don't want it, none of it," Shelby said so low that Mr. Queria had to ask her to repeat herself.

"I'm sorry, what did you say?" Shelby looked up at him and spoke louder.

"With all due respect, Mr. Queria, I said, I don't want it. None of it, not the house, not the money, *none of it!* If I thought any of it could bring Paula back… give me back her laughter, her smile, her text messages, I would take it, *all* of it! But you and I both know all the money in the world will never bring Paula back." Mr. Queria nodded his head slowly in agreement with Shelby.

"If I may ask this of you, Mr. Queria, this is how I would like the money from the sale of Paula's house, and all other monies left to me by her, to be divided—three ways, please. I would like 50 percent to go to a shelter for the homeless of your choice, 25 percent to go to a home for battered and abused women, and 25 percent to go to one of the many organizations fighting for gun control." Silence hung in the air before he answered.

"Are you sure about this, Shelby?"

"Yes, sir. I've never been more sure about anything in my life. I will sign whatever papers are necessary, giving you permission to do as I've instructed with the inheritance."

"Very well then, as you wish, my dear. If you ever need anything, Shelby, anything at all, the firm has my contact information. You just let me know." Shelby walked over and knelt down beside his wheelchair before taking one of his hands and patting it on the back.

"Thank you, thank you so much. You take good care of yourself. Ms. Savoy, please take care of him and call me if you need me."

"I will. I will take very good care of him. Mr. Queria is like a father to me. Ms. Paula was like a daughter. You can believe I will let nothing happen to him."

Mr. Queria motioned for his caregiver to prepare for them to leave. Shelby hugged him and kissed him on the head.

"Thank you again, Mr. Queria."

"You are welcome, Shelby. Have a good day." Ms. Savoy smiled and rolled Mr. Queria out into the sunshine. Shelby closed the door behind them and leaned her back against it before saying softly to herself, "Thank you for the inheritance Paula, I put it to good use, you did not die in vain. I love you." Shelby's spirits lifted, she smiled, and for the first time in a very long while she felt truly happy.

About the Author

Linda McCain is a new author presently working on her second book. She enjoys decorating, renovating, and gardening. She feels that her daughter, affectionately called Toots, is the best gift she has ever been given. A friend once said to her, "No matter what happens to you, you seem to have the ability to move forward with a positive attitude." Linda's response was "Life is too short to allow triviality to diminish your happiness." She simply doesn't allow it to but chooses to focus on the positive.

There were times she felt, while writing *One Bad Decision*, that the endeavor would never work. She focused on the words of her friend Tim Pool "to finish it" and the words of Maya Angelou that says, "Nothing will work unless you do."

CPSIA information can be obtained
at www.ICGtesting.com
Printed in the USA
BVHW031927231118
533780BV00001B/35/P